THREADBARE

MALCOLM HOLLINGDRAKE

Book Nine in the Harrogate Crime Series

ISBN 978-1-9160715-9-9

www.malcolmhollingdrakeauthor.co.uk

Praise for Malcolm

The opening pages had me completely gripped and I read and read, reaching the end of the story in just two sittings. I was immediately drawn to the lead character, Roy, and found myself torn between feeling empathy for a man suffering as he was following his time spent fighting in the Gulf War and anger towards him for planting bombs which would more than likely cause death or injury to innocent members of the general public. The author has pitched this story perfectly and it is a work of fiction that could so easily be real-life. I was completely blown away by the authors ability to lead the reader into Roy's head and understand why he felt he had to do this.

MoMo

My wife and I had to fight over who was going to read it first. She won and I had to take my turn. Certainly well worth the wait, I couldn't put the book down. An excellent read; suspense all the way.

John Michael

Full of twists and turns … never quite sure whodunnit…love this author and the Yorkshire setting … keeps you guessing up to the end

Kathy B

Book 8 in this series didn't disappoint! I really liked the escape room/ gaming side to the crime story and thought it was clever and a bit different and I always love 'catching up' with Bennett and Owen. As always, a well written and thought out book and the characters are as engaging as ever. After that ending, I can't wait for the next one!

Donna Dee

Something that kills people in three breaths? Something that leaves no trace. Cyril Bennett has his work cut out here. There are several victims and they seem to be linked together by coincidence. Do you believe in coincidence? We have an unusual killer with what seems to be a random selection of victims and it's interesting to see how the pieces fit together. I enjoyed the further delving into Cyril's past life, his bequest from his father, and Julie and his stepmother Wendy's continuing relationship. There's the most unusual murder method I've ever read about, combined with some delving into Cyril's past relationships which give a balance of head and heart that I really liked. Engrossing and satisfying.

Ignite

Malcolm Hollingdrake has done it again with a great book. He manages to show a killer who uses a very surprising way to murder. Great characters and storyline throughout the book. I so enjoy how DCI Bennett continues to grow with each book in series. I look forward to reading next book in series.

Susan

Also by Malcolm Hollingdrake

Bridging the Gulf

Shadows from the Past
Short Stories for Short Journeys

The Harrogate Crime Series

Only the Dead

Hell's Gate

Flesh Evidence

Game Point

Dying Art

Crossed Out

The Third Breath

Treble Clef

Dedicated to

Bill O'Brien

Barbara and Jim Ashcroft.

True friends

When humans act with cruelty we characterise them as ‘animals’,

Yet the only animal that displays cruelty is humanity.

Anthony Douglas Williams – Inside the Divine Pattern

I must be only cruel to be kind;

Thus bad begins, and worse remains behind.

William Shakespeare

Prologue

Heading north out of Harrogate, Julie slid along the bench seat and rested her hand on Cyril's knee. Neither spoke as the sun dappled the road before them. At Ripley they turned off the Ripon Road. In no time Cyril manoeuvred the Bentley into a car park and collected a bag from the boot.

"Fountains Abbey?" Julie asked, confusion and a faint disquiet evident on her face.

Cyril smiled. "You'll have to trust me, doctor."

They soon reached the ruins of the Cistercian Monastery. He walked over to the bridge spanning the small river, the Skell, before putting down the bag. Removing a blanket he threw it over the bridge's low wall.

"I take it this seat will be okay and the view to your liking?"

"Cyril, you know I think it's the most beautiful place in Yorkshire but then ... so is Brimham Rocks and Ramsgill and ..." she laughed. "Only kidding. This is my favourite, honest."

He moved towards the bag, removed two flutes and a box, lifted the lid and presented it. "Would this be to the lady's taste?"

She read the word *Krug* and a date. "Have you solved the murders, Cyril Bennett?"

He removed the cork, the popping noise loud and sharp, making her smile. He poured the two glasses.

"You have, haven't you? Clever man."

He stopped her from taking a sip. "Just a minute."

Putting his hand in his pocket, his fingers felt for the small box. He took it out and knelt before her. "Dr Julie Pritchett ..." He opened the lid of the small blue box revealing his mother's engagement ring. "Will you ... please ... marry me?"

Julie put her hands to her lips, looked at the ring and then at Cyril, as a tear swelled in her eye.

Chapter One

July

You could almost feel the tension as so many people crowded onto the railway platform, each seemingly jostling for a space in which to say their farewells and prepare for their journey. In some ways the scene was familiar; all large Victorian period stations seemed to be made the same way. The skeletal ironwork designed and constructed at Paddington Station by the engineer Isambard Kingdom Brunel was strong and powerful. Cyril Bennett could almost smell the atmosphere, he could conjure the smell, the heady mix of coal steam and oil he enjoyed when travelling on the Skipton to Bolton Abbey line. He could hear the excitement as he let his eyes wander along the row of passengers eagerly preparing to board the train; unembarrassed he observed their embraces, saw them check their luggage in anticipation and start to climb aboard.

It was as he panned the group from the left to the far right that he saw what he was looking for and he leaned forward, concentrating his gaze on three people; one, an officer in plain clothes, was prepared and had already removed his handcuffs as his colleague laid a firm hand of the law on the shoulder of the man about to board. Cyril moved a little closer and smiled as he surveyed the suspect's expression of total surprise and horror and Cyril could only speculate as to his next move. That conclusion, however, he would never know as this moment was frozen in time, set for posterity, oil paint on canvas. It was at this intense moment of concentration and speculation that he was startled himself as a hand firmly grasped his shoulder. He jumped instinctively and turned to be greeted by Julie's smiling face.

"Sorry I'm a little late, phone call just as I was leaving and you know that curiosity always gets the better of me. Besides, knowing that we were meeting here I knew that time would be an irrelevance and not be something that concerned you."

Cyril leaned over and kissed her. "Do you know this painting?"

Julie turned and looked at the huge canvas hanging in an elaborate gilt frame. "I don't. Didn't ever know William Powell Frith existed until you mentioned this exhibition."

"It's from the Royal Collection but it's this that draws me in."

Julie looked in the direction of Cyril's pointing finger and immediately smiled. "It's your day off, DCI Bennett, and you come and drool over a painting depicting a crowd of people that includes what we can only guess to be two plain-clothes police officers arresting some poor chap about to board a steam train back in another century."

Cyril brought his hands up to his face and allowed his fingers to massage his eyes. She could almost hear his thoughts ... *give me strength* probably followed by *pearls before swine*. Julie smiled inwardly before slipping her arm over his shoulder. She sang in whispered tones, "*Wind me up, let me go.* You make it so easy my lovely man ... it's absolutely wonderful, Cyril." She giggled and took a seat in the armchair positioned in front of the painting. "Okay, my house-trained art critic, tell me all about it."

It would be an hour before they descended the steps of the Harrogate Mercer Art Gallery. The sunlight reflected off the polished brass handrails that curved gently away from the door like welcoming arms.

"Coffee or a drink?" Julie said as she slipped her arm in his.

"All forms of life are depicted in those paintings, Julie, from the highest of the high to the lowest form of humanity. All you need to do is look. You can see it in their expressions by simply reading their eyes. Goodness, William Frith could paint and that painting of The Railway Station was stunning. Did you know that it sold for £4,500 in 1862? Believe me, that was a fortune then."

Julie stifled a yawn. He had pontificated long enough and it did not go unnoticed. Cyril led Julie up Swan Road.

"It doesn't get better. A couple of hours surrounded by outstanding art work and a beautiful companion." He kissed her cheek. "Then we have *The Old Swan* and a beer outside. What more could a man ask on a summer's day?"

Chapter Two

August

Looking at the carpet he knew what the future held. It was laid out there beneath his feet like his life before him; a woven maplike pattern, a two-dimensional family tree – it had seen better days and happier times but then, had not he? He recalled a poem by Yeats.

Had I the heavens' embroidered cloths,
Enwrought with golden and silver light, the ... he paused and looked again at his feet, *... Tread softly because you tread on my dreams.*

Even after all these years in situ the carpet was still a fashion statement from the past; they had much in common – a past.

A mirror hanging on the chimney breast briefly drew his attention. He stared at the white hood and blue mask, all marks of his profession, one he had toiled over for longer than he cared to remember; it camouflaged a great deal. The eyes returned the same stare, there was no emotion, they seemed dull, tired and yet there was defiance. He immediately looked away and down at the blue covers that wrapped his shoes and then at his gloves; he wiggled his fingers as if checking each still worked. If only he had a pound for every time ... he shook his head, glanced back at the mirror, he had been distracted long enough.

Moving towards the chair positioned directly to the right of the television, he allowed his foot to touch a threadbare patch, a marker where the same feet had rested hour after long hour. It was, he thought, the indelible mark of time lost in pursuit of mindless, soon forgotten pleasure. To him it seemed a wasted life but to others it was life itself. *One man's meat*, he said to himself as if justifying his stance on the matter. Here, on this spot, the carpet's pattern was long gone leaving the coarse, inner, criss-crossed threads like bleached sinews in a decomposing corpse. Turning, he considered the carpet's surrounding pattern. It was faded; brown diamonds ran diagonally to the edge of the carpet, a wrapped border that deliberately failed to reach the walls but was positioned away exposing a moatlike barrier of brown stained floorboards. In 1971, there had obviously been no need for a fitted carpet.

The room was quiet apart from the melodic, metronomic sound of the clock sitting on the mantelpiece; the only audible beat within the room's walls that signalled progress, a sense of future and time progression and yet here, within the four walls, the space showed none of that optimism. It was dead, without character or warmth, a time capsule separated from the outside world by the unnaturally yellowing net curtains and grimy glass. To the observer, the world was there but beyond the glass; if you listened carefully you could hear it, but it was a generation away.

On closer inspection, even the walls were tinged with a hint of brown. He allowed his eyes to follow the ceiling's edge. There the nicotine stains were darker, jaundiced. Occasionally the paper was trying to slough off the anaglypta separating, sliced, crisp and curling. It was hard to believe that once, for a brief period in time at least, this room had been the height of fashion. It was valued and loved but now in the semi-dark it seemed to be a mere shadow.

A siren, way off in the other world was barely audible but it prodded him briefly out of his introspection before he returned his eyes to the threadbare patch which seemed to have a greater connection than any part of the room to the person or persons who had occupied that chair. It made him realise what his next course of action had to be, after all, he was growing threadbare too, no longer the person he once was but that would change.

Removing a craft knife from his pocket he cut one of the exposed threads from the worn area. It now sat, curled and lifeless on his outstretched, gloved palm before his fingers closed over it. Within seconds it was safely stored within a plastic bag which he placed in his pocket. Walking over to the wall, he took a set of keys from a hook and left. He allowed himself one last glance back at the scene, his eyes lingering on a small picture on the far wall. It brought a smile behind the protective mask.

***

Owen went through the doors of Tennant's Auction House and stood by the staircase that ran in a majestic curve on either side of the stainless steel balustrades, contrasting with the marble and glass. This was not what he was expecting and he had whistled on first seeing the auction house building when they had moved off the road. He turned to Hannah and raised his eyebrows. "Bloody posh this, love. I thought these businesses were in old, damp churches or schools. This place must have cost a fortune. It's more like a stately home!"

Hannah sought advice and registered before going to look at the items on which they wanted to bid. It had been Julie who had asked them to bid on one specific item for her – the Herbert

Whone painting was perfect in many ways. She had handed the catalogue to Owen and assured him that Cyril would not be bidding on any of the items within the sale. It was as he flicked through the catalogue, more out of boredom than interest, that he saw the photograph of the small bronze statue entitled *Liberty.* He could visualise it standing on Cyril's desk, even if only as a paperweight. It was the title that made him think it inappropriate; after all, he was getting wed! Hannah suggested they look and if they liked it then the decision was made.

They went up the stairs and through to the viewing gallery. The Whone was the first thing they saw: a painting, a palette of greys depicting a Yorkshire stone farmhouse in the snow, set with what appeared to be a gas type lamp in the foreground.

"Bloody hell, that's as miserable as sin, would make more sense at a funeral than a wedding! Mind, have you seen his Theodore Major and that one by the Frenchman, Valette? He seems to like the dark and moody stuff, that's what comes with a life working in the shadow of life's underbelly."

"Stand back a bit and it might look better," Hannah suggested.

"Put a concrete wall between me and the painting and it'd be perfect." Owen grinned, stooped and kissed her head.

"When we have coffee, I'll tell you something about the artist that might make you understand the reason Julie wants it at any cost," Hannah replied squeezing his hand.

"She's not from Yorkshire, is she?"

Soon they found the bronze. It stood no higher than eight inches; a tag was wrapped around the lower part detailing the lot number. Owen did not know whether he was allowed to handle it so he asked one of the porters. He gently weighed it in his hands, turning it and holding it away. "That's gorgeous!" He smiled at Hannah. "We have to try to get that."

Checking her watch, she saw they had half an hour before the start of the sale and went into the café.

"So why the miserable painting?"

Hannah took out a piece of paper from her bag. "Herbert Whone was born in Bingley. His parents were both musicians and they encouraged him to play the violin. Getting any clues, detective?"

Owen nodded. "Go on, Sherlock."

"He studied in Paris after the war and then played at the Royal Opera House and then," she paused, "played for the BBC Symphony Orchestra and who else do we know who ...?"

"Cyril's mother."

"Strangely enough, on his retirement he lived in Harrogate. One of his paintings is in the Mercer Art Gallery."

"They may have played together. He might have known ..." he stopped. "I now see why she wants the painting."

Within the hour they had secured both items and were heading back home.

Chapter Three

Owen peered under the chair allowing his hand to run blindly along the cold of the laminate floor covering. He thought it had bounced off his shoe and then disappeared quickly from sight. It had to be there. Goodness Cyril had only given it to him the evening before with the firm instruction, 'Don't lose it!' He could still hear the order ringing in his ears. Pulling out his phone he turned on the light. It was clear from what he could see that this part of the flat was a stranger to the vacuum cleaner. Myriad masses of fluff, like miniature tumbleweed, moved with the strength of his breath. He found a fifty pence piece, a wrapped mint and a bottle top. He removed his jacket and was now totally prostrate, his head as close to the chair as possible. It could not be anywhere else.

"Hannah!" The high-pitched plea carried his desperate plight to another room.

***

Cyril checked his watch and shook his wrist before taking another glance. Butterflies bounced around his stomach as he looked in the mirror again. He had dressed far too early and he knew it. The noise from the bedroom made his nerves even worse. He turned and watched Wendy, his stepmother, appear. She looked amazing. The deep blue of the dress, the small contrasting bolero jacket and the hat screamed *wedding*. Cyril felt so proud. Walking over he bent and kissed her hand.

"You look beautiful, mother, simply beautiful." They stood momentarily, their eyes smiling and proud.

"Your mother is here in me, Cyril. I know it, feel it. When I close my eyes, I see her, hear her voice as I have done since the day she died. I've been proud to be your stepmother."

Cyril watched as her eyes closed and her hand gripped his. Her expression fluctuated, her mouth twitched as if she were in conversation with an invisible being. She lifted Cyril's hand and kissed it.

"She'll be with you today." She paused and smiled. "Believe me, we are closer to her than you think." She opened her eyes and the small tear swelled like a tiny jewel before bursting. Cyril raised his finger and caught it before bringing it to his lips.

"Bless you, as I now realise I have been blessed with having two mothers."

***

Hannah was standing to Owen's side.

"You're going to be filthy, look at your trousers!"

Owen brushed a hand down his thigh. "I'll sort that when I find the ring."

"Where did you say you saw it fall?"

"It struck my shoe and then just ... well ... vanished. I'm sure it shot under here."

Hannah ran her hand around the cushion of the chair until her fingers felt the metal's contrasting cold. It was the ring.

"It's here, on the chair." She held it out. "It's here."

Owen looked up. "Give it to me, Déagol," he whispered, changing his voice to give a more sinister edge as he sat up dusting himself off.

Hannah frowned but stepped back as she held out her hand to help him up, not that her petite size would help. Owen's build and strength would probably pull her over.

"It's not your birthday!" she answered, using the script she recalled from the film they had recently watched, as she handed him the ring. "You really need to take a lot more care. Leave it in the box and the box in your pocket." She held out the ring.

Owen took the ring bringing it close to his face before mumbling, "My precious," mimicking the film character before staring down at Hannah and then returning the ring to the box. "Frightened myself to bloody death, imagine if I'd lost it, Cyril would strangle me! Thank you."

"Well?"

"I found this fifty pence and this." He held up the wrapped sweet.

Hannah hung her head before pointing her hands to her clothing, her face growing red, more out of frustration than anger. "I neither care about the money nor the sweet. How do I look, for goodness sake? And if he doesn't strangle you by the end of today, I might."

Owen pulled a face realising he had been thoughtless. "Lovely, sorry, lovely, yes. Is it new?"

Hannah shook her head. "Bloody men!" She checked her watch and then moved to the window. The taxi was waiting.

"Give us all strength!" she mumbled, turning back to Owen who was perched on the arm of the chair, his head down. "Owen?"

"I was just thinking about Cyril." He looked across at her. "I don't think I know anyone else who has such inner strength and personal commitment in everything he does. Being divorced from his family for so long because of the courage of his conviction must have helped him become the person he is; the same strength and fortitude his mother had when she knowingly handed over her husband and then her son to her best friend, Wendy, knowing she was soon to die."

Hannah moved across and put her hands to each side of his face. "I know, I've talked to Julie about it. His mum and Wendy are truly remarkable women."

"I don't know whether I'll keep it together when they play *The Lark Ascending*. It's the strings and the thought of …" He did not finish. The sound of the taxi's horn interrupted him. "That's why her wedding gift is so right. It's as if it were meant to be."

"You'll be fine."

Cyril's mother had played the piece of music to Cyril as a child and he had requested it be played during the ceremony.

Owen smiled. "Yes, fine. I'll be fine and to think he asked me to be his best man, Hannah. Imagine, best man!"

"Remember how special *you* are in all of this."

***

Cyril was already standing outside the door of *The Boar's Head*, Ripley. He watched as a wisp of white vapour from his electronic cigarette played briefly in the warm air before vanishing like a dawn ghost without trace. It was as if it were exorcising the memories and the internal angst that had tormented him since that day, the day he saw his father with another woman. Finding her to be his mother's best friend, Wendy, brought confusion and uncertainty to his young mind. Only later did he realise that it was his mother's plan to ensure he grew up with a mother and a woman who would love and cherish both him and her husband. However, even the best intentions go astray, and as far as Cyril was concerned, the action had brought trauma and fear, especially where forming relationships with members of the opposite sex was concerned.

He smiled inwardly as a robin landed onto one of the wooden benches just to his side and began to sing. *Not the lark*

I was expecting but you'll do, he said to himself. He inhaled again and allowed the white vapour to leave his lips. It curled before forming a small yet almost perfect ring; it seemed so apposite, a sign and he naturally looked towards the heavens.

Wendy had nipped to the toilet; she seemed so nervous. He looked across at the church. Its ancient grey stone was the colour of elephant skin and equally as rough and it was nestled nonchalantly behind trees, the strength of its tower dominating the surrounding area. There was something special about Ripley; the quiet, the history, the birdsong. Positioned a few miles from Harrogate, church and castle offered the perfect wedding venue.

His peaceful reflection was disturbed as Owen's taxi turned off the road onto the cobblestones bringing a deep, rhythmic rumble. Cyril could see Owen's hand waving from the open window and he wondered just what sartorial elegance would greet him. Surely Hannah would have ensured that his shoes were clean, that he had a handkerchief and a new tie. At that moment Wendy appeared. Other cars began to muster and fill the car park. Cyril turned to his stepmother and smiled.

"Here we go, but before we do, I just want to say …" He paused as his hand went to his pocket, "I want to say thank you for a mother's love." He took out a box and held it on the palm of his outstretched hand before opening it. Wendy looked at the diamond and sapphire white gold bracelet before lifting her gaze to Cyril. She could not hide her surprise.

"I thought it would match your outfit and your eyes." He smiled.

Wendy paused before looking back at the jewellery. "My eyes aren't blue, Cyril, surely you know …"

Cyril put a finger to her lips. "The happy tears we will both shed will be the matching diamonds."

He winked at her. They both laughed. Cyril wrapped it round her wrist and then he kissed her.

"Morning." Owen's eagerness and enthusiasm were tangible. He touched Cyril's elbow. "Morning, Wendy. Well how are we both doing? Legs of jelly and stomachs a bag of bees?" Owen asked as he lifted his hand and slapped Cyril on the back before smiling at Wendy. "You've met Hannah."

Wendy smiled at Hannah.

"Come on, sir. We should go in."

"Cyril, Owen. Sir will do from tomorrow but for today, it's Cyril."

Owen could not recall a time when he had ever referred to his boss as Cyril. It had never been suggested and never presumed. Even when they had a pint together the one-sided formality remained. He felt a warm glow of emotion well up inside his huge frame as he wrestled the word to his lips. "Er … Cyril, sir ... we should go in."

Chapter Four

There was little sound but the lights from the several different glass tanks created unusual patterns across the walls and ceiling. Some tanks were covered, their own internal light, set to a timer, brought the change of the day. The strip light, mounted centrally within the room, was off and the blackout curtain closed permanently blanking the small window. In an upstairs room the radio was on and the shipping forecast could be heard. *Forties, Cromarty, Forth, Tyne, Dogger – south or south west four, five decreasing three at times. Showers decreasing – good occasionally moderate.* Apart from that and the occasional movement from one of the tanks, there was nothing. Even the outside traffic did not seem to penetrate. The room remained like this permanently, as if cocooned. Only in the morning things changed but the familiar smell remained. It was unusual, but not unpleasant.

The peace was broken as the door swung wide allowing a dagger of light to stab the darkness, silhouetting a figure in the open doorway. A hand found the switch resulting in the fluorescent tube spluttering into life with the occasional click and quickly illuminating every corner of the room. Carrying a highsided tray, the figure went to each vivarium in turn, made a selection from the tray and after lifting the lid or the cloth cover and lid, dropped in the item. Later, water bowls would be changed but initially, food was the requirement. Removing her thick gloves, she checked her watch. It was five thirty in the morning. The shop would not open for another three hours. She would, as usual, go back to bed.

***

The call had come into control at eight. The early morning carer had arrived at the house late; traffic had been at a standstill on Forest Road in Knaresborough, making it impossible for her to meet her appointed time. Nothing had been moving down Forest Moor Road. She was told that the police were investigating a fatal traffic accident and from what she could make out, it involved a young woman cyclist. Barbara had moved her car to the side of the road allowing the emergency vehicles through before being directed towards a diversion.

On arrival at her client's home, everything appeared normal. Retrieving the key from the safe mounted on the wall she had entered the compact bungalow. George would almost certainly be in bed. She moved through to the kitchen to make him a pot of tea and prepare the table for breakfast. The daily routine was the same: wash the few dishes from his evening meal, prepare his breakfast, usually cereal and toast and marmalade, then straighten the living room before nipping along to his bedroom to help him shower and dress. She checked her watch against the cooker's clock; she had skipped some of her routine as time was now against her.

Even though she had done this for the past four months, she failed to notice the subtle changes. The kitchen door was ajar, normally it would be closed, the curtains in the living room were not drawn, the glass that held his usual nightcap was not on the coffee table by the armchair and if she had looked, certain tablets in his daily medical box remained. Had she noticed any of these things, she might have been suspicious but the morning delay meant she had to work quickly.

It is never easy finding a client dead. It would not be the first time and she knew that it would not be the last, it was the nature of the job. *You can't work with eggs without finding the odd one broken in the box*, she had been told during her training and it had made her giggle before the gravity of the statement hit home. The thought of being alone in a house with a body, to be the first to find a corpse made her shudder. However, she quickly looked on the positive side of the job and tried to keep the cracked egg analogy separate from her daily work. After her first experience she seemed to grow a second skin and be able to detach the person from the lifeless body.

It depended too on the person. Somehow this was different and therefore difficult. She was fond of George and she knew that he liked her. He was kind and considerate, not like some. He often showed his gratitude by way of offering small gifts; the odd fiver now and then. It was usually in an envelope with the words 'Thank you' in spidery font. She always made a note in her private diary when this happened adding the date. She had also asked the others in the group if they too received similar gifts and it appeared that George was grateful for all the help he received.

She found him, sitting on the toilet, his pyjamas lodged around his calves, his head slightly to the right. The red line running from each nostril, the left seemingly stronger than the right before reaching the edge of his slightly gaping mouth, was shocking. The fresh blood still shone. It was then that she saw the twitch, the movement that caused her heart to bounce in her chest and for her to step back, an audible gasp escaping from her mouth.

"George?" Her voice was wavering and desperate, she moved closer to the old man. It was then, even in the dim light of the confined space, that she noticed the swelling to his right foot, it appeared blistered and bleeding, positioned just below the bottom of his pyjama leg. "George!" Leaning forward she touched the flaccid arm that hung to his side; the pale skin was old and wrinkled like translucent dried parchment but it was warm. She moved closer, noticing that one eye was partially open yet the other closed. Moving her right hand to the side of his head she gently moved it to the vertical and his lips moved, releasing a gurgle followed by what appeared to be a mix of blood and vomit.

Without hesitation she turned and ran back to the kitchen, picked up her phone and dialled the emergency services.

"Ambulance, please hurry ..." She went through the questions trying to keep calm. Had George been dead on her arrival she would have taken it in her stride as she knew the procedure, but to see him like this, neither one thing nor the other, brought with it a degree of panic. The room seemed unnaturally quiet as she settled herself. She knew she should have remained with George but she could not stay within the confines of the toilet. The amalgamated stench of vomit and faeces was too strong. She would keep the door open and listen for any further movement.

"Tea, Barbara, that's what you need, tea," she said out loud as if trying to reassure herself that she had done all that she could. Her hand was shaking as she brought the mobile phone down and placed it on the table. She knew that she could do nothing for George. "You're a carer not a nurse. You've done all you can." Checking her watch, she expected to hear a siren within minutes.

The small teapot was still where she had placed it and the kettle was full. She flicked the switch and sat at the kitchen table, the plastic floral covering cold and sticky to the touch. She stared at the phone. She needed to call her supervisor to advise her that she might not get to her next appointment. The day was rapidly going from bad to worse. It was then that she heard it, like water on a hot plate – surely the kettle had not splashed water onto the cooker and if it had, the cooker should not be on. She stood quickly to check and felt something under her foot; it was then that she felt the pain in her right calf.

Immediately she moved her hand down to the site of the discomfort only to feel the same agonising pain strike her hand. Straightening, she brought her clenched fist near her face. She screamed as she saw what had caused the pain. Two growing jewel-like beads of blood swelled, bursting and running to the end of her index finger and falling together before splashing in unison onto the linoleum tiles. What started as drops became a single stream. Barbara moved to the worksurface and grabbed the kitchen roll, swiftly wrapping the absorbent paper round the wound before pulling her hand close to her chest. Slowly, to her dismay, the wet blood began to bloom through the flowery patterned paper. Suddenly she felt her temperature rise but it was the pain in her calf that seemed to focus her mind as she squeezed her wrapped hand more tightly with more of the roll. It was then the nausea came, suddenly in waves and her head began to spin. Steadying herself she managed to sit and lean her upper body on the table. She heard the kettle switch off but darkness was quickly closing down her senses.

The sound of a distant siren played somewhere in her head and seemed to enhance the severe pain that she felt ravage her entire body; everything seemed to throb with the fast beat of her heart and she allowed herself to succumb to the darkness that brought some relief. She neither sensed nor saw the figure standing in the hallway who mimicked in a whisper the sound of a siren. The intruder watched as Barbara slipped into unconsciousness. Now was the time to move, collect what had caused the damage as carefully as possible and put it in a small sack. A quick check ensured that there was not a thread of evidence to bear fruit for Forensics, apart, that is, from two casualties. Moving quickly to the shed he lifted the lid of the metal box and removed what he needed before adding a thick thread from a plastic bag and allowing the snake to fall in. The lid was closed leaving a small gap and the latch partially locked. He was done and soon he would be gone. He could hear the sound of a siren. There was no more time.

***

The first responder's Skoda Octavia parked behind Barbara's car. Within minutes, Peter Holgate had pulled a large, medical bag from the boot of the estate vehicle. The blue strobe lights continued to flash, reflecting from the yellow strips that ran around the lower legs of his trousers. As he dashed up the path his extended hand banged on the door. He noticed that the key safe was open to the left of the entrance and the key was in the door. Turning it, he immediately tried the door. It opened. It was then that he saw Barbara, her upper body spread across the table. Blood flowed from her nostrils and the corner of her mouth. He also saw the kitchen roll, now almost totally red, tucked under her right breast. The report he had received was for an elderly male not a female and Pete's inner alarm sounded as he assessed the patient. There was a pulse and he detected that she was trying to move and speak. He signalled for her to remain still and stay just as she was before he investigated the other rooms in search of the original patient.

Seeing George and the similarity of their symptoms immediately alerted him. The attack by the nerve agent Novichok in Salisbury came immediately to mind and he called Control. He could clearly see that the victims had vomited, they were both showing signs of a distressed mental state. He smelled the air. From what he remembered from the training that had been put into place soon after the nerve agent attack, another key symptom was involuntary faecal incontinence but there was clearly no sign of that or at least not currently and not that he could detect. With the victim within the confines of the toilet it was to be expected and it was this that brought the uncertainty.

He called Control. "Just be aware. I'm going to monitor the patients but we could be dealing with an unknown hazardous substance. Operation Plus Five, I say again Operation Plus Five as a preliminary precaution. I've been present," he looked at his watch, "four minutes. Still feeling fine. I've activated my bodycam so you can monitor the room, patients and my condition."

The person receiving the call in Control repeated his instruction. "Operation Plus Five is now activated. Stay where you are and monitor the patients. We can see that your bodycam is live."

Operation Plus Five would bring the North Yorkshire Hazardous Area Response Team (HART) who, whilst co-ordinating with the resilience and specialist team, would organise the safe extraction of the victims before checking the site and identifying the reason for the patients' condition. If the first responder failed to show signs similar to those first victims whilst being in close proximity to the two casualties, the scenario might not be as serious as was first thought. However, a moderate exclusion zone would be brought into play and any neighbours immediately checked and quarantined.

Peter Holgate knew he had to voice his thoughts in order for those back at Control to gain as much information as possible. Both could have been affected by vapour or gas. He smelled her clothes and her hair but there was nothing. He continued to talk through his actions, knowing it was monitored on his chest cam, as he took hold of Barbara's wrist, feeling for her pulse whilst scanning her hand, particularly the nails. There was no sign of a struggle; there had been nothing out of place either so he doubted there had been a robbery.

Carefully he lifted her body and retrieved the hand wrapped in bloodsoaked kitchen roll. The paper was saturated and began to disintegrate as he unwrapped it. He could now inspect the running wound; coagulation was clearly not happening. He immediately mentioned the possibility of a joint suicide. He checked the teapot but it was empty apart from two dry teabags. The sirens still continued to be audible as they approached. It would not be long before the specialist HART team arrived and removed the casualties and himself. He checked Barbara's handbag for drugs but found nothing and then checked the bathroom cabinet. It contained just general items. However, the bedroom held a collection of prescribed medicines and he held each one and stopped at Warfarin. Only a few of the tablets had been removed from the blister pack and he doubted that they were the cause.

The door burst open and Peter Holgate faced two colleagues dressed in full hazmat suits. One went to Barbara whilst the other followed Peter into the toilet. They would see if they could identify the toxidromes within each patient and therefore make an accurate assessment of their needs. It was Peter who pointed to the wound on Barbara's hand. The wound to the leg was then checked.

"These are snake bites and that would account for the lack of coagulation." He immediately looked around the floor area, particularly to freestanding cupboards. "What about the other?"

"Similar wound to his leg, severe blistering," the call came back. "Snake bite, I agree."

Chapter Five

Cyril stood next to Owen as he stared at the stained glass that flooded the building with light, changing the pews, the stone columns and the floor to a mosaic of blended colour, the pattern both intricate and strong. Cyril's mouth was dry, his palms, sweaty. Even though the day was warm there was a welcome cool air in the church. The music from the organ seemed almost inaudible as he mentally wrestled with the magnitude of the occasion. Cyril knew Owen could sense his discomfort when he felt his left hand round Cyril's shoulder and pulled him a little closer.

"It'll be fine, sir, sorry, Cyril. She's not late, not yet at least. I'll marry you if she fails to show." He winked and smiled. "Kidding!"

Cyril looked up at Owen. "That's just what I was afraid of, Owen." Looking at the hand around his shoulders, he realised he had made the right choice in picking his best man. He rubbed his palms together and felt the perspiration.

The organ changed pitch and *The Arrival of the Queen of Sheba* filled every corner and crevice of the church. *George Frederic Handel* Cyril said to himself. He forced himself to keep looking at the vicar who now appeared before them, all smiles and reassurance.

***

Quinn looked at the report and then at his computer screen. The office was quiet, the majority being at Cyril's wedding. He had watched a live stream sent from April Richmond as Julie arrived with her father in the maroon Bentley but it had been only a glimpse. She would be back along with others on this shift. The job did not stop, not even for DCI Cyril Bennett.

***

The toxicology results had been convincing. Viper, all the evidence suggested. He quickly checked Wikipedia:

Russell's viper *(Daboia russelii) is a species of venomous snake in the family Viperidae[1], the family which includes the venomous Old World vipers. The species is found in Asia throughout the Indian subcontinent, much of Southeast Asia, southern China and Taiwan.[2] The species is named for Patrick Russell (1726–1805),[3] a Scottish herpetologist who first described many of India's snakes, and the name of the genus is from the Hindi word meaning "that lies hid", or "the lurker".[4] In Bengali this snake is called* ***chandroborha*** *since it carries lenticular or more precisely lunar marks all over its body. Apart from being a member of the big four snakes in India, Daboia is also one of the genera responsible for causing the most snakebite incidents and deaths among all venomous snakes on account of many factors, such as their wide distribution, generally aggressive demeanor, and frequent occurrence in highly populated areas.[5]*

Daboia russelli is commonly known as ***Russell's viper*** *and* ***chain viper****, among other names.[6][7]*

"Bloody hell!" He allowed a low, slow whistle to escape from his lips. "*The lurker* – responsible for more snakebite incidents and deaths – aggressive. The chain viper … chain. That's some enemy but why would it be in Knaresborough? Where is it now?" The report clearly stated that the house had been thoroughly searched. A call had gone out for people to be extra vigilant in the location but so far nothing had been seen. The autopsy had concluded that it was a bite and not an injected poison, so both victims had come in contact with *Daboia russelli.* But why? Quinn skimmed the report again. George had never even kept a cat let alone one of the world's most venomous snakes. He wanted to know more. In two minutes he was on the phone to the Liverpool School of Tropical Medicine as the centre for snakebite research but also a herpetarium holding a Russell's viper.

***

The music slowly faded as he sensed Julie move to his left. He could smell her, that familiar perfume, and his stomach tumbled like it did when he was excited as a child. Turning to look he was met by her warm smile. Owen looked at Hannah, who stood just behind the bride, before giving Cyril a small shove and they both moved closer to the bride and her father, Fred.

For Cyril, the next twenty-five minutes seemed a blur. Yes, he heard the hymns, he joined in but it was as if he were an intruder looking in. Was it really happening to him? Did he deserve such a special, warm and kind woman? His life only seemed to refocus when they were signing the register and within minutes the sound of a violin made the hairs on his neck stand … he felt Julie's grip squeeze his hand. He knew this music was coming, they had planned it as it meant so much, the music his mother had played to him throughout his childhood until her early death, but nothing could prevent the bittersweet memories returning. The strains of *The Lark Ascending* made him momentarily close his eyes and picture his mother, violin in hand, a smile on her face. "Cyril Vaughan Bennett, do you …?" The vicar's words came to mind as if spoken by his mother.

Vaughan, his middle name given in homage to Ralph Vaughan Williams, "I do!" he said out loud. "I most certainly do, Mother."

Wendy slipped a hand onto his arm. She knew just what he was going through at this crossroad in his life. He felt Julie squeeze his hand again and he was back, surrounded by the two females he loved most in the world.

As they walked down the aisle, smiling faces greeted them from either side. On reaching the main door Cyril laughed out loud. Four officers lined either side, their batons raised across the path followed by four members of Julie's team dressed in their scrubs. He stood momentarily and two rows of Police tape fluttered by the gate *POLICE – DO NOT CROSS* clear for all to see. There was a loud cheer and a number of photographers moved closer capturing the moment perfectly. Within ten minutes, Cyril and Julie were in the Bentley and her father drove them the few hundred yards to Ripley Castle.

***

April Richmond carried her heeled shoes and deposited them by her desk. Quinn looked up and smiled.

"Thank you for the live stream. Julie looked marvellous. Glad to get them off I see." He pointed to the red shoes.

April looked across to him and smiled whilst rubbing her feet. "Killing me. Never thought he'd do it. Men get to a certain age and they don't usually bother. Just shows how wrong you can be. Cyril looked like a lamb being led to the slaughter. I think I saw him smile at the end when he saw the guard of honour. Anything on the snake deaths?"

Quinn raised his eyebrows. "While you were all captivated by the charms of romance, I was searching out the truth. Ninety percent chance the toxin that killed both was from a Russell's viper, one of the worlds most venomous snakes. What we need to find out is why, and where the bloody thing is now. We've had no more reports."

"They're sure it was a number of bites, plural? ... Brew?"

"Yes, and please. The autopsy's clear. Barbara Perry was bitten twice, the right calf and on the hand whilst George Lyons was bitten only the once. I spoke with a Professor Victor Moodley."

April paused and turned to look at Quinn. "Who?"

"Moodley is an expert on these things. Tracked him down in Liverpool. There are a number of factors as you can imagine, not least the strength of the *envenoming,* I have a new word." He broke the word down into syllables. "Sounds less frightening than bitten don't you think?"

"And those factors are?"

"The age and size of the victim. What's interesting also is that they took blood tests from both patients and looked for certain factors that would determine their chance of survival from the outset and therefore the correct course of care. It was too late for George as he was dead on arrival. Barbara needed dialysis as the venom caused kidney failure and we know from the evidence when they were discovered that their blood wouldn't clot, it had become incoagulable. But what's exciting is this. The evidence suggests that he was bitten first, probably a couple of hours before the 999 call was received, whereas she, on the other hand, received both bites after the call." Quinn looked up at April and she could see the enthusiasm in his eyes. He was a keen copper.

"Exciting? Really? And your point is?"

He stood and turned to a whiteboard. There was an eagerness in the way he moved as he started jotting times down the left hand side.

"Let's say the call came in here." He pointed to the time. "So, we work from the point of the call as that's a definitive ... Barbara envenomed here." He turned and smiled. "Love that word! George here. Now, what's crucial to all of this is the fact that Professor Moodley mentioned that considering the samples taken, she would've been conscious for only about fifteen minutes after the first bite." Quinn marked it on the board. "So?"

April moved closer to the whiteboard, a clear frown etched on her face. "According to the evidence she made the call?" She looked at Quinn who nodded his head.

"If the science is right, yes. The bite occurred immediately afterwards. If that were the case, we add the time the paramedic arrived." He added that to the board. "He first believed it to be some kind of gas or biohazard but once his colleagues arrived according to the recording from his chest cam, they confirmed snake bites. He searched for the snake once he realised what he was dealing with, probably more out of self-preservation than curiosity."

"Forensics?"

"They found no snake."

"We need a more thorough forensic search of the house and gardens. Something's just not right. You mention the key factors for people dying from snake bites are linked to age and size of the victim so I get the effects on Lyons, but a young woman?"

"Well, the autopsy on Barbara suggests an unidentified heart condition. We checked her medical records and it was clearly never diagnosed. There's evidence of high blood pressure too."

"What do we know about George Lyons?"

Quinn drew a file from the tray on his desk and tapped it with his finger. "All here, what there is of it."

***

The wedding reception, although not large, was perfectly organised. Julie and Cyril had decided on only a few close friends and colleagues but the venue within the old castle itself was breathtaking. In his speech, Cyril had brought tears to the eyes of many as he spoke warmly about his stepmother and he even had a few kind words to say about his father. He believed and had observed that his speech did not need to be eternal to be immortal and sincerely hoped the Best Man's speech would follow the same principles. However, he had one card up his sleeve that he hoped would take a little wind out of his friend's sails and as he was about to sit after toasting Julie's parents, he returned to his feet mid-applause.

"Sorry, I almost forgot to mention that yesterday I received a phone call from a colleague and friend with some wonderful news. As some here will know, my best man and sergeant, DS David Owen, has heeded advice and made the necessary steps to progress to the next level in the force. It appears, from what my friend has told me, that he obviously spelled his name correctly on the necessary test papers and is now no longer Detective Sergeant Owen but Inspector Owen. I wanted to be the first to congratulate him and I ask you all to stand and raise your glasses to my best friend and colleague. Owen, we've always worked on the well-known police premise, *Job satisfaction – role not rank* – I know you're staying put with me so the job satisfaction flies straight out of the window." Cyril winked at the guests. "To Inspector David Owen."

Over laughter, the combined voice in the room repeated the words, "Inspector David Owen," followed by loud cheers. Cyril sat down and waited for Owen to make his speech; it would be a while.

***

Quinn thumbed through the notes. "George Lyons. Born 1936 in Hull. Evacuated as a child to Masham and then to a village closer to Hull – both in 1941. That's not unusual according to my research. Something to do with either over-protective parent or some kind of abuse. And we think that the sexual exploitation of minors is a recent phenomenon! Says here after bombs fell on the town many were evacuated. In 1945 he went back to Hull. First job was at the National Radiator Company but quickly left going to work at the Hull Knacker's Yard, I prefer the term abattoir." He paused as April put a mug of tea on his desk. "Married in 1968. No kids. She died in 1992."

"Knacker's yard is a tad different from an abattoir, Quinn. I believe it to be a place where animals, usually horses and dead farm animals are disposed of. How did she die?"

Quinn flicked through the page. "Doesn't say." He made a note to check further. "Knacker's yard closed in 1984 and he moved to Coalcut Abattoir, just outside Knaresborough, until he finished on health grounds in 1991. That would make him ..."

"Sixty-one."

"According to this, he's been on benefits ever since. Interestingly, Coalcut was known as *The Knackery* as they dealt predominantly with horses. According to what I've been able to discover, and I've not had long, they dealt with injured and unwanted animals."

"Is it still active?" April sipped her tea.

"Nope. Closed down about 2010. There was an investigation into the trading of horse meat to France, samples of which were later found to contain traces of bute. That's phenylbutazone, an anti-inflammatory drug. Some of the exported meat was destroyed but there's evidence to suggest that from France it went to different European countries. There was even talk that it filtered into the manufacture of beef-based products. Also, and I find this staggering, April, the industry went underground. There was still a market as people needed to get rid of horses and ponies cheaply and so isolated barns became knacker's yards."

"Was George Lyons involved in that?"

"No evidence but I guess it would depend on his needs at the time. According to the latest bulletins it's happening today out in the open, in the bloody fields. Last month farmers in North Yorkshire and Northumberland discovered a good number of their flock slaughtered and butchered. Professional gangs, quite possibly from Europe." Picking up his tea he looked directly at April. "Is it me or do you see the irony? A man who killed and butchered all of his life is killed himself by an animal. Okay, divine retribution would have been to see him trampled by a harras of horses."

There was a slightly awkward silence. April was impressed by the way Quinn went about his work. He was diligent, enthusiastic but also unsure and it was that uncertainty she liked. It made him question and look again and again.

April cleared her throat. “We need to find out more about George Lyons. We also want a closer look at his home. Has anyone questioned his neighbours?”

“There’s a brief note here as they were moved temporarily until the HART team knew just what had caused the injuries. All speak highly of him. There was genuine concern.”

“I’ll check with the duty Inspector to get a Forensics team back in. In the mean time I want as much information on George as possible. Pay particular attention to his wife’s death and I need a better understanding of his place within the community. His friends and his enemies … that’s if a man of his age has enemies.”

***

It took a while for Owen’s face to return to its normal colour and as he stood his knee caught the edge of the table leg causing two glasses of wine that were sitting near the edge of the table to fall. Fortunately, they contained white wine and neither glass broke. He went to retrieve them but knocked the table again.

“Leave them, Owen, before you create a domino effect,” Hannah whispered. “Just get the speech over, you’re a bundle of nerves.”

Owen removed some crumpled sheets of paper from his breast pocket and tried with shaky hands to straighten them. “I’m sorry but if truth be known I’d rather be arresting a bunch of baddies from the dark streets than standing here. You lovely people scare me more than most villains do.”

“You tell ’em Inspector!” a voice from a table to his left brought a ripple of laughter.

“Firstly, I want to say that if promotion had meant moving from the present team in which I now serve proudly, I wouldn’t have applied. Although we see changes to that team there is one constant, and my friends, that constant is sitting here; my boss, a man I’m proud to call sir every day but he’s also my true friend.”

Owen surprised many by his speech, a collection of anecdotes that brought both tears of laughter and moments of reflection.

Cyril and Julie's leaving in the Bentley was traditional. The clatter of tin cans on strings followed the car through the gates of the castle before turning towards the road. Julie laughed on seeing the police motorcycle. They would be escorted only a short way to the ring road but the gesture made both Cyril and Julie proud.

"It's been wonderful, Cyril. A fortnight away." She rested her hand on his thigh as they drove towards Harrogate.

Chapter Six

The talk within Harrogate police station had centred on the wedding and the fact that a number of people doubted whether Cyril could stay away for the duration of the honeymoon. He would use some spurious reason to get in touch if only by phone. Owen had felt nervous about looking after the department but he had been reassured that his concerns were only natural. As they said, he had done it in the past as a DS so as an Inspector, it would be plain sailing.

Quinn stood with Smirthwaite in Incident Room Three. The initial Forensics results had been added to the second board; the first being reserved for the personal details of the two victims.

"So how long had Barbara Perry been a carer for Lyons?" Brian Smirthwaite looked at the photograph of the young woman.

Quinn let his finger follow the list of key events on the board. "Just over four months."

"She can't be the only carer?"

Quinn shook his head. "No, we'll have completed interviews with the others in the team shortly but from the results so far they'd not a bad word to say about George Lyons. What's interesting with Barbara's appointment that day, and it may hold some relevance, is that she was late by some forty minutes. There was a cyclist killed at the junction on Forest Moor Road, young woman, teacher. All traffic was diverted as investigation work took place."

"If it were murder and it was planned then the killer would have believed that the carer would be well gone. She was normally there for ... what? Twenty minutes?"

"Twenty to thirty according to the Head of Care and I quote. 'Yes, he liked to chat. You must remember our clients may not see anyone during their day other than the carers we put in place, but it means these vulnerable people can stay in their homes, that is what they want and that is what George wanted.'" Quinn added a high-pitched, matronly tone and pulled a face as he read it. It brought a smile.

"Our killer would have known that the carer hadn't been as George was still in his pyjamas." Smirthwaite tapped his fingers on the board.

"Going back to collect the *weapon*? Took longer than planned? Interrupted by the carer? What if the snake had been released the day before, let's say for argument's sake, popped through the letter box ..." Quinn did not finish as Smirthwaite's laughter at the thought stopped him mid-sentence.

"Bloody hell, Quinn, where do you get this stuff? A snake would have vanished down a hole or gone in search of a mouse, and there must have been a few of those knocking about. How do you make out a snake could be a weapon?"

Quinn flushed bright red.

"If you want to kill someone, Quinn, you bring a gun, a knife and even a plastic bag. If you want to do it subtly you can scare the old bugger to death ... but a snake ... I can't suspend my disbelief that far, my friend." He laughed again. "Superman, flying cars, James Bond, yes, but this theory?"

Quinn raised a finger. "Un moment s'il vous plaît." His annoyance was evident as he moved to the nearest computer, tapped in his password before trawling for the file he required.

"Take a minute and read this. It might show you the holes, Thomas."

"Bria..." He stopped himself but not before realising he too was now red-faced. Smirthwaite reluctantly moved in front of the screen and started to read.

"These are reports stored at The School of Tropical Medicine in Liverpool. As you can see the Russell snake is neither the most aggressive nor is it the most lethal but it can be both of those. The first report tells of one being planted in a villager's hut and the snake, trapped within the confines, attacked the occupant. It was later discovered that the victim was owed money and the man in his debt had placed the snake in the belief that it might attack. There are three or four cases. What can't be guaranteed is death but what can be seen from studying the symptoms of this specific snake's bite and venom is that it causes traumatic and painful injuries. Depending on the age and infirmity of the victim it could result in death. Considering Lyons's age, it can be correctly assumed that whoever brought that snake to the house had murder on their mind."

Smirthwaite continued to read.

"If you also look at the initial findings reported at the crime scene the place was secure apart from the front door. That had been opened by the carer and also the paramedic had used the same entry point. The only other possible entry point noted was the toilet window, it was open and where was our main victim found? The toilet is separate from the bathroom and is literally the smallest room in the bungalow. Assuming the door was closed and the snake dropped in there ... man meets snake in the dark ... Bingo!"

"So how is the snake collected?"

"He or she knew the code for the key safe holding the key to the front door? Let's assume male for now?"

Smirthwaite nodded.

"Let's consider that he opened the door before popping the key back in and then closed the door. He would then look for the snake. Had Lyons closed the toilet door it would be there but if not, it could have been anywhere in the house. Had the snake been located quickly he'd have been gone, but my guess is that he was distracted. The problem came with Barbara's arrival."

"Do we have evidence of all of this?"

"Nope! We do, however, have two bodies in the morgue and the initial autopsy results tell us they both died from bites from a Russell's viper and as far as I'm aware this snake is not native to North Yorkshire. As you know, anyone keeping this type of snake has to hold a licence under The Dangerous Animal Act of 1976."

"Not supposed to breed fighting dogs but people do."

"True."

"I rest my case." There was a degree of uncertainty in Smirthwaite's voice as he asked the next question. "So, we've checked all the licence holders of such creatures, Quinn?"

"Within a fifty-mile radius and we have exactly ..." He let the pause linger and could see from Smirthwaite's face that he expected it to be none. "Three are registered licence keepers."

"Zoos?"

"No, two individuals and a pet shop owner."

"Your average man in the street can keep these things?" Smirthwaite whistled before walking back to the boards, his demeanour had changed within the last few minutes. "So, have we checked them?"

"All present and correct. None was near the crime scene on that day and, we can assume, neither were their pets."

***

The technique was well-rehearsed as the squidger forced the yellow wink to fly across the felt-covered table top before falling directly in the red, wooden cup. There was no indication of success showing on Leonard's face. It was expected, essential that he achieved one hundred percent accuracy every time he played. He went to the green, then the red. His mother glanced in and smiled; the net curtains shaded the sun and cast dappled patterns across the wall. He would be there until he failed to hit the target and then he would let her know with a cry of anguish that would shatter the peace, a stubborn recalcitrance that had developed the older he had grown.

Leonard looked too old to be playing this solitary game with such enthusiasm, just as he had yesterday, the day before, and would do tomorrow. At thirty he should be working; possibly teaching his own children the rules of the game – but a freak accident at birth had deprived his brain of oxygen and his mental and emotional capacity was locked at the age of seven. Strangely, the nurse had said that he had had his breath stolen but whichever way they expressed it the consequences were the same. To compound matters, being an accident, the result of a drunken fling, the father had left not long after the repercussions of the birth difficulties had been fully explained. His mother had raised him with a strength of love that could only be admired; it had been a struggle but one she had faced bravely. Penny, the young mother, had taught him the basics one would teach to any child. He could go to the toilet, wash and dress himself with little difficulty, use a knife and fork with great dexterity and although he could not tolerate children or dogs, he enjoyed the company of the elderly. However, it was inevitable that throughout his life he had been overly protected. His early venture into the care of a special school had been a disaster and his mother, although never completing her teacher training, had deemed it sensible to homeschool him.

Even now he was completely protected as they would always walk hand in hand. His anxiety was apparent as he shunned the contact of others, particularly the young. On seeing another child, he would be heard repeatedly shouting, "He's looking at me!" There would be genuine fear in his voice as this man, six feet tall, tried to hide behind his diminutive parent. As a consequence, his mother would pull his hat below his eyes to make them disappear, and he would calm and be led away. The local children found this both amusing and exciting if a little worrying and therefore trips out for Leonard were carefully planned.

Earlier in his childhood, his mother had been given a puppy by a neighbour and she believed caring for the dog would help his emotional development as he would take responsibility for feeding the animal. She also felt that he would enjoy its company and he would bond with it as it grew. However, to her amazement it had the opposite effect. He had been fine when the three of them were together and when the pup played, but when he was alone with the dog, she witnessed his cruelty for the first time. Within weeks the dog was returned and pets and animals were not brought into the house. Life quickly returned to normal and Leonard neither asked about the dog nor missed it.

Being alone or with the elderly was all he craved and tiddlywinks proved to be his sole achievement even though it was only witnessed by his mother and very close friends. There was one anomaly. Leonard had a fixation about the elderly. It had started when he visited his grandparents and it had continued until the last had been placed in, what his mother told him, was a retirement home. Karl, a gentleman they had met a while ago when walking back from town, had an apartment there. He had been kind to Leonard allowing him to stroke the dog he was walking. The building held a number of different private apartments, a restaurant, pool and a gym. The twice weekly visit for Leonard was special owing to the fact that the house was a short walk away and it was unlikely he would meet children on the journey. His mother was careful to ensure their visits did not coincide with the start and end of the school day as the Primary School was situated next door to the retirement home. She often noted that he would become agitated if he could hear the children in the playground during the school break but more often than not, he would be engrossed in the company of the elderly.

The lower floor of the retirement home was as familiar to Leonard as his own home. The resident's lounge and the television rooms were his favourites but he also liked to sit in the large conservatory that clung to the rear of the building; the pool and the gym were out of bounds. Over the last few months, Karl, a sprightly gentleman in his mid-sixties, had formed a particularly strong bond with her son after their early meeting.

Karl had smiled confidently, reassuring her before approaching Leonard. He bent and whispered in his ear. Penny watched with interest, confident that Leonard would stay put. She was amazed to be proven wrong. Leonard stood and followed Karl. It was what Karl kept in his apartment that attracted Leonard and very soon visiting him were the highlights of his week. These times gave his mother precious breaks where she could enjoy an hour away from him, when rekindling her love of intelligent conversation. They had also given Leonard newfound confidence.

It was during a Tuesday visit that his mother first witnessed a change in Leonard's behaviour. He seemed more eager than ever to visit, displaying an assertiveness she had never witnessed before. Normally she experienced his reluctance to leave the house, the pavements had to be checked just in case a passer-by might be close, but on this day, he led the way down the short path giving her little time to lock the front door. It was the same when it came to crossing the roads. He almost took the initiative. She released her hand from his.

"Leonard. Stop. Look at me!"

Leonard rubbed his hand and pulled a face she had seen so often but there was something in his eyes she had not noticed before. There was a coldness, an anger, similar to that she had witnessed when he had the puppy, but then the expression vanished as quickly as it had appeared as he mouthed the word, *sorry.* She lifted his hand and kissed it. "Come on. Your friend, Karl, will be waiting."

***

Karl had been sitting in the conservatory and the drizzly rain had greyed the windows. He read his paper knowing within the next ten minutes Leonard would arrive. He heard the fuss before he saw Penny holding Leonard's coat and hat.

"Good morning, Karl, although it's a poor morning as far as the weather is concerned. He'll not walk with an umbrella, as you can see from the state of his coat."

Karl smiled. "Let's get those wet things hung up. Where's he gone? Don't tell me, the toilet?"

"The third time! I don't know what you two are up to today but he's been like a cat on hot bricks all morning, wanting to know when we could leave."

Leonard appeared and waved at Karl as he hung the coats by the door. "Now Karl, please, now!"

"Go on, I need some peace. Thank you, Karl." Leonard's mother settled into the chair previously occupied by Karl and picked up his paper.

Within minutes they had arrived at Karl's apartment. "You need to sit and wait, Leonard." Karl had been firm with him from the outset and Leonard had responded, eager to see. From another room Karl brought a box. "You must not touch, only look. If you listen, and do as you're told, then one day you will be able to hold him. Do you understand?"

Leonard nodded and shook with excitement. His eyes never left the box. Karl removed the lid and Leonard knelt staring at the spider. He had never seen anything quite like it. He had seen spiders at home but never one so large. Giggling with excitement, he moved his hands to his mouth, his eyes like saucers; saliva trickled from the corner of his finger filled mouth.

"This is Tony, Leonard. Tony is a Chilean Rose spider. He can tell that we're here from sensing us, those hairs on his legs will pick up the vibrations. They are movements like this." He tapped his fingers on Leonard's hand. Karl never adjusted the way he spoke to Leonard where others did, some even changed the tone of their voice as if talking to a very young child. Karl picked it up and let it slowly move along his arm. Each leg deliberately made its move giving it a sinister appearance.

"Spider," he emphasised every sound. "Spider, Incy Wincy spider," Leonard said as he moved his fingers along the carpet, imitating the creature before moving forward in an attempt to touch it.

"Not this time ... soon, Leonard, soon. This is our secret." Karl put his finger to his lips. "Can you keep a secret? Can you, Leonard, I need to know that?"

Leonard frowned but then nodded. “I can keep a secret. I have secrets.”

“What secrets do you have, Leonard? Surely you can tell Karl all of your secrets.”

There was a pause before Leonard brought a finger to his lips and shook his head.

Karl smiled and patted his friend’s shoulder. “Good. Now remember, we’ve come to see Tony the spider. Tell your mum we saw Tony, not a spider. She might not let you come again; might not let you touch him or hold him and we don’t want that do we? It’s our secret.”

The following week Leonard handled the spider and his confidence grew. He counted the legs and learned the word *arachnid*. They watched a video of them in the wild. Leonard could not remember being so excited to see anyone as much as meeting up with Karl.

“I have more surprises, Leonard. More secrets but not just yet.”

***

John Gornall had been on edge all day. It was his only day off in the week and what with the need to shop early, friends calling for dinner and builders expected later in the week, he had a good deal on his plate. The intermittent rain did nothing to enhance his mood. One stop he needed to make was to pick up a prescription. The chemist on King Edward’s Drive was always convenient. The parking spaces along the road were full so he pulled down Albany Road but struggled as a red Vauxhall was parked on double yellow lines. To his amazement it had not received a parking ticket. He shook his head in disbelief. *No coppers on the street and now no wardens. People just do want they want,* he said to himself under his breath.

The car was still there when he returned. On passing it he noticed an elderly lady using a mobility scooter crossing the road, and he stopped to make sure she was safe and able to get up the kerb as the Vauxhall blocked the lowered edge to the pavement. She moved down the road to the next one.

He smiled. “You’ve faced inconsiderate drivers before?”

“Is it yours?” Her tone was pointed and critical.

“Certainly not. If I parked on yellow lines, I’d have a ticket on the windscreen before you could say Jack Robinson.”

“Been there two days.” She slipped past him and disappeared around the corner.

John wiped the mud from the rear registration plate and took out his phone. He intended to report it to the council but soon changed his mind as he had to register on their website and then log in. He would do it later.

Chapter Seven

The Parking Enforcement Officer left his moped just behind the Vauxhall. The car had already been checked and it was neither taxed nor insured and probably did not have an MOT. He tried all of the doors; it was locked. There was no damage to the locks or the windows. Whoever had parked it must have had a key. It had been reported stolen a week before from the back of a farm near Bedale. The number plates had been covered with mud, probably the reason that ANPR had not discovered the vehicle on the road. Checking the car's history, it was registered to a Samuel Peterson of Drover's Cottage who according to the DVLA had owned the car from new. He tagged the car with two large adhesive posters to show that the Police had acted and left.

Samuel was seventy-six, a retired farm labourer. The car had been left at his employer's farm. He had decided to stop motoring when it needed road tax, a test and insurance, so to find it gone had been a mixed blessing. Not hearing from the police after five days, he believed it to be burned or broken up. However, that was short-lived as the police had telephoned to inform him that the car had been located. He had been given a collection address and a warning about not taking the vehicle on the highway until it had been taxed and insured. Samuel had slammed the phone down in disgust, not because it had taken so long to find, but because now he would have to put his hand in his pocket.

Within an hour of receiving the call there was a knock at the door.

"Mr Peterson?"

Samuel was a little taken aback. "Aye. How can I help?"

"The police have located your stolen car."

"I know, they rang. I need to get it collected. No tax nor nowt see, so I can't drive it. I could do with it scrapping to be honest. Never use it like."

"That's why I'm here. I work for a company called *Car Returns*. We specialise in returning stolen vehicles. Normally our fees are covered through your insurance but I've been informed that your car is uninsured."

"Don't use it as I said." Samuel nodded. "So how much?"

"£200 in your case, Mr Peterson."

"It's not worth that … it can go for bloody scrap. I'll ring 'em. They'll give me £100 and I'll be done with it. So, you've wasted your time coming here. Do you always wear gloves when it's warm?"

"Dermatitis unfortunately. I cover them with cream and then wear the gloves. It helps. The car is locked but undamaged as far as the locks and windows are concerned. Do you know how it was stolen without a key being used?"

"Aye. I leave the key in the barn. Likely whoever took it, found it."

"Do you have a spare key?"

Samuel nodded. "On the hook."

"When the scrap people you are going to call come, they may need it. You might get more for it if there's a key. May I use your toilet?"

Samuel pointed the way before looking at the hook. There was no key.

"Bloody key's not there. It's always bloody there!" he grumbled to himself, lifting his cap and scratching his head.

Within minutes the visitor was back. "Sorry did you ask me something?"

"No key. Should be there. I'll be beggered, it's always there!"

"You probably put it somewhere else. I'm sorry to trouble you. Good luck with the scrappers. Please remember you have a short time to retrieve it."

Samuel escorted him to the door.

"Without a key it will be worthless." He paused at the door and turned. "I have a friend who could help. I know he would give you the hundred, if that's what the slaughtermen of the car world will offer for it. He'd pay now." He chuckled. "I know that for sure as I have the money with me."

"What? Slaughtermen? What are you on about?" Peterson flushed a little and stepped back, unsure as to how he would proceed.

"The scrap men, Mr Peterson, the scrappers, the killers of cars. You just sign over the V5 registration document and ..." he fished in his pocket and brought out some cash. "One hundred pounds and the car's off your hands."

Samuel thought for a while as his eyes focused on the money being counted. "One hundred and twenty and it's a deal."

There was a pause as the stranger stopped counting and was about to return the cash back into his pocket. He looked at Peterson and waited. "Okay. Providing you have the documents to hand. I can't be here all day."

***

The Forensics Officer moved to the back of the garden to inspect the arched, corrugated metal shed that was slowly being strangled by ivy. A common approach path had been established by the CSI and had been clearly marked along the overgrown, crazy paved flagstones. The paint-peeling door hung twisted at the top hinge, causing it to pull away from the frame. The edge of the metal surround was simply a filigree of rusty, jagged edges; how it remained standing was anyone's guess. To her surprise the door opened freely, breaking the silence with a deep screech. It made a shiver run down her neck and reminded her of finger nails running down a blackboard. She giggled behind the mask; it brought back memories of her school days.

The inside was dark but the large hand lamp she held powered light into the furthest recesses. The entry had been checked previously and the only partial print found had been lifted earlier. Internally it was a mish mash of rubbish. A spider hurriedly crossed a web that spanned the upper doorway. From what she could see, whatever was no longer used in and around the house, but might one day come in useful, was stored in here – if *stored* were the correct term. Her father had the same mentality with his garage; he would throw nothing away. The job was going to be like archaeology, but on a vertical scale, as she progressed from the front to the back. The oldest objects would probably be at the back unless of course, now that it was full, items were just tossed in. Whatever the case, it was going to take some time to sift through. She had placed the lamp on the shelf and tapped together her gloved hands. "In for a penny," she whispered.

It was the unusual sound breaking the silence that first attracted her attention, a brief and almost inaudible *sizzle* that seemed to emanate from somewhere near a metal box that was sitting on one of the cluttered shelves to her right. She paused and listened but heard nothing. On closer inspection, the box appeared to have been touched recently, many of the other items along that same shelf were festooned with cobwebs and dust, but this, to her experienced eye, contradicted that. She was confident that it had recently been moved. Bringing extra light and the camera, she began to photograph the object and its surrounds. Even though there was a web attached she knew that could have been woven within the last twelve hours. Carefully, with her colleague now next to her, she moved closer.

The box had the appearance of an old green ammunition tin. There were markings on the lid next to a thin metal handle but they were worn, scratched into the surface and from the angle they viewed it, illegible. However, along the side she could see the initials GL painted in white. "George Lyons," she said out loud. The lever lid catch to the front was not fully locked down leaving a small gap along the front edge. She took a mirror from her box and leaned forward whilst extending its telescopic arm. Once positioned, she angled it close to the narrow gap. Fine LED lights positioned around the mirror shone through the fine gap. Tilting her head, she saw it.

"Snake!" she squealed. "It's in there. Bloody hell, bloody hell, bloody hell ... big one ... hate snakes." She moved backwards towards the Forensic Manager who was standing in the doorway.

When she had calmed down, they discussed their next move. The folding handle on the top of the ammunition box was upright.

"If the clasp-type lock holds, we can lift the box out into a secure space and get the contents removed." She deliberately did not say the word *snake*.

Collecting an extending gripper, the manager moved and locked onto the handle before taking up a forward stance. He checked the weight and looked to see if the lid would hold on the unsecured latch. It did.

"When I have this outside, I'll secure the lid temporarily and swab it. Check your phone for the RSPCA, they, I know, have a snake specialist and we'll need them here ASAP. Let them know it's probably a Russell's Viper if it's the same one that killed Lyons. Mention also that some cruel bastard's locked it in a tin, it might be relevant as we need to keep it and us safe."

The CSI frowned on removing her phone. Some guy uses a snake to kill and her colleague has sympathies for the snake.

Once the call was made, they were advised to cover the box with a ventilated container and leave well alone as it would be fine. Snakes only eat once a week.

On completing the task, the manager lightened the mood. "When I was a kid, I kept a grass snake for a couple of years. Bloody thing escaped more than once but I remember I lost it for days. It was only by chance we found it. My mum flippantly said there could only be one place it could be as we'd looked everywhere; she was right, it had managed to get inside the piano. Me and my dad had to strip the antique to pieces to get it out. As you can imagine after that episode it had to go. I swopped it for a pond yacht."

"The piano or the snake?" she giggled.

"Both. The piano was ruined."

"Pond yacht? For a piano and a snake? Doesn't make sense."

"That small boat nearly cost my brother his eye but that's a story for over a beer."

***

Quinn put down the phone and walked over to Smirthwaite's desk. Brian looked up.

"Apparently one of the carers had a visitor during their time at Lyons's house – Tuesday morning he thinks it was. As the carer was getting ready to leave, they noticed someone try the door and as the carer was at the door, he opened it to be confronted by a bloke in his mid-sixties. Said he was just checking on George as he was an old friend. The carer asked him to wait and went to inform Lyons but as they both returned to the door the bloke was nowhere to be seen."

"What did George say?"

"Said it was a pity it wasn't a lady friend and that the carer had been working too hard and needed a holiday. Made light of the situation."

"We need a full description, Quinn."

***

The smile spread across Samuel's face as the stranger agreed to his price. He had done well.

"V5 and everything you have for the car and," he paused, looking Samuel directly in the eye, "when you've collected all that I've a simple question for you to answer."

Samuel moved to the hallway and began to rummage in the understairs cupboard. He was almost invisible apart from one boot. Pulling a cardboard box towards the entrance door, he settled in the confined space before blowing the dust away from the surface. He immediately began to cough.

"Are you alright, Mr Peterson?"

"Fine."

There was a rustle of papers and the occasional cough.

"Bingo!" he spluttered and started to move out backwards.

"Hang on. Wait. Pass them to me first." A quick check showed they were the documents. "Now for that question before we go any further." Samuel stopped, turned and something cold touched his temple.

***

Once the snake had been removed the box could be searched, further swabbed and checked. Inside was a small plastic bottle of oil, some brass caps and a thick piece of old thread. It was all photographed, measured and catalogued.

"Blank cartridges. Old too. Look like .22. Possibly a starting pistol." He held up the bottle against the light. "Looks fine enough for gun oil."

"It is, after all, an ammunition box."

"No gun though, unless it was eaten by the snake, making it twice as deadly!" The Forensic Manager winked and smiled. His colleague pulled a face. The items were bagged and tagged and the rest of the shed was searched.

Chapter Eight

Control received the call at 14.23 and April Richmond and Quinn were parked outside the cottage within the hour. The familiar blue and white tape fluttered, strung loosely between various vertical objects. A single police officer stood by the gate and a CSI van was parked close to the cottage. Quinn noticed a photographer, probably from the local paper.

"They're like vultures, ma'am. They must communicate with death in a similar way. They find it first!"

April laughed. "You learn quickly, my friend."

Light flecks of rain hit the windscreen immediately changing her mood. "Perfect, talk about timing, Quinn. It'll make the CSI's job interesting if they're hoping for evidence outside." As she spoke a pop-up gazebo-type structure was erected between the gate and the porch.

When they left the car, the farm smell was particularly pungent. They checked in with the officer on the gate before donning overshoes and gloves. Both ducked beneath the tape and walked on the step plates that led to the open front door. The Forensic Manager looked across and signalled. It was clear from the sign that he needed two minutes. April scanned the room taking in as much information as possible. Most of the activity was out of view in the hallway.

She stared at the clock on the mantelpiece and heard the rhythmic tick, each sounding tired and slower than a second, complementing the look of the room. The space seemed claustrophobic, the yellowing walls and the heavy net curtains appearing to keep natural light at bay. "Darkness and dirt make good bedfellows, Quinn."

"Picture missing off that wall," Quinn announced. "These walls have neither seen a duster nor paint for a few years. There's been some smoke and nicotine deposited too, enough from a lifetime of smoking!"

April had not noticed the picture; she had been too focused on the clock. She turned in the direction of Quinn's finger and saw the albino silhouette stain on the wall where it had obviously hung for many years. She was soon interrupted by an introduction.

"DI Richmond if I'm not mistaken?" The manager smiled, his voice declaring his uncertainty. "I remember you from that case with the bloody remembrance crosses. Strange affair. Anyway, I digress. The body, male, we know to be a Samuel Peterson, seventy-six years old. He's lived here for approximately twenty-five years. Farm labourer and still does a bit, or did according to the cottage's owner. He found the victim at about 13.00 but he can't be accurate as to the exact time. He was positioned under the staircase, partly in the cupboard, his head resting on a damaged cardboard box. First responder has been and gone. Didn't request an ambulance. The farmer who found him thought he'd banged his head badly when coming from the cupboard."

"The police doctor?" enquired April whilst trying to look further into the hall way.

"Requested immediately by the paramedic. She's with the victim now. As you're aware, Samuel has been shot. Unusual weapon too."

April waited as the CSI laboured the point as if to create tension. Both she and Quinn stared in anticipation.

"A captive bolt gun." Collecting a camera from a box on the side, he flicked through until an image came on the small rear screen. "It's a *Cash*, probably fifty years old. Serial number has been removed so we can assume it was stolen or held illegally. It was filed away a number of years ago and may well have belonged to Peterson. Many farms at one time killed their own animals but now they're no longer permitted to hold and use this type of weapon but that doesn't mean to say they don't have them. It's either a .22 or a .25. We'll know shortly."

Within minutes the doctor came through from the hall, her mask, head covering and safety glasses still over her face. Sweat gleamed in droplets on her forehead. She pointed outside. Quinn and April moved onto the path. The cool air had an immediate effect on the doctor as she pulled the mask below her chin and lifted the glasses. She rested her case on a step plate.

"Goodness me it was warm and tight under the stairs, glad to breathe fresh air."

Quinn breathed in and frowned. He did not consider the air particularly fresh as all that filled his nostrils was the pungent odour of manure.

"Time of death about 11. Possibly suicide using a humane killer, a captive bolt gun. The gun is to his side. The bolt destroyed a considerable part of the temple and forehead area and death may not have been swift nor immediate. It could have been slow from the evidence I've collected. Suicides can be like that. He had obviously gone under the stairs for something and it can only be assumed it was the gun. This one fires using power load blank cartridges so they make a bang but considering the location of the body within the property and the house itself, nobody would have heard it but it's worth asking. The other type of captive gun, as you may well know, is fired using compressed air … they're relatively silent." She picked up her bag. "I'll have more for you once we've had a much closer look. Will anyone be joining me or my colleague? If so, I'll send the details."

Quinn looked at April and pulled a face.

"DI Owen may well. He seems to have grown somewhat accustomed to the more involved area of your work, doctor."

"DI and not DS? He's done well. Pass on my congratulations. Must fly." The doctor was careful how she passed and made her way to the gate. She turned and called. "Forgot to ask. How was the wedding? Who'd have imagined it. Never thought Flash would marry. I tried to snare the bugger but … another lamb to the slaughter!"

April raised a thumb.

"An old flame! Who'd have thought it? Must have been close to know him as Flash. Come, Quinn, we need to have a long chat with the farmer. Do we have a name?"

Quinn smiled. "We can walk, five minutes tops or we can drive."

"I need the air and the rain has stopped."

"Why do people say the stench of the farmyard is good for the appetite? Destroys mine!" Quinn replied in all seriousness.

***

The red Vauxhall started first time. He tossed the picture from the cottage wall onto the passenger seat. He would now stick to the side roads and avoid any unnecessary contact. Checking the rear-view mirrors, he moved off from the double yellow lines. A large pool of engine oil had collected where the car had been sitting. Things were going well for him.

"Two questions, two answers, two dead – one hundred percent. Go to the top of the bloody class."

Chapter Nine

The farmyard looked deserted as they walked through the gates. A building constructed of breeze blocks and rust-patterned corrugated sheets faced them. There was a general air of neglect. Two border collies barked repeatedly, the sound amplified by the metal sided building. Quinn and April paused, ensuring the dogs were secure. Reassured, they watched momentarily as the dogs paced within the confines of the large mesh kennel deliberately positioned to be facing the gate. Each dog was eager to get closer to the strangers. Chickens moved along the edge of the barn, ignorant of the intrusion and commotion as they scratched the dampened soil before pecking the soft ground. April walked over to the battered Toyota pick-up and made a note of the registration. The curtain in a window of the whitewashed farmhouse moved to one side; a face appeared briefly. Seconds later the door to the farmhouse opened and a woman appeared; her facial expression was firm and yet puzzled.

"Can I help you?" Her voice was as sharp and threatening as the dogs.

Quinn already had his warrant card ready and held it up for her to see. "Sorry for this intrusion. Mrs Bostock?" He waited to see the recognition dawn on her face as she read the card before continuing. "DC Quinn and this is DS Richmond. I think you know why we're here."

She took the warrant card and held it closer before inspecting the photograph and then Quinn. "Look too young to be in the police, lad. You sure your mother knows you're out?"

Quinn was about to answer when he noticed the hint of a smile.

"Come in, DC Quinn. Is she coming in too? Tell her the pick-up's not for sale." She winked. "Ted's in the kitchen. All the kerfuffle meant he's missed his lunch and he's running late. He's not happy, mind he never is these days what with Brexit and grants, environmental issues. I could go on!"

Quinn waved at April. "Bark's worse than her bite. Quite a sense of humour actually. Think she likes men in uniform." He raised his eyebrows and chuckled.

"You're not in uniform, Quinn, and she's old enough to be my mother!"

"Sorry, yes. Good point."

"He'll only be a minute, got sheep to check in the top fields what with all this rustling going on. The other week our neighbour had four slaughtered not half a mile from the farm. Brass necked these people and probably dangerous too. I shouldn't say this but I will, you people don't do much. You can't even find Peterson's stolen car for goodness sake … mind, in my opinion it's better off not being found. Bloody eyesore. I'm making him a brew, do you two want one? Sit in the lounge." She opened the door to the left of the hall.

"As you can imagine, Mrs Bostock, we have much to do … cars and killers to catch." He could not hide his sarcasm. "Thank you but no."

At that moment Ted Bostock came in, mug in hand.

Bostock recalled the discovery of Peterson's body in a matter of fact way. There was neither empathy nor sorrow in his tone considering they had known each other for twenty plus years.

"Why did you go to the cottage this morning, Mr Bostock?"

"Rent. It was due last week and he asked for a week's grace. Always skint – that's why his car was off the road most of the time, cluttering my bloody yard. Liked a flutter on the horses. Always said he had a system but they all say that. Never see a poor bookie but know plenty of skint gamblers. Hard worker though and was frightened of nothing or nobody."

"Just explain how you found him please, Mr Bostock."

He emptied his mug and wiped his mouth on his sleeve. "The cottage door was open when I arrived; open as in ajar which seemed strange as it had been warm but not that warm and so I called his name. There was no answer so I took a look around the outside first, thinking he might be in the garden or yard. There was nobody about. I went in. His door was never locked and if it were, the key was always under the mat. There was nobody in the kitchen so I went through into the hall. I could see his legs sticking out from the understairs cupboard. It was dark under there but I could see he had some blood on his head and neck and I thought that he'd banged his head. There was a pulse and he seemed to hear me, but didn't respond. His left foot was constantly twitching. Said nothing. You hear all these things about strokes and the like. I immediately rang for an ambulance. Only after I'd made the call did I see the bolt gun. I knew money was tight but not enough to ..."

For the first time April saw some emotion that might be interpreted as guilt.

"If I hadn't pushed for payment he might still be here." Bostock looked at each officer in turn as if searching for some consolation. None came. "He wasn't dead. Those things are meant to stun a beast but with a human? When the paramedic arrived, I knew by then that he was dead. His foot stopped moving. There seemed to be nothing."

"Did anyone take your prints and a DNA swab to eliminate you from the enquiry that's taking place?"

Bostock nodded.

"Have you seen the captive bolt gun before or did you know of its existence?"

"No, don't know why he'd have one. If we ever had to dispose of an injured animal or one of the dogs, we wouldn't involve the vet. We'd shoot it, put it out of its misery, like."

"And simply bury it?"

"It's all classed as fallen stock. You're not supposed to but you can with horses. But we do bury dogs and the very young lambs. The main animals over a certain age have passports and have to be accounted for as they'd be entering the food chain. What with mad cow disease and foot and mouth you have to follow strict rules for everyone's sake and that's that. No, the big stuff doesn't stay on the farm. We'd call for the carcass to be collected. That's usually a Thursday when they come so I wrap it and leave it in a certain spot by the road, in a container to keep wild animals from eating it. Then either the knacker comes or the maggot farm, we just let them know. The animals are tagged so they know the history. If we had to destroy a beast and we needed to do it quickly we wouldn't fanny about with a captive bolt. I'm surprised Sam did as he has two guns, a .22 and a shotgun, in the house."

"Do you know where he kept them?"

"They should be in a gun safe and they should be registered but Sam was old school. Probably under his bed or even in the boot of hi ..." Bostock paused, realising what he had said. "Something else, too. He knew how quick a shotgun would be if he wanted to top hisself. A bolt gun really only stuns the beast. You then have to pith it ... you stick a rod through the hole you've made and jiggle it about like. Bloody hard to do to yourself after you've put the bolt gun to your head!"

Quinn stood, made his excuses and left. The thought of pithing turned his stomach but his immediate excuse was that he needed to find the guns. He would run back to the cottage and no matter what the aroma he enjoyed deep gulps of air. They needed to discover if the firearms were there. The same officer stood by the gate and smiled on seeing Quinn, lifting the tape in anticipation. The door was still open and he was greeted by the CSI Manager.

"Two guns are reportedly stored somewhere in the house. Not sure if they'll be in a gun safe. The farmer suggested looking under the bed!" Quinn pulled a face, spread his hands and raised his shoulders to convey his thoughts on the matter.

"We have one shotgun positioned on the top of the kitchen cabinets near the door. Box of cartridges too but as yet we haven't seen another gun."

***

Bostock showed April to the door. "Thank you. We may need to chat again, Mr Bostock, but at the moment we'll leave it there." She smiled but merely received a nod in response.

"Give us notice. Can't be hanging around waiting and then you don't turn up."

She walked across the cobbled yard; the dogs protested at her presence but soon were silenced by Bostock and she heard the door slam.

"Christ, what did he go and do that for, the daft bastard?" It was as if he were talking to himself but he looked directly at his wife. There was silence.

"I should have told them, Ted, it might be vital."

"And it might not. You just keep that mouth of yours closed. He was a daft bastard at times, Peterson. I warned him, no I told him but he had to do everything his way. You sow the wind and reap the whirlwind. How many people do we see around the farm and the farm lanes? We're keeping a bloody eye out for these bloody rustlers so we take note of more now than we normally would. You said he seemed nice enough."

Belinda Bostock wiped her sweating hands on her apron. "He did but ..." She paused again. "He was asking for Peterson. Said something about his missing car. I thought he was from the police, a plain clothes officer even though he seemed too old so that's why I checked Quinn's ID thoroughly and whatever her name was, but that was before all of this happened, his death like. Could he ...? Was it just as you told them, Ted?"

"That's for me to know and them to find out. I'm off checking the top fields so just keep that shut." He touched her lips. "Especially when you're having your hair done!"

She nodded, knowing she often repeated things there she should not. She could not help herself.

***

As Quinn left Peterson's, he saw April coming up the road. They met by the car. "We'll wait for Forensics to do what they do," April suggested. "Need to find that missing Vauxhall."

"Anything else from Bostock?" Quinn asked as he opened the car door.

"He told me that they'd use a vet for most animals that needed putting down and it was only in extreme circumstances that Peterson would do it."

Quinn looked across. "If they could save money, I'm sure they would take the cheaper route."

"You went a funny shade in there. Were you alright?"

"I'm a sensitive soul, ma'am."

"For a man who'd just found an old colleague and tenant dead from possible suicide, he wasn't really in a state of shock. Yes, he showed some distress but to come in and eat lunch especially after seeing what he'd seen … there may be more to him than meets the eye."

"Butchers, ma'am, they've a switch inside their heads that must be attached to that part of the brain that controls compassion, sensitivity, empathy and they can distance themselves. How else could you spend part or all of your day killing, surrounded by the sound and smell of death and then go home without a second thought and eat your tea? Farmers have a degree of that too but in a different way. They care so much for their animals they don't want them to suffer and can, if necessary, kill without hesitation, not for killing's sake but out of compassion. Maybe his switch isn't as general as the others and that's what Bostock did, he just flicked his particular switch."

Quinn said nothing else for a moment before turning to April. "Bostock or Peterson?" He then turned and stared out across the fields and watched the sheep clustered near a large oak tree.

April observed his expression. Maybe Quinn had a point.

***

DC Harry Nixon stared at the collected snippets of information held to the whiteboard by small, coloured magnets. It was clear Cyril was not on the case as there was no logic to the colours. He would have ensured that separate information or photographs would be held by the same coloured magnet. He studied the photograph of the thick strand of material that had been found in the box containing the snake. It was set against a small ruler. Beneath was a description: *Warp or weft from an Axminster carpet or rug. Testing for colour shows leaching of brown dye – dye used pre-1973. Probably from a worn area. Both ends cut using a sharp knife.* He tapped the photograph and made a note before letting his gaze fall on the next image, the collection of five blank .22 brass cartridges. These were small, crimped at the end and badly tarnished as if they had been in the box for some time.

He made a call to a friend in firearms and after pleasantries posed the question concerning the effectiveness of blank cartridges after long storage. He was amazed to learn that ammunition did not really have a shelf life as it was dependent on how it was stored and could realistically last decades – a closed, airtight ammunition box kept in the dry was as good as it got.

"How dangerous are they as they are, Spud?" Nixon used the man's nickname.

"People have died putting a gun containing a blank to their head. The superheated gas is forced down the barrel. There's the famous case of the actor putting a Magnum to his head thinking he was safe and that he was having a laugh. The pressure penetrated his skull sending fragments of bone into his brain. Harry, never underestimate the power of gunpowder."

"Thanks, Spud. I owe you a beer."

Nixon carried on reading the forensic results taken from the container. It appeared that two further cartridges had been stored, owing to the cylindrical staining to the bottom of the box. It had also held a larger item and there was clear evidence of minute rust and oil deposits, deposits that matched the oil in the small bottle, plus some traces of hardwood fragments found to the sharp lip of the box. It had once held a weapon of some kind but what and when it was removed was at this stage still unknown.

***

The CSI had made pleasing progress at Peterson's house. The second gun had not been located but an additional box of cartridges had. If he owned a gun safe it certainly was not within the four walls.

During the routine close inspection of the floor their attention was drawn to the worn patch of carpet situated between the chair and the television.

"This carpet must be donkey's years old. It's certainly like my granny used to have. She too had a gap around the edge and most weeks, until she was well in her eighties, she polished on her hands and knees." The CSI looked at her colleague who took a few samples from the balding patch before slipping them into plastic envelopes, noting the photographic reference and the room co-ordinate.

"This character was nothing like your granny. You could plant spuds in the crap that's around the edge of this room. Never seen a brush nor broom for some time. Mind you, that helps us."

***

Owen put his head round the door to Cyril's office. It seemed to hold his very DNA, and in some ways he found that comforting. However, he was surprised that Cyril had not been in touch, not thinking being on his honeymoon would matter but maybe he was wrong. He had noticed many positive changes in his boss's demeanour. He placed the beautifully wrapped box on his blotter pad, a pad Cyril had *rescued* from Newby Wiske, the old Police Headquarters before they transferred to a purpose-built station in Northallerton.

DC Shakti tapped him on the shoulder. "Apple for the teacher? Missing him, sir?"

Owen turned. "Goodness, yes." The word *sir* swam in his head for a moment. He had always been Owen when he was a sergeant but now it was to be *sir*! Owen raised his eyebrows. "Like toothache, Shakti." They both laughed. "Our wedding gift; wanted it to be a surprise when he gets back, Hannah's idea."

Shakti smiled. "A woman's touch, sir. Is that a new suit and tie?" She did not wait for the answer. "Very smart, goes with the new position. Shoes shiny too. Bennett has rubbed off on you."

"You can't sit in a hot bath long before your skin turns pink and wrinkly!" Owen said as he turned to walk back to his desk.

Shakti frowned trying to understand the analogy. "Right, yes, wrinkly, pink. If you say so, sir."

Owen wanted his desk to remain in its position for the time being; some things he did not want to change immediately as he enjoyed being amongst the team. He fished into the mug for a sweet, letting his fingers fumble through the empty wrappers until he found one. There was something about *Uncle Joe's Mint Balls* that he liked, probably the sugar. He had a meeting within the hour and he needed to get up to speed; he called in the team and April was to lead. Although he had only taken a day out, he felt disadvantaged. He had read the reports and case notes and he was familiar with developments in both cases, but new forensic evidence was coming in all the time and that had to be assessed and evaluated.

Owen was the last person coming into the briefing, holding his *Harrogate Festivals* mug. Although he had reluctantly moved up another rung on the professional ladder he had not changed, and after some thought considering his present team, he should not. He was just the same dog but with a different name, and after all, if things were not broken, they did not need fixing! To compound that thought his mug still seemed to be leaking as droplets of tea splashed down the lower part of his suit jacket onto the lower leg of his trousers before occasionally hitting the floor – it was ever thus. As he entered the chatting stopped and a light ripple of applause took over momentarily. He raised his mug and smiled. "Cheers everyone."

April had set his place next to her and the necessary paperwork was laid out neatly. She looked at Owen who smiled, a signal for her to start.

"There's a common thread to Lyons's death and that of his carer, Perry, and that of the latest death, Peterson. It might only at this stage be cotton thin but it's a strange coincidence. Nixon has the details."

Harry picked up the remote and the blue screen saver displaying the North Yorkshire Police logo vanished to be replaced by a photograph of the ammunition tin found in Lyons's shed. "As you can see it contains a number of items. You'll of course all be familiar with those. It was suggested by Forensics that it may well have held a firearm of some type. Now look at this." He brought the second photograph to the screen. "This is the weapon found next to Peterson. It's a Coles and Shelvoke Cash captive bolt gun. You can see that written here in block capitals. Below that should be a serial number but it's been ground off at some point in its history. I'm assured that has not been done recently. You'll also note the initials RSPCA and the manufacturer's name and their patents. This one was made in Birmingham."

The next picture followed. "This is the fired blank cartridge removed from the gun. As you will detect it is identical to those found at Lyons's house. We're assuming, therefore, that this once belonged in that box. Considering this item would be vital equipment to the slaughterman's trade, we can assume that it belonged to Lyons. What we need to know is when and how it found its way into Peterson's possession. We've asked the owner of the cottage, a farmer by the name of Bostock, if he knew Lyons or whether he'd been seen near or around the farm. It'll be some time before we can determine, using touch DNA testing, whether either visited each other's property so we have to make rational judgements."

April's phone signalled that she had received a message. She knew it would be relevant. The room fell silent awaiting her response to Nixon's brief. "Forensics have a match on the thread found within the ammunition box. It comes from the carpet at Samuel Peterson's." She let the thought linger before speaking again. "So, a piece of Lyons's property finds its way to Peterson's and something of Peterson's finds its way to the home of George Lyons."

"One piece of evidence seems to have replaced the other," Quinn astutely pointed out. "And the object from the later killing was placed there before or just after the first death. Coincidence?"

Brian Smirthwaite stopped chewing his pencil. "Doubtful, Quinn. Don't believe in coincidences. What about Lyons's friends? How did his wife die?"

"Cancer. We've tracked a friend with whom he'd meet for a drink. Will be interviewed tomorrow. He's away on holiday at present."

It was Owen's turn to speak. "Surely a countryman would know that putting this weapon to his head might not result in death, if we work along the theory of suicide. So, why not a shotgun in the mouth or a .22 to the head as he'd know the immediate repercussions of either of those? And if it were a murder attempt with a captive bolt and you were left with a live victim, you'd shoot again surely?"

"The murderer was disturbed? Didn't realise that it might not kill immediately?" Shakti added.

Owen was tapping the top of his pen to his lips. "Someone didn't want him to die quickly? Lyons died slowly too. That's what that venom does. Can cause dreadful injuries. So too would the captive bolt. Maybe he wasn't out to kill, just maim. Inflict suffering and pain but not kill."

"Failed on both counts there then, sir!" a voice from the back of the room added. "That's all we need, an incompetent nutter who might now have a .22 gun."

"Let's not forget that according to Bostock, the gun could be in the boot of the missing car," April suggested tentatively.

There was an immediate silence as her words were considered.

Nixon was the first to speak. "According to a friend in firearms, to kill an animal, slaughtermen use the captive bolt against the skull and then pith it." He immediately saw the looks of enquiry and explained in some detail. "It's humane and the animal is killed painlessly."

Owen saw that Quinn had turned a shade of grey. "Add that to the whiteboard please, Quinn. As April rightly identified, there's a common thread here, the mixed items from both houses and possibly the slow deaths. Am I grasping at straws ladies and gentlemen or am I simply keeping an open mind?"

April turned. Owen sounded just like Cyril. The master was there within the student.

"If there's a connection between the two murders, items left in each house before the killings took place, we should presume that there could be further killings planned. Is there anything in

Peterson's home that shouldn't be there? We know that the picture and the gun may have been missing from the time of the murder. Whether that's relevant cannot be verified as yet. What we do need to do is find out what the missing picture depicted. April, if you'd talk to Bostock again. Take him to the house. Take Shakti with you. A new pair of eyes."

She made a note.

Chapter Ten

The gloved hand moved the sheets of newspaper cuttings one by one. All appeared old and dogeared as if they had been there a lifetime. Some still contained dates which confirmed their age. The sheets were momentarily scanned before they were inverted and stacked neatly ready to be returned as found. Where there were a few photographs attached to an article, the page was checked with more care. They had been saved for a reason, that was very clear. Occasionally one was placed on a white sheet that had been spread on the table and the copy photographed. The barrier mask covering the mouth, like the rest of the barrier suit, was always an inconvenience but rules were rules if you did not want to contaminate a scene.

***

DC Stuart Park sat opposite Peter Finch. He looked tanned after his holiday and was only too pleased to help. The news of the death of his friend George Lyons had come as a total shock.

"And how did he die?"

Stuart batted the question, immediately asking one of his own. "How long have you known George Lyons?"

"Goodness, how long have I known Sniggy? I suppose thirty years on and off. Worked with him for a while and then our paths diverged. We were both at The Knackery, that's a slaughter house at Coalcut but he suffered with some respiratory disease I think it was for a while, and he finished on medical grounds.

Wasn't that old either. As far as I'm aware, he didn't work again. Come to think of it we might have been about the same age."

"What did you call him? Sniggy?"

"His nickname. Always called Sniggy or Snig by his mates. Don't ask me where, when or why but he was always called that, even by the boss and some clients."

Stuart scribbled notes. He should be adding it to an electronic tablet but he wanted the chat to seem informal and less threatening. "How often did you see him after he retired?"

"Hardly ever. I bumped into him about three years after leaving; he had packed in well before I finished. I'm seventy-seven now you know." He paused waiting for a compliment that did not materialise. "Anyway, we had a beer and chatted about the old place. He told me he missed the lads and the banter."

"Do you know if George did any work on the quiet?"

"What kind of work?" Peter Finch flushed a little and suddenly seemed on the defensive.

Stuart deliberately kept quiet as the induced silence was designed to ensure his interviewee would feel uncomfortable and need to speak. It worked.

"We would help out farmers on occasion, humanely I have to say. We used our experience and our skill to minimise the suffering of the animals." He looked at the beer mat as he fumbled it nervously in his hands. "I don't think it was illegal."

"I take it you were cheaper than the official process?" Park's tone was sympathetic as he added the notes.

"It was better than leaving it to the farmers, that's for sure. Some only balanced sympathy with the contents of their wallets, I can tell you, and animal welfare was not their number one priority."

"And after that?"

"The carcass you mean? We advised incineration, and burning well away from any public place for obvious reasons. We didn't want them buried."

"So, it was all down to cost?"

"And embarrassment. The vanity of the rich and the famous drove much of it. We were approached by an important person of the area. He took his hunter for a ride out on a particularly frosty morning against his better judgement. Metal shoes and iced cobbles are a recipe for disaster. Luckily, he hadn't got as far as the public roads and we were called in to help. He wasn't too bothered about saving a bob or two, just didn't want the neighbourhood to know about his incompetence. Mostly though, it's all about money. To come and put down an animal and remove it would cost the thick end of two hundred pounds – they go by the size of the animal. We'll do it for less than half that. Granted, we don't take it away."

"So, for a big animal you'd use the captive bolt?"

"No, we'd use a thirty-caliber pistol and if it were really unapproachable, as some can be when hurt, we'd use a forty-four Winchester. You needed a quick kill."

Stuart Park stopped writing and looked at Finch. "Say that again." He did not give Finch time to respond. "Who owned those two weapons?"

"Neither of us. We'd used them at work when called to a job. Most times a vet would do the job but on occasion it was too dangerous and we would have to dispose of the injured animal as quickly as possible. He borrowed the pistol and the Winchester. You knew an animal wouldn't suffer any more if you used either."

"From whom?" The incredulity in his question was clearly evident.

Finch just raised his shoulders. “Never asked. Always best that way. I didn’t handle them. That was George’s forte.”

“When was the last time you worked together?”

“About five months ago.”

“So, Mr Finch, the question is, who owns the tools of your trade?” Park deliberately did not name the gun, he wanted everything to come from Finch.

“George had his own humane killer. He’d had it throughout his career. When they changed to compressed air guns, they kept some as back up or field work but got rid of the older pieces. He’d bring that in an old ammunition box. Standard old fashioned stuff but effective.”

“What about the pithing?”

Finch paused hearing the officer mention the word *pithing*. It took a moment for him to collect his thoughts. “Long screwdriver, nothing fancy. That’s kept in my car. George was reliant on me after he got rid of his old jalopy; he had a three-wheeler Reliant for years. We’d never take that as they were prone to roll on corners and in my opinion, it was a bloody death trap. It drew a good deal of attention too. It wasn’t what we nor the customers wanted, believe me.”

“So, five months. Do you have a record of the work?”

The look on Finch’s face told him everything and he did not pursue that line of enquiry. “Did George Lyons ever work on his own do you know?”

“Probably, always happy to make a bob or two. How often? I couldn’t say. All I can be certain about is what we did together. Besides, we chatted about carrying the tools in the car. What with all this terrorism stuff and the possibility of being stopped by you fellas or breaking down which was more possible. Mind, saying that, you police are like that old Reliant, as rare as hen’s teeth these days. Never see any and if you do, they're usually in twos in a car, never on foot."

Stuart was only too well aware of that.

Finch watched as Park made further notes. He seemed to be writing for ever. "Look, DC …"

"Park." Stuart looked up and then back to adding the notes into the pad. "Just want to read this through and make sure that I've written everything in your statement."

"Statement? You wanted a friendly chat you said." He took out his handkerchief and blew his nose. "He was a bloody friend and nobody knows everything about their real friends let alone a work mate. Just look at the number of families who have skeletons hidden in the cupboard. Married for years and people have shadowy and hidden pasts so how I'm supposed to be able to talk about this bloke … have a friendly chat you said and now it turns out to be a statement. I don't know anything he did when we weren't together. As I keep saying, he was a work mate who I occasionally had a beer with and that's it."

"You worked together – tax man know, did he?"

Finch noticed that Park did not write anything further but put his pad into his pocket. Finch stood.

"Next time I want a solicitor. Bloody statement."

"Next time, Mr Finch, you might require one. Thank you for your co-operation."

***

The Forensics results on the captive bolt gun had returned a positive match with the tests carried out on the ammunition box. They had their connection. Shakti stared at the arrows drawn on the white board showing a connection between the two death sites. There was an obvious thread between the two male victims and it was still believed Barbara was the unfortunate victim and that she was in the wrong place at the wrong time. The results clearly showed that DNA from Lyons, Peterson and Bostock were on the wooden handle of the weapon but it could not be determined who was the last to handle it. It was presumed to be Bostock. All enquiries as to any long-term links with either Lyons or Peterson proved negative.

The call from Stuart Park after his interview with Finch had added two more weapons to that missing from Peterson's cottage. A search of the specialised firearm licence records should track those in the locality holding a pistol and the Winchester that matched those described, as well as confirming their working together. Having to get a licence for such weapons would limit the number of owners, but there was the chance that these weapons were held without the necessary paperwork.

***

Leonard loitered by the hallway. The sun's light penetrated the coloured glass within the transom window above the door and the shadows from the leaves of the roadside tree played and danced in varying strengths along the wall. He tried to tap the moving shadow with his hand and giggled momentarily; it occupied him for a short while as he waited for his mother. His coat was fastened and he had been ready for ten minutes. He hated to wait, it made him cross.

"You're an eager beaver, Leonard. Has Karl got more secrets to share with you? We're early and there might be children still walking to school." She raised her hands and carefully placed them on each of his cheeks. "We don't want you upset now do we, my precious boy?" She slipped on her jacket.

Leonard had smiled on hearing the name Karl but his expression changed when it was followed by the word children. His mother's gentle touch briefly comforted him. He frowned and moved away from the door the instant the sun went behind a cloud bringing darkness to the hallway. Leonard approached his mother and took her hand. "Now, please, now. Karl is kind. I do like him. We have secrets."

His mother knew about the secrets. When she had first heard Leonard talk about their secret, alarm bells had gone off in her head. She had always feared people might take advantage of his disability and naivety, and that she would guard against at all costs. Unbeknown to her son, she had chatted with Karl and asked for an explanation. He had told her about the spider and the other animals he was allowed to keep in his apartment but also talked about himself. Over the week they realised that they had much in common.

Not originally from Harrogate, he had moved into the apartment when he retired having always had accommodation linked to his profession. Karl had spent time in Belize, a country first visited when he was in the forces and a place that drew him back. The fact that English was the main language and the chance of working and studying at Cockscomb Basin Wildlife Sanctuary allowed his enthusiasm for the biodiversity of the area to develop. He moved then to work in zoos within Britain, mainly Chester and Blackpool, predominantly with reptiles until retiring early and moving to Yorkshire. Karl had never married. Penny liked him and she appreciated the fact that he could not only help Leonard, she saw that he also knew that it helped her. The insistence on secrets, she realised, was a way of keeping his interest and maintaining discipline. He needed Leonard to follow instructions, abide by rules that would safeguard the welfare of his pets and using the knowledge that his mother would find out and prevent his going to Karl's apartment had worked. She had also seen the logic and was only too grateful for the respite his kindness afforded.

"Come on then, but no shouting if we see any children."

Leonard shook his head. "No shouting, no shouting." He moved eagerly to the door before pulling his hat down lower until it reached his eyebrows. The short walk passed without incident and soon he had disappeared to spend an hour in Karl's company whilst she settled down with a cup of tea and some adult conversation.

"Now remember, Leonard, we don't touch unless you're given permission, nor shout when I bring your friend Tony out here," Karl instructed, his voice firm but fair.

Leonard rocked on his knees and smiled. He had held the spider on a few occasions but was as eager now as he had been on the first day. "Incy wincy, Tony," he muttered to himself. He still squealed as Karl freed the spider from the box but he was controlled, his excitement palpable. He watched as Karl placed it on his arm. Leonard now knew the terms for the various parts of its anatomy. He counted each leg. "They are the *metatarsus*, Karl, your legs Tony are *metatarsus*." He would then go on to list the parts he knew, like a young child fascinated by the complicated names of dinosaurs: *spinnerets, cephalothorax, pedipals, chelicerae.* Each word would trip off his tongue in the same sequence. He relished his newfound knowledge and he loved being in Karl's company.

"I'm going to bring another friend of mine to meet you when we put Tony to bed. It's another secret, Leonard. You must promise not to shout or touch when I bring it. Do you understand?"

Leonard nodded and immediately brought his legs to the side and his index finger to his lips like an infant. He was demonstrating he would comply. Karl removed Tony and within minutes brought another plastic box back into the room. This was larger. Around the upper ring he could see rows of perforations. Karl placed the box on the floor in front of, but away from Leonard who was about to move closer. Karl raised a finger and he stopped.

Leonard's eyes were wide open and again his hand went to his mouth. The box lid was removed and Karl withdrew a snake.

"Kaa! Kaa!" Leonard shrieked as he watched the snake coil on the floor, its tongue shooting back and forth. "*Jungle Book*. I love *Jungle Book* and I love Kaa. I see Kaa in the park. He's on the benches. I like to go and see."

"You can call him Kaa. It's a Corn Snake, Leonard. It has a longer name too, *Pantherophis guttatus,* but we won't worry about that."

"Guttatus, Guttatus." Leonard's smile grew.

"Another of our secrets." Karl put his finger to his lips before picking up the snake.

***

April sat opposite Owen as they read through further Forensic results from the homes of both Lyons and Peterson.

"They discovered a number of documents relating to the stolen car located within the box Peterson had been retrieving, old service records and the like but no registration details. There was also this." She handed it over.

Owen looked at the news cutting in a plastic, forensic bag. It showed a black and white photograph that was now faded and yellowed through age, taken of four men, each holding a gun, a deer at their feet. Each face had been removed leaving four rough holes where their heads had been. Owen held it to the light and then put it back on his desk. There was nothing else on the cutting and the rough torn edges of the newsprint showed its hasty removal. "This was in the same box you say? We know what it's of but do we have any idea as to when it was taken, where it is and whom they might be?"

"No, but we know it was the top item in the box. What's interesting is there's no forensic evidence on that linking it to Peterson but the fact that it's there suggests there should be."

"Unless of course ..." Owen did not need to finish.

"Whoever placed it there could easily have added Peterson's prints or DNA before, during or after but they chose not to ... come into my parlour said the spider to the fly!" April whispered and she beckoned him with her finger.

"So was the box open or closed when he was found?"

April passed across further photographs of the crime scene. "As you can clearly see from these, the box was closed."

"There's a tiny opening where the folds don't meet and you say there's no blood or brain spatter showing?"

"There isn't on the magazine that was stored directly beneath but on the one below that there was."

Owen realised that April was leading the conversation. She knew that this cutting had been positioned. "And the magazines?"

April pushed photographs of the box's contents across the table. "Lonely farm labourer?"

"Didn't think they produced top shelf mags these days. Thought the internet was bursting with the stuff." He turned the photographs. "I suppose he's broken no laws and even if he had it's too late. So, April, someone is playing with us, maybe even leading us by the nose."

She waited a moment and then passed over some more photographs.

Owen flicked through them. They showed Peterson standing next to a variety of animals. Each had been strung up on a branch. They varied from stags to foxes. Some showed him holding just the heads. “Makes me want to become a vegetarian. So, I wonder who took the photographs?”

“Another point of interest. I said that Peterson’s DNA wasn’t found on the top photograph but DNA from a person, as yet unknown, was. Remember we’re looking for threads connecting the dead with the dead? Maybe that DNA is a link to a future victim.” She paused, uncertain as to whether her logic stood. “They’re checking the database and I’ve also requested an international link. Urgency is the key.”

Owen nodded. “Thanks. If the carpet thread and the captive gun are anything to go by, whoever did this was in their houses well before the crimes were committed. They had easy access and they had time. They may have been known to each other, be mutual acquaintances, an old friend or enemy, but I have a feeling they’ve planned this thoroughly and this is only the start.”

April leaned across the table and tapped the photograph. “We have four there just for starters and who’s to say that two people photographed there could be our dead men? Both are linked with guns and both with animals in their professional life.”

“One cared for animals and the other slaughtered them. That’s not a balanced connection, April.”

“With respect, sir, according to Bostock, the farmer who employed Peterson said they both slaughtered animals. Have you read my interview?” She selected the file and pointed to the whiteboard. “It’s referenced on there.”

“So, we have no DNA links from the DNA findings on the specific item from the box.”

“I checked with Forensics regarding touch DNA and as you know it’s not an exact science as we’re often led to believe.

Firstly, about forty-four percent of people may not leave any touch DNA. It depends on various circumstances. So, if we went into the same room and touched a certain object, you might not leave your cells but I might. It's to do with your *shedder* status. It can depend on whether you wash your hands frequently, your personal habits – whether you touch your eyes, hair, nose or ears where you'd collect DNA. That's known as *loading."* She noted Owen's face flush. "Maybe I'm teaching my grandma to suck eggs?"

Owen felt uncomfortable as he knew his personal hygiene was not like that of his boss.

"Sweat too can increase the chance of leaving positive samples as does the surface type you might touch; rough surfaces will have a better chance of holding data. It's also to do with the lab process of retrieval but that part went over my head."

"How long can it last?"

"That's difficult for them to say, but interestingly, if you have a number of DNA samples, it's almost impossible to determine the order in which an item was touched. So, the captive gun has a number of known and unknown links but they can't be definite about the last touch sample."

"As yet."

"We now know that Peterson and Lyons were in both houses at some stage in the past."

Chapter Eleven

The pick-up was parked in front of the kennel when April drove into the farm yard but the dogs began to bark as soon as she pulled to a halt. She told Shakti to wait and see if they appeared but they were, as she had hoped, locked away. A chicken appeared from beneath Bostock's vehicle, looked and then returned out of sight. The door to the side of the barn opened and Bostock appeared. He checked his watch.

"You're late. Eleven they said and it's fifteen minutes past the hour. Now what's this about a picture?" He wiped his hands on an old cloth as he spoke.

"We'd like to take you to Peterson's as there are a couple of elements of this investigation we need to get straight so that we can move on and eliminate some queries to save time and money." She emphasised the word *money* knowing it would be important to the Yorkshireman. "Seeing you know the house better than anyone, we need your advice."

Bostock lifted his flat cap and scratched his head; the idea of saving money struck a chord. "I'll follow you up, need to nip into town afterwards. I found these hanging in the barn." He held up a key ring and keys. "Peterson's. He left them in the barn in case I had to move that car of his. Forgot all about them until today."

Shakti took an evidence bag and let Bostock drop the keys into it before sealing the top.

At Peterson's, April opened the door. A safe pathway was still in place inside the cottage and they followed procedure.

"If you look carefully, Mr Bostock, you can see a mark where a picture once hung. Do you remember what it was and the last time you saw it?"

Bostock leaned forward, a look of recognition on his face which immediately turned into a frown. "Bloody hell! Do you know, I'm not sure!" He took his mobile from his pocket and dialled. "It's me, lass. I'm up at the cottage. Do you remember what was in the picture on the far wall of the lounge? It's now missing. I remember one being there but for the life of me I can't remember what it was."

Shakti and April watched Bostock.

"You're right, bloody hell, how did I forget?" He turned and looked at the two officers, a smile across his face. "Ben, the wife knew. It was a picture of him at Ripon races. He'd won that day for a change, quite a bit of money too."

"How long ago was it taken and was it just him in the picture?"

"Over thirty years but I can't be sure. When you get to my age, love, time flies. He was with a few of his mates. A Bill was in it if I recall, Billy, if I remember rightly and the name *Sniggy* and of course, Peterson whose nickname's always been *Nutter*. As I said, he'd do anything for a dare. The other one I couldn't say, wasn't really registering it all. I think it was taken by the local press, went in the paper and he bought it from them like you could. No expensive smart phones then." He held up an old Nokia phone. "And some of us won't spend hard-earned brass on them now. Just need to make calls, none of this internet crap."

April immediately thought of the men's mags that had been in the box as the words, *internet crap,* rang in her ears.

"And the last time you saw it?"

Bostock shook his head. "If you want an honest answer I can't say. A couple of ..." He paused as a look of surprise appeared across his face. "Funny, a couple of months ago when I called for the rent, he wanted to show me a problem with a window frame. Bloody hell, rarely did he want work doing so it came as a shock. Rotting window frame. That's right. He took the picture down and we chatted about it. I turned it over and he'd scrawled something on the back. He did say but I was too interested in the window frame and getting the brass from him. He was a bugger for not paying on time. Took it from his wages on occasion and he'd get really up tight, fucking angry ... Sorry forgot myself ladies."

April smiled. "We hear worse, Mr Bostock. Did he have a temper?"

"I think I told you he was like a terrier, frightened of nothing or nobody."

"Did he have any particular friends or enemies that you know of?"

"He worked for me and rented one of the cottages. He wasn't really a friend, more a neighbour if that makes sense. Is there anything else?"

"When you found him through there under the stairs you said that at first you thought he'd bumped his head, that's why you rang the ambulance. We have the recording. You then say that you saw the weapon by his side. Did you touch it?"

Bostock frowned and his tone became defensive. "What are you saying?"

"I'm asking a simple question. On that day did you touch the captive bolt gun? Now before you answer this, I could caution you. That doesn't mean arrest you, it means that what you say next could be used in a court of law. However, you've been honest and helpful so far and therefore I simply want to know if you touched it."

Bostock nodded. "I moved it to one side with my finger and thumb and then dropped it. Sorry!"

"Had you seen it before that day? Had you handled it before that day?" She emphasised the words *before that day.*

"As I told you before when you were with the lad, no."

Shakti touched his elbow. "Thank you, Mr Bostock. One last question. What can you tell us about the men in the picture, Bill and the one you called *Sniggy*?"

Bostock shook his head. "Sorry, he mentioned the names but for the life of me I can't recall if he said anything else."

"We have a similar picture, a news cutting, but there are no faces to the four men. Have you seen this before?" She handed him a photocopy of the cutting.

Bostock moved his head from side to side. "Never seen it before. Just a hunt. Four blokes though. Why no faces?"

April said nothing and took back the picture before handing him her card. "If you think of anything, no matter how trivial you think it is, give me a call. Talk it through with your wife, it might just jog your memory."

***

Gill Cunningham had checked her flock of Swaledale sheep the night before, one of twelve hundred flocks within the north east. She had been brought up on the farm and had taken over the running at an early age. With a family of four and an Airbnb cottage to run she was one of the youngest shepherdesses in the country.

Looking down the valley she admired the early morning haze and the colour of the sky seemed to bring a warmth to the scene. No matter how often she looked at her surroundings she never ceased to believe that she was fortunate to live in the most beautiful part of Britain. The quad started first time disturbing the solitude and shattering the magic. Her eldest daughter, Maisy, sat behind alongside Ned the border collie. Of her four daughters, Maisy was determined to follow her mother's career path and took every opportunity, when holidays from school allowed, to work with her.

Cloister Hill Farm was situated a mile from Middlesmoor below Scar House and Angram reservoirs. Although close to the villages and large towns and with that schools and amenities, it was, to some at least, considered isolated. They would take the road to Ramsgill before turning off through Lofthouse. She had a hundred sheep on fields just off Topping Hill, a narrow road that meandered to the moors and the high road. This was her furthest flock from the farm.

Once negotiating the steep bend, she turned left along the track and it was here that her suspicions were aroused. The steel bar gate was open. The chain that would normally secure it to the post hung loosely. Stopping the quad, she leaned to take hold of the chain. It had been cut. Gill scanned the field. A fox moved across her line of vision and Ned immediately leapt from his secure space to give silent chase, causing a murder of crows, a collection of gulls – from the nearby reservoirs – and a solitary buzzard to rise from one area of the field, their call shrill and haunting. Gill allowed her eyes to focus on the black and white cloud of birds as they reluctantly took flight, like a moving chess board before settling a distance away. Her gaze then followed the gradient until she stopped at the copse of trees to the left. Around the base of the tree she could see fleeces. She cautiously approached but Ned had other ideas; returning from chasing the fox he was now ahead, stopping just before the tree. He crouched before moving stealthily forward as if stalking.

Maisy was the first to see the evidence, a sheep's head to the left of their path, and another, and then a bloodied fleece. She leaned across and touched her mother's arm whilst pointing with the other. Neither spoke nor climbed from the quad. The detritus of the rustlers' trade was now evident. From the stout tree branch Gill could see two thick steel wires hanging. It was here, whilst the captured sheep were supported, that the butchers had performed their nocturnal trade. As Gill looked over the aftermath, she knew that the killing had been done systematically and professionally. Gill concluded the process; it had been highlighted in the farming press; her flock was not the first to be attacked and neither would it be the last. There had been a twenty-five percent increase in rural crime and in particular the rustling of sheep. They had been collected and killed in the night, the whole process well-organised and planned. Once the meat was removed the rest was discarded.

Gill wrapped a reassuring arm around Maisy and was pleased to see Ned rounding the surviving sheep from the far corner of the field.

"We need to count them my brave lass. Okay?"

Maisy smiled and nodded as Gill moved the quad away from the temporary slaughter area.

"We must keep that free for the police to collect evidence."

The birds were disturbed again but soon settled back to their original spot. They would not stay long, however, if Ned had his way.

"We've lost thirteen. Thirteen in one night and nobody sees nor hears anything." Gill knew there were any number of routes they could take to leave the site. Removing her mobile from her pocket she checked the signal strength and dialled Tony

Calderbank, a friend and the local community police officer. Dialling 101 could take a while and 999 was, for this, inappropriate even though to her it was an emergency. Maybe as these incidents became more common it might bring some urgency. What she did need was an immediate response.

"Tony it's Gill from Cloister Hill."

***

The gloved hands turned the framed photograph over. Scrawled in block capitals were the words:

Ripon Races – 1986
Billy, Sniggy, Charlie and of course, Nutter.
Great St Wilfred's Stakes
Catherines Well
I told you so!

Turning the picture back over he ran his gloved index finger along each face and said the names out loud before finally coming to Samuel Peterson. It took a minute to bend the clips that held the back and the picture against the glass. Removing the photograph, he carefully pushed a screwdriver through three of the faces and moved it to obliterate the facial details before returning it to the frame.

Putting it down, he picked up the .22 rifle. The weapon's condition was poor and clearly Peterson had neglected its appearance but on inspection it was clear that the mechanism had been cared for. Slipping the bolt, he checked the chamber and was satisfied; the action was smooth. Everything was nearly ready. Taking the framed picture, he placed it against the sugar bowl that was on the kitchen table ensuring it faced the door before moving into the porch. The late afternoon sun was sitting along the top of the garden wall and the sky had turned a soft and mellow orangey blue. The garden was neat and organised. Taking a minute, he admired the setting. He was surprised that the rented property was immaculate both inside and out, a stark contrast to Peterson's cottage. They were chalk and cheese – you had a farm labourer, a man who cared little about his home and his appearance. He would always make do. He could see no point in spending for spending's sake unless, of course, it was on a racing certainty. The problem had been that certainties did not seem to be that certain these days. Bill Hurst, always known as Billy, had been a friend of Peterson's for some time. They both enjoyed the horses and the odd shoot, rabbit, fox and pigeon mainly but there had been bigger game. Unlike Peterson, Hurst had not always been Hurst but Humphrey. At that time of his life he had been a successful butcher, learning his trade from his father before leaving to work in the greengrocery trade. He had never taken out a mortgage nor a loan. Cash had always been king and property was one means of sheltering illicit earnings.

His father had insisted on early mornings and late evenings. The business had thrived, but the growing regulations for meat storage from Europe and the ever-increasing onset of the supermarkets had brought the need for an alternative career. It took a while and after the greengrocery trade he found one. Concrete patterned driveways had suddenly become the fashion and for little outlay and even less training, he'd started *Driveways Direct*. Initially it had enjoyed a smooth three years of highly profitable work but then things quickly changed and the disappearance of his business partner with some of the profits and the equipment left Billy feeling sorry for himself. He was also being hounded by a number of dissatisfied customers who had paid a high price for shoddy work and now realised the written twenty-five-year warranty was worthless. A contact suggested a move to North Yorkshire with a change of name to Hurst, and his new lease of life was started. At forty he was lucky to have money in property that was quickly sold.

Three hooks held various items of outdoor clothing and below that a rack housed a selection of footwear, wellington boots, some stout hiking boots and in contrast, a pair of slippers.

The visitor looked down; the mail trapped beneath the blue protective overshoes brought a smile. Within the hour he had walked every room, there was no need to rush as Billy Hurst was on holiday for another few days. The same order was to be found everywhere. He found the item he was looking for and slipped it in his bag. The gun he placed on top of the kitchen cabinet. He would come back when the owner returned home and hopefully he would be tired from travel. Besides, he had another visit to make.

***

Quinn had identified three firms which held the weapons described by Finch; one was a working knacker's yard in Lancashire and the others were a Wildlife and a Safari Park. He noted that they all had personnel trained in the use of the guns and they had kept records logging when and where they were if off site. Local officers had visited each venue and could confirm that their holding the weapons met the requirement of the licence so it was likely that the guns used by Finch and Lyons were unregistered.

The names from the back of the photograph had been added and link lines drawn on the whiteboards but no further information had yet been forthcoming. He had set the computers within a fifty-mile radius, looking for all residents by the name of William and Bill along with those called Charlie and Charles. The tedium of police work could often reap the greatest rewards but the list was endless. It was then just a case of narrowing the search parameters and simple police work.

In his office, Owen sat at his desk as Quinn looked over his shoulder at the screen. The list comprised two hundred and twenty-seven names for Bill, Will, Billy and William.

"This is too wide. How far apart in distance are the two deaths?" Owen looked on Google maps. "See, Bedale to Knaresborough is about twenty-five miles. Let's say for the moment thirty as a maximum and we'll guess Knaresborough to be the central point. How many names will we have left?"

Owen moved sideways to allow Quinn full control of the keyboard. "Knowing from where we draw the circle is critical but it reduces the number to one hundred and eighty-four. Interesting, we have females here too giving their addresses and electoral link. If we get rid of those … we have reduced it by sixteen!"

"Select them in alphabetical order and then age categories. Let's assume that Bill is within ten years of Peterson. Now what do we have?"

"Thirty-seven, sir."

Owen smiled.

In the Incident Room, Stuart Park checked the latest additions to the whiteboards in the Incident Room, suddenly paused and felt his face flush. "Shit! Shit! Shit!" He slammed his fist on the wall and three officers turned to look. He shook his head and held up a hand as if in apology and left. Owen was still at his desk when Stuart walked in, Quinn was leaving.

"Sir, Sniggy. Just been checking the boards and I note we have reference to a person called Sniggy, possibly written on the back of a missing photograph from the crime scene at the farm."

Looking up, Owen said nothing but dropped his pen and sat back.

"When I interviewed Peter Finch, Lyons's friend, he mentioned that he had a nickname … Sniggy. I added it to my notes but forgot to add it to the bloody report." Park raised his eyebrows in embarrassment.

"Sniggy?"

"Sorry. As I said, just forgot."

"You've spotted it, you've followed procedure and checked the boards. That wouldn't have slipped through HOLMES had you …" he stopped himself making the officer feel any worse. "But we humans are simply that, human and we get there in the end. So, Stuart, if the name refers to Lyons then Peterson should be on there too. The key now is to find the others before they possibly go the same way."

***

Leonard watched as Karl took the snake and carefully walked to another room. He stood to follow and went to the door. "Can I see where he lives, Karl?"

"Stay there, Leonard. Remember our promises and remember our secrets. If you do as you're told when you come again, you'll be able to hold the snake. Do you think he'll be wet and slimy or dry and smooth?"

"Kaa in the park is cold." Leonard could see the open door a short distance up the corridor. Karl's voice seemed so close yet so far away.

"Are you sitting down, Leonard, or are you in the wrong place?" The voice was firm but nonthreatening.

Leonard immediately moved back to the lounge and sat on the carpet, his finger on his lips. "I'm being good, Karl. Promise."

"What was my question, Leonard?"

"Forgotten, Karl."

"When is your birthday, Leonard?" Karl asked as he entered the room. He had washed his hands and was wiping them on a towel. He could see from the blank expression on his friend's face that he was unsure. "I wonder how old you are Leonard. I'll talk to your lovely mother. You never know but if it's soon I'll see if we can make it a very special birthday."

Leonard moved his hand to his mouth, failing to control his excitement. Saliva dribbled off his chin and onto his knee.

On returning to the resident's lounge, Leonard and Karl spotted his mother. She was in the conservatory, her eyes closed, the sunlight spreading across her legs like a blanket. Karl looked at Leonard and put his finger to his lips. "Let her sleep, Leonard, we'll just walk in the garden for ten minutes as there's something I want to show you."

They moved towards the French windows but Leonard in his excitement knocked a chair that clattered on the tiled floor. Leonard squealed, it brought Penny to her senses. "You're back."

Leonard turned and went to her, eager to reveal that he was to get a surprise on his birthday but it was a secret. Karl promptly laughed as he picked up the chair.

"Secret you say?" Penny ruffled Leonard's hair and they both laughed. Karl stood to the edge and said nothing.

Chapter Twelve

Cyril Bennett lay on the lounger. The sea lapped the white sand metres from his feet. The umbrella offered perfect shade but the white fedora pulled over his eyes momentarily blacked out the world and soon he drifted to sleep. A large catamaran breezed past, the sail full. A large white tarpaulin tied to the boat's thin, steel shrouds formed a horizontal sunshade giving protection to the passengers who were enjoying the coastal trip. The music, a rich reggae beat, seemed to drift along the turquoise water. To some it was a brief moment of pleasure, to others an annoyance but for the moment it was neither for Cyril. It filtered into his dream turning it into a nightmare.

He heard the noise as he approached his office, the beat penetrated the building accompanied by shrieks of laughter but the onslaught was nothing to what he faced on opening the door. His office was full. People seemed to fill every space as Owen and Hannah danced on his desk whilst others clapped and laughed. He scanned the room. On a chair near the centre sat Liz Graydon. A girl wearing a Venetian mask lifted her head as if presenting an award. Cyril, amazed, focused on her face. How could it be? She was dead. At first she was laughing but from the corner of his eye, at the far side of the room, he noticed a huge man in tight pink trousers. It was Charles. He pointed to Cyril and then he withdrew a hat pin from his shirt collar. Cyril tried to shout, *Charles, stop!* but no words came. He tried again as Charles bent to kiss Liz; she slumped forward, lifeless. Both she and Charles immediately turned to smoke and drifted towards the light. There, in their place, was Wendy, his stepmother. She was on all fours and naked, his father was kneeling behind. He was laughing and staring directly at Cyril. *I'll make a man of you yet my son,* were the words that seemed to drift above the music, quickly followed by everyone's laughter.

All of Cyril's emotional and traumatic past was played out here in what seemed like some bizarre theatre. He was getting hotter and felt like a child again. It was at that moment Owen kicked the computer screen with great force. Cyril dashed towards it. *Owen!* he screamed at full volume. The authority in his cry carried back over the sea to where the boat had long since been. A number of heads had turned to see from where the plea had originated and they watched as Cyril sat bolt upright with some force as if trying to catch the screen. People continued to watch, a moment's entertainment in what had been a long and lazy day. Julie, sitting on the next bed, reacted instinctively; she had experienced his dreams in the past. Dropping her book, she thrust a hand across to grasp Cyril's arm.

"Cyril, stop. Cyril! It's a dream." Her voice was calm but assertive and she felt the rigidity drain from Cyril's body. She could see the sweat running from his forehead.

Cyril stopped and saw his own feet, the sand and then the sea. Immediately he turned to look at Julie, his eyes red. He rubbed his face with the palms of his hands and shook his head before looking at his hands. They were shaking.

"Bloody hell that was so real, so real." He explained what he had just witnessed and Julie at first laughed but then moved closer and wrapped him in her arms.

"You're not used to doing nothing, Cyril. For the first time in years you've laid ghosts to rest and occasionally they will fight back. They will try to win and weaken you. It's because you're worried about the station and your team. That's expected, the dreams or nightmares are natural. It's all part of the catharsis. Remember what Caroline, your counsellor, told you after Liz's death? She told you that Liz might return and she did, but she also told you that over time she would slowly leave you and ..."

Cyril nodded.

"With the reunion with your family and your father's death, the wedding and the planning we've had to do, all of those things will dredge those fears and anxieties from deep within, no matter how far down you believe you've buried them. This is not the first, neither will it be the last nightmare but we will beat it together, my darling. Ring Owen if you're concerned. Have a chat, not necessarily about work. Let your Best Man know you're thinking about him and the team and how proud you are of him and of them. It'll put your mind at rest but you must learn to trust them and open up more, allow your emotions to surface. They've never let you down yet and besides, there'll come a day when you're simply driving a desk and others will be at the sharp end so you'd better get used to it." She acknowledged that he found showing and expressing his emotions a major problem. It had taken him an age just to tell her that he loved her. She presumed correctly that he had been emotionally starved as a child and taught that males were expected to be strong and demonstrate a stiff upper lip.

Cyril looked at her. He knew that everything she said was true but in real terms he had brushed his feelings and emotions under the carpet. "There was one thing that was even more strange. They were all there, the people from my past, apart from one person."

Julie knew immediately to whom he referred. "Your mother, Cyril?"

He pulled a face. "How did you ...?"

"Was I in this dream?"

Cyril shook his head. "No."

Julie just held his two hands. "And why is that?"

He smiled. That thought was a step too far, although he accepted it was because they were the two people who meant the most to him. To hide rather than to surrender that thought, he allowed the barrier to begin to fall again and his expression swiftly changed. "I need a beer, and for you my beautiful wife?"

"*Sex on the beach* would be lovely."

Cyril looked askance and giggled. "Sorry?"

"Cocktail, not a demand, Cyril." She chuckled. "It's killed your sense of humour, that dream, hasn't it?"

Cyril frowned and bent before kissing her forehead. "It was frightening and too real. Too real."

***

It had meant a very early start for Stuart Park as he researched the local papers for reports on the races held at Ripon, in particularly the Great St Wilfred's Stakes, the richest race on the calendar. If the Bostocks were correct the picture should be within the archive and it was the photograph that he really needed to locate and then any editorial that supported it. His early error made his quest even more critical, and he knew it was going to be slow work. Most copies were held on microfilm but there might still be details held on file. Contacts he had built up over the years had directed him and he now had two papers – the rest were on microfiche and an original copy detailing the day and date of every race. It was a piece of luck but within minutes he had the photograph for which he had been searching. It was taken in 1986. It showed four individuals all grinning at the camera. There were also others in the shot but it was clear that the four were together. Two horses stood behind and beyond the sign, *Ripon Races – Yorkshire's Garden Racecourse.*

"There can be no doubt where this was taken," Stuart said out loud and he read the editorial accompanying the photograph but his language soon changed. "Shit!"

'*Samuel Peterson and friends enjoying a successful day at the races …*'

He photographed the image and sent it directly to Owen partly out of uncertainty, but mainly out of guilt.

Studying the photograph carefully he could see that there was no acknowledgement as to who the others were, only a description of the winning horse and jockey. He needed to check the other two local papers, maybe they were more detailed. Once he had familiarised himself with manipulating the computer containing the microfilm, he could understand its value. Again, however, there was only the photograph and the same article beneath on one copy, and only the photograph on the second. There was, for Park at least, a glimmer of hope – the article was attributed to the reporter Frank Fitzpatrick. He jotted down the name.

Three phone calls later Stuart had tracked down the reporter. Fitzpatrick was now employed freelance in London and working as a news reporter for a major television company. Park was also heartened to hear that Frank had kept all of his notebooks and recordings of interviews from his early career and that there might be a chance that further details that did not make the editorial would be somewhere on file. It was this sense of achievement that fed his love of the job, the sleuthing; it made it challenging but also so worthwhile. All he had to do now was await an evening call from Mr Fitzpatrick.

***

The report of the rustling should not really have arrived on Owen's desk, it should have been handled by a lower rank, but he had glanced at the content before passing it to Quinn to direct it to the relevant department. He had informed Quinn that the killing of thirteen sheep was not on his radar as the deaths he was dealing with seemed more appropriate to his new office. Within the day and to Owen's astonishment Quinn had brought it back with good reason.

"Sir, I'd like to put this back on your *radar* I think you said. I strongly believe that in some way it's relevant to the case."

Owen looked up and frowned. "Rustling near Ramsgill, relevant, right … How?"

"Sir, it has a certain ring to it and there's a connection; slaughtermen and a farm labourer who was constantly short of money, experts who knew how to handle sheep and how to kill and possibly butcher." Quinn stabbed a finger on the file. "I had a quick word with the community officer who went to the scene. Thirteen killed and the meat taken. But, sir, that's not the real issue. There's a greater problem that we and those outside the farming industry would fail to spot. All farm animals are treated with medication. Sheep are no different and owing to the way that food entering our food chain is monitored and logged, this is taken into consideration. If they're killed too soon after they've been treated there is a possibility of those medicines or chemicals entering humans. There is no way of knowing where it's come from once the meat is removed during one of these clandestine collections. The passport system only works on the full carcass. People will always buy if the price is right."

"Lyons and Peterson are dead, Quinn. They didn't rise up and come back to slaughter sheep in Ramsgill."

"No, no. Not them. They were probably involved in the past, small fry, but it may have got them killed. This new attack. Is someone clearing the way?"

Owen tapped his finger on the desk. "Did Crime Scene Investigation take place?"

"Indeed. It's on file. There are more incidents like this occurring nationally, usually a secluded spot close to a road, possible trees to conceal the activity and from which to hang the animal."

"How do they see? Catch the sheep? After all, farmers need dogs."

Owen's phone signalled a mail. He checked. It was the photograph from Stuart Park. "Sorry. Go on."

"Red lights I'm told, but as to the capture …"

"Red lights, Quinn?

"The ones you strap to your head." He could see his boss had been distracted by the mail.

Owen looked again at the image and checked he had a connection to the printer. He heard the machine come alive before spewing the picture to the side. "Samuel Peterson." He flicked the paper's edge. "But who are the rest?" He handed the picture to Quinn. "1986, The Great St Wilfred's Stakes, Ripon Races. This was the picture taken from Peterson's house. One looks like Lyons to me, the one on the left. According to Bostock one was known as Sniggy, and Lyons's mate and colleague informed us that he'd had that nickname most of his life."

"Sniggy and death by snake," Quinn proffered. "And Nutter, if I remember the notes from our trusty farmer was Peterson and his death …"

"Cracked the nut," Owen whispered. "Some bugger's playing bloody games and I mean bloody. We need to know who the other two are and we need to know pretty damn quick."

Owen rang Park. "As soon as you know anything, Stuart, I need it immediately. Upload too, in case there's a link we fail to see."

Within minutes of hanging up, his phone notified him of another message. It was Cyril. If nothing else it brought a smile to his face.

***

The shop bell rang as the door opened and the familiar smell seemed thick and pungent but also reassuring. The noise from the fish tanks, the sound of air bubbling through water, was relaxing and potentially soporific – the very reason aquaria are to be found in places where human stress may be present; hospital waiting areas, airports and schools. There is something about watching fish to alter the mood. The owner entered from a door behind the counter. Karl turned and smiled.

"And how is Miss Taylor this fine evening?" He moved away from the tank he had been inspecting and leaned on the counter; finding a space amongst the plethora of merchandise spread in no particular order, from dog treats to wild bird feed, was more difficult than he thought and he pushed boxes to one side.

She watched with interest before moving the box back. "I'm fine thank you. There is a structure to all this. You might not think so but everything has a place. Hope you're looking after your menagerie, Karl. Come for your usual feeds and things?

You seemed more interested in the fish than usual. Thinking of keeping fish, are we?"

He let his finger draw circles on the counter as if considering the question. "I'm negotiating with the retirement complex to get a large aquarium installed in one of the lounges. Some of the residents think it's a good idea. Need to be a bit bigger than these, mind. Maybe one of those that sits in the centre of the room. That would be in keeping with the place. It has to go through committee and Health and Safety raises its ugly head I'm afraid."

"Posh!" Joanne chuckled. "Never marked you as a snob, Karl. Would need a floor power unit, couldn't have people falling over cables. Best to keep things simple if you ask me."

"I wouldn't say *posh*. I'm lucky to own an apartment in the complex that comprises a mix of accommodation from private to …" he paused. "Let's say those needing more direct intervention. Comes to us all in time and that time seems to be fast approaching. Being central to town is so convenient and if I want to go on holiday …" He said no more.

Karl had been coming to the shop in Cold Bath Place since his arrival in Harrogate. Joanne had a broad knowledge of the pets in which she specialised as well as having an outstanding reputation for their welfare. She had weathered many a storm from those who considered her type of store unacceptable in the twenty-first century but she had not let the doubters win. She had developed strong links with her customers as well as local schools and public offices, and had even supplied the local bookshop with a small fish tank, often popping in to ensure all was well. She ran a boarding facility for certain pets, especially those needing specialist care and handling, a service that allowed owners time for holidays and to recover from ill health. Over the past few years she had specialised in the more unusual reptiles to counter the competition from the larger pet stores. So far, her business was surviving.

"Turn the closed sign on the door, love. I've had enough of this day and need a little attention myself." She winked at him, made minor readjustments to the counter and left the shop.

Karl smiled as he moved to the door. He turned the sign. Shopping at *Joanne's Small Pet Store* he had soon discovered that she enjoyed his company; there was no pressure as they were both single and both had a love of animals. On leaving the front of the shop he put his head into the back room. He looked into each of the various transparent boxes, every one seemingly holding a different small world of its own. Here was an interesting collection, some of the creatures were staying short term whilst others were for sale. Finally he went over to the largest glass tank and admired the python, curled round a large branch. It was an impressive creature. The word *Lilith* was written on a card and stuck above the tank. He thought for a moment before shouting to Jo. "You have some wonderful specimens, Jo," he called as he walked round the room.

Jo, now upstairs in the apartment, shouted her reply. "I bet you say that to all the girls in your life. Are you staying with the ones in the tanks who are safe or are you coming up here to the one who is free and dangerous?"

Karl said nothing but chuckled before climbing the stairs and in his eagerness found himself taking the first few two at a time.

***

Owen dialled Cyril's number and waited. The tone seemed so distant and dissimilar to when he called him locally. After four rings Cyril answered. "Thank you for your message. All's well here." Owen felt clumsy and uncomfortable, as if he were intruding.

"Over a week done, Owen. Not the kind of person who can lounge about all day. What's happening?... And Owen, I want the truth."

Owen went over the case as briefly as possible and occasionally reminded his boss that he was supposed to be on his honeymoon and leaving work behind but he was encouraged to reveal all and be questioned about it. Although he was delighted to hear Cyril's voice, he was angry with himself for calling. He looked at his phone after hanging up. Cyril's words rang in his head. *Find those in the photographs.*

Moving through to the Incident Room he stared at the whiteboard. *Sniggy and Nutter. So, who the bloody hell are you two?* he whispered, stabbing a finger onto the board. He felt his phone vibrate just before it rang. He immediately thought it might be Cyril and was relieved to see it was Stuart Park.

"Fitzpatrick has just been in touch. He's found the notebooks for 1986 and although he had little recollection it was noted in his diaries. George Lyons, Sam Peterson, Bill Hurst and Trevor Bostock."

"Bostock, isn't he the farmer who owned Peterson's cottage?" Owen suddenly felt excited as he scanned the board looking for the name. "We have a Ted Bostock. What's the connection?"

"Only have the names. I'll start digging tomorrow. We need to know if they're both still with us and if so, where they're now living."

Owen stretched and checked his watch. He should have been home an hour ago but he felt restless. The conversation with Cyril had unnerved him and he wondered what Cyril would do right now; the *Coach and Horses* came to mind. Within twenty minutes he was walking down the passageway that linked West Park with Robert Street. Speaking to Cyril had reminded him he needed to check Cyril's home.

The pictures of the wedding in the local paper would notify all and sundry that he would be away. Standing in the empty lounge seemed strange. He could understand the term *a woman's touch* as Julie had certainly changed what was the bachelor's home into something special. There was a mix of their furniture, the paintings were displayed with more structure, a better designer's eye had been cast over everything but the place, as usual, was immaculate. Sitting on the side were some of the gifts they had received but one remained unopened, it was the Herbert Whone painting. Julie wanted it to be a surprise on their return. After a swift check of all the other rooms he was heading back the way he had come. Within minutes he was in *The Coach* nursing a well-earned pint. It would seem so strange when their new home was ready; Robert Street was synonymous with Bennett. They were undecided as to whether to keep it and rent it or sell. Owen thought they were in the fortunate position to have the choice. He wondered if Hannah might like it but then looked at his beer and shook his head.

Chapter Thirteen

Karl heard the alarm, a shrill, intermittent noise and he immediately pulled a pillow over his head as his arm stretched to the bedside cabinet to silence it. He could see that the early morning light in thin sharp beams, was piercing the slight gap in the curtains. The side of the bed to his left was empty but still warm and he could still smell her. It was then that he heard the shipping forecast. Why she had this fascination for the bulletin no one knew. As far as he was aware, she had never been to sea nor had she any intention of buying a boat. He doubted whether she had put a toe in the briny in the last thirty years but the shipping forecast was a morning ritual. He knew that it was 5.20 and that German Bight had storms. However, where German Bight was located was anyone's guess. Climbing out of bed he pulled on his trousers and went to the top of the stairs.

"Morning, Captain. Would you like tea?" He waited for the response. "Jo, are you there?" He moved down the stairs more slowly than he had taken them the previous night. The radio was no longer on. Normally, once the radio went on in a morning it stayed on until the shop opened. The back room appeared to be the same as usual, the dim lights, the few noises from the creatures; the blackout curtain was doing its job changing day to night. He turned and entered the shop. The morning light mixed with the coloured glow from the tanks brought an eeriness that made Karl feel uncomfortable. "Jo, are you here?" He spoke almost in a whisper. He turned to go back. There was now only the store room, but surely she would not be in there at this time in the morning. It was an old, small shipping container out the back and across the small yard. Suddenly the sound of the doorbell rang, followed by the shop door opening. It made Karl jump and he immediately turned to face the door; it was a sound he was least expecting. Jo walked into the shop, her dressing gown wrapped tightly round her.

"You may well look startled. Did you lock this bloody door last night, like I asked?"

Karl was nodding before he spoke. "Turned the sign and dropped the latch. I'm sure."

"Top and bottom bolt too?" She could tell from his expression that he had not. "It was open this morning, ajar. I've done a quick check but there seems to be nothing missing. Someone was obviously in a hurry to climb the stairs last night." As she spoke, she let the dressing gown fall open exposing her breasts. Karl stared before a smile broke on his lips. "Now, did I hear someone mention tea? Afterwards, Karl, if you're a good boy, mummy might forgive you!"

Had she looked carefully she would have seen it, but they had other things on their minds.

***

The farmyard was quiet. He had watched as Bostock loaded the two dogs into the back of the pick-up along with some interlocking aluminium hurdles. There was little finesse as the four sheets were slid along the back until they hit the cab. The dogs bounced excitedly, their heads to the side as the vehicle moved towards the farm entrance. Bostock saw the person walking along the road but paid no attention. The dogs barked momentarily in protest as they passed but were soon relishing the wind brushing their faces and quietened. He leaned on the wall watching Bostock's pick-up disappear before checking his watch. On time, Belinda Bostock closed the door, checked it was locked and walked to the small four by four. If it was Thursday it was hair day, the one luxury she afforded herself. Strangely, Thursday had been the day Peterson's Vauxhall had gone missing from the yard but she neither thought about that nor cared. On approaching the gates to the yard, she too noticed the man leaning on the wall and felt a moment's hesitation as she considered if she'd locked the door. She stopped, climbed out and walked back to check. She had. On her return to the car, the man had gone. She would be about an hour.

Belinda nipped for a coffee after having her hair done. She had gossiped too much about the police incident and she knew it. Even though she had reassured herself and Ted that she would say nothing about the incident, Franco, her hairdresser had teased it from her. She was disappointed in herself. Ted, however, did not need to know. She collected a paper and some flowers and a large pie for Ted's lunch. It would be a peace offering of sorts. She had no intention of telling him what she had said and there was little chance of his finding out.

The rain started as she approached the farm. It was steady at first but then the sky darkened and it came, large drops that turned quickly into a downpour. Her wipers worked hard to clear the screen and she was relieved when she turned into the farmyard. Parking as close to the house as possible, she pulled her jacket over her head and made a dash for the door. Inserting and turning the key, she entered. She quickly checked her hair. It had survived. Moving to the side she took the kettle and approached the sink. Glancing through the net curtains, she dropped the kettle. At the far side of the yard stood the red Vauxhall. It was positioned as it had been before it was taken. "What the …!" She rooted her phone from her bag.

***

The briefing was just that, brief. Owen quickly directed the investigation. They now had two new names but only one address.

"We have our missing men from the Ripon Race. Two are dead and we can assume the others might follow or might be responsible. It seems that Trevor Bostock is the elder brother of Ted Bostock. He wasn't a farmer like his father or his brother and it appears he moved away, bit of a scallywag from all accounts. Womaniser and drinker. Fell out with his father over some issue and joined the army. Have his record here." He slipped one to each person and they glanced through it.

April read it out. "Belize, Northern Ireland. What did they always advertise? *Join the army and see the world."*

"Where the hell is Belize?" someone asked.

"Central Americas," retorted April. "Used to be British. The Queen's the head of the country."

Owen turned to Quinn. "You need to chat with the Bostocks and discover more. Find out where he is now. Take Shakti with you. Hurst is a bit of a problem. We've run a check on *Quest*. We added his name and what we consider might be his physical description and personal features after professionals looked at the photograph but none meets the criteria of age and location. Bit of a long shot if I'm honest."

"Desperation, more like," Quinn shot back, aware the computer database would require a more accurate input.

"I've given Dan Grimshaw the challenge of locating him."

As Quinn drove ... the call came through to inform them the missing car had suddenly materialised in the exact spot from where it had been taken. CSI had been notified and should arrive at the farm shortly after them. Quinn brought the car to a standstill. The two dogs leapt from the back of the pick-up and came towards them. "Stay where you are Shak."

The barking started and Ted Bostock immediately appeared at the door and whistled before gesturing. The dogs were silenced and ran in the direction of the pointing finger. "Stay there!" He walked over and closed the kennel gate before waving to the officers.

"Sorry, rushed home when the wife phoned about the bloody car. Can you believe it? It's as if it's always been there. That's just where it was. Whoever took it brought it back, otherwise how would they know?"

"Have you touched it, Mr Bostock?"

Bostock cringed. He had been asked the same question up at Peterson's. "I looked through the windows. Had a strange feeling, but touch it? No. Neither has the wife. She locked the kitchen door and wouldn't open it until I came home."

"Can we go inside? We were on our way here for another reason but we received details of the call you made to DS Richmond."

"She gave me her card. Thought you'd want to know immediately."

"Indeed, Mr Bostock, indeed." They walked into the kitchen. Belinda Bostock was nursing a mug of tea.

Both told the story of their morning and it was only when Belinda mentioned the man leaning on the wall and her returning to check the door that Ted seemed to come to life. He explained that he had seen someone walking close to the gate upon leaving fifteen minutes earlier. They shared their impressions of his clothing and height. It was the same man.

"He was obviously waiting for you both to leave. He couldn't be in the car as you'd both have noticed. Have you checked the barn and the house?" Shakti asked and watched the worried expression spread across Belinda's face.

"No, bloody hell." Ted looked around the kitchen as if he had suddenly seen someone hiding in one of the cupboards. The dogs started to bark and Quinn stood, leaned on the sink and moved the net curtain. It was the CSI.

"It's only our people coming to check over the car. Can we go and look around the barn and the yard for anything unusual?" requested Quinn as he moved towards the door. "My colleague will take a statement from your wife and then we'll take yours, Mr Bostock, and talk about the reason we were coming out here in the first place."

Bostock collected his flat cap from the peg and followed Quinn outside. Immediately the dogs went quiet. The two CSI were already donning their protective clothing in preparation for the task ahead. They would perform a quick but thorough inspection of the Vauxhall in situ before having it removed for a more in-depth investigation should they feel further investigation was necessary.

Quinn had a quick word before joining Bostock at the entrance to the barn. It had to be said that structure and order were not Bostock's priorities. Old equipment, bales and sacking seemed to fill most of the space. Bostock pointed to the far wall. A wooden rail containing a number of nails held leather straps, rope and the odd old jacket.

"The keys. That keyring shouldn't be there. I found Peterson's on that nail when you people were round. I gave them to the lass who came before, the lass with you today, DC Misery. She held open a plastic bag and I dropped them in."

"Misra, Mr Bostock, DC Misra. We know that those keys held your DNA, that of Peterson and strangely, that of your wife, but no other. When we first spoke with your wife, she said she wasn't aware of any keys in the barn linked with the car. She informed us that Peterson had just left the car there. However, now we know she knew of the keys, touched the keys. Did she drive the Vauxhall?"

Bostock lifted his cap and rubbed his head before raising his shoulders. "Maybe we should just go and ask her rather than standing here guessing, not that I bloody know. Why would she? She has her own car and she drives the pick-up." There was now a tone of defiance, of frustration in his answer. Quinn moved over and inspected the keys. It was obvious that they had not been there long.

"Come and look around here but touch nothing. Is there anything else you see that wasn't here the last time you were in or that's been moved or ..." he paused considering what he was going to ask next ... "is out of place?"

Bostock came to stand by Quinn and he went along the line of nails. Shaking his head he turned, then stopped. "There, that wasn't there this morning. I came in to collect some hurdles." He pointed to a stack of straw bales that had been there some time as they were now grey with dust and cobwebs. Protruding from one was a knife handle and wrapped between the hilt and the straw was a butcher's chainmail glove. From its appearance it looked as though it was a recent addition. Quinn looked at Bostock. "Was it here before and just been moved or did it come with the keys?"

"Never seen it before." There was an uncertainty and confusion in Bostock's voice. "What the fuck is going on?"

Shakti had noticed the worry in Belinda's eyes when on their arrival she asked if they had checked the barn. She had seized the opportunity to question her when her husband was with Quinn. The information was sensitive and Shakti had assured her that she would not mention it when the men returned, informing her that she could not withhold evidence and that her husband would find out as the investigation proceeded. Shakti's insistence that they were investigating two murders and not car theft seemed to bring her a greater degree of understanding but also anxiety. The door opened and Belinda jumped, looking towards it before returning her gaze to Shakti. She leaned over and touched the officer's hand as if reminding her of their agreement.

"Did you know about the keys in the barn, the ones to Peterson's motor?" Ted walked quickly over to his wife and towered above her. "Well?"

"No. I thought you kept them somewhere but exactly where I couldn't say." There was a long pause as Belinda's complexion reddened.

"So how come I'm told that your DNA was on the keys? Yours, mine and Peterson's. Funny that, if you didn't know where they were. Have you been in that car?" He raised his voice and Belinda seemed to try and inch a little further away. She looked at Shakti and then Quinn before turning her gaze to her husband.

Quinn was the next to speak. "Remember the photograph removed from the wall at Peterson's, the one you rang your wife about as you couldn't remember certain names?"

"What's that got to do with this?" Bostock turned. Spittle flew from his lips as his eyes narrowed. Quinn noticed his fist begin to clench.

"Funny how you couldn't remember that your brother, Trevor, was one of the four."

He quickly turned back to Belinda. "Just what have you been bloody saying?"

Chapter Fourteen

It would be nine thirty before Karl left the shop. He checked his watch, knowing Leonard would be coming later in the day and he had errands to run first. Jo had collected his order whilst he showered and they had kissed as he left the shop.

"Next week?" Jo asked as he left.

"Are you sure the door to the shop was ajar this morning?" Karl sounded guilty.

"It's a good job it was a calm night otherwise the bell would have warned us. I've checked the main stock and nothing's missing. You were worth the trouble." She kissed him again.

It was only when she was serving her first customer that it was brought to her attention. The customer had spotted it on the floor to the left of the door. "Is this yours, dear?" the elderly customer had asked. She stooped uncomfortably to pick it up.

She placed the item onto the counter next to the RSPCA charity container. It appeared to be a photograph. Jo looked at it. *Looks like someone has dropped it or it's come through the letter box*, she mumbled to herself as she adjusted her reading glasses. "Maybe this man with …" she paused looking closely at the people in the picture. On recognising one of the men she laughed. "If I'm not mistaken. What am I going to do with that man? Firstly, he leaves the door unlocked and then … drops this. Pity it wasn't his wallet! I know who's lost this. Thank you, I wouldn't have seen it until I cleaned or the post was delivered."

The customer smiled, collected her change and her purchase and left, the doorbell sounding its familiar ring.

Reaching for her phone, she dialled Karl's mobile but it went to voice mail. She collected the photo and put it on the shelf below the counter top. She would call again later if he did not respond to her message.

Karl had left his phone in his jacket pocket as he was to prepare for Leonard's visit. Having given a great deal of thought to a suitable birthday gift, he realised that both a spider and a snake would be too difficult to manage. He was also unsure as to whether his friend would handle the creatures appropriately when unsupervised. Although Leonard was compliant most of the time he was in the apartment, he had witnessed some disturbing outbursts when he was leaving and on one occasion when he had seen him in public. It was when looking at the fish at Jo's that the idea had come to him. His conversation too with Penny had a strong bearing.

He checked the animals in his care, grabbed a biscuit and his paper before going down into the conservatory. Checking his watch, he had forty minutes to himself.

***

"When's my birthday?" Leonard asked for the fourth time that morning.

"It's on the 30th. We'll have a cake and candles. We'll take it to Karl and his friends. Would you like that, my precious boy?"

Leonard ran his finger along the calendar until it rested on the red cross marked in the square of the thirtieth. Penny came over, moved his finger to the day's date and they counted together.

"One, two, three, four. Four days, three more sleeps." Leonard hugged her and bounced up and down. He squeezed tightly until Penny felt as though she could not breathe.

"Stop now!" she gasped. "I can hardly breathe." She looked up into his eyes and saw the same look she had witnessed in the past, when he was particularly cruel, a look that seemed to be coming more and more frequently.

"Say please, mummy, say please." Leonard squeezed a little more and she felt her feet lift slightly off the floor.

Penny began to struggle and she grew angry. She slapped his legs with her trapped arms. "Stop this at once or there will be no visit today nor will there be cake and certainly no birthday. Stop now!" The final two words she screamed louder than she had ever shouted at her son before. It had an immediate result. He let her go and he ran to a corner of the room. Penny, thankful to be able to get her breath, grabbed the nearest chair and sat. Her legs felt weak. She began to cry. For the first time in all the years she felt as though she were losing her son. Maybe she was just getting too old to be his mother and his full-time carer. At times like these she loved him but she did not like him.

Leonard turned and saw Penny's discomfort. He thrust his fingers into his mouth and he too began to cry, but he was unsure why. "Will I still see Karl, mummy?" was all he could repeatedly ask.

Penny looked up wiping the tears from her cheeks with her hands. "What do you say to mummy, young man?" her voice now calm, but still unsteady. She looked across at him. "Well, what do you say?"

"Please, like you should say." She saw it in his eyes again and for the first time felt frightened of her own son.

***

Quinn and Shakti looked across the desk as Owen read through the notes they had taken whilst at the farm.

"So, the car was in exactly the same position as when it was taken?" He did not lift his head but carried on reading. "The keys, or should we say a set of keys, were in the barn and yet we have the original set in forensic storage. We can safely presume, if we should ever make presumptions in our line of work, that whoever took the vehicle brought it back, borrowed it for whatever purpose. We do, however, know that Peterson reported it missing but it was not located until it was discovered illegally parked and without tax or insurance on Albany Road. That was a good number of days after it was reported missing and there's some uncertainty as to when it was actually taken as according to the Bostocks each thought Peterson had driven it away when they were out. If you check that day, you'll also see that too was a Thursday. Are you seeing the connection I'm seeing?" Owen looked up at both his officers and smiled. "Once it was reported found, Peterson was notified and the car was moved. We know that this couldn't have been him because he was dead by then."

Quinn quickly raised a finger. "Belinda Bostock told Shakti that the day after the car went missing, a man came to the farm asking about Peterson's whereabouts. She said he was looking around the barn area when she first noticed him. Smartly dressed, quite elderly but she thought he was police. It was the way he spoke, his dress and his shoes. Clean and shiny."

"Not Flash, I hope," Owen quipped, as both laughed at the thought. Cyril had always carried the nickname *Flash.* Many new officers believed it was because of his immaculate dress sense and highly polished shoes, but it had originated owing to his name. Originally, as a young copper, he was known as Gordon after the billionaire Gordon Bennett, famous for the races trophy. It did not take someone long to link Gordon with *Flash Gordon* and so the name *Flash* stuck. Even after working with Bennett for a number of years, Owen had never heard many call him that to his face and those that dared usually received the worst from his tongue.

"As you see, sir, this all came about after I mentioned that traces of her DNA were found on the keys that Peterson left hanging in the barn even though she had denied any knowledge of them being there. It blew up when Ted Bostock insisted on knowing how that could happen. Let's say further tests will be taking place once the car is back at the forensic garage." Quinn raised his eyebrows and smiled. "The games people play, sir!"

"So how did Bostock respond to that?" Owen asked, probably knowing the answer.

"It wasn't pleasant but she mentioned that she'd also forgotten about a bloke who called, let's say in the days after the car went missing. Bostock put two and two together and got six thinking that he too might have been, let's say, enjoying his wife's alleged hospitality."

"So, where are we with them? And how come there was no mention of his brother when questioned about the photograph?" Owen closed the notes.

"According to Ted, he's not heard from his brother for a number of years. Fell out over the inheritance. After all, we're talking ten years' age difference and it seems the sudden arrival of a younger brother caused upset from the start. Bostock even suggested that he probably drank himself to death!"

Owen, concerned by the brevity of the statement, looked up but Quinn continued. "He still maintains that he'd forgotten he was in the photograph and protested his innocence. He seemed relieved to direct the questioning away from himself onto his wife when the DNA was mentioned."

Shakti swiftly continued the discussion. "I feel sorry for the woman if I'm honest. She's coming in today to look through some photographs of possible suspects but we've also planned *Efit-V*, if she doesn't identify anyone."

Owen nodded. "Good. Owing to the potential links with animals and their welfare make sure you drag images of hunt saboteurs or the animal rights brigade. From recent experience you might find one of those capable of just about anything, even though the hunting of foxes by hounds has been banned since 2004."

"The newspaper photograph Park sent will go live on the North Yorkshire Police website today and we've planned for media coverage. We're also asking for witnesses in the area around Peterson's and the farm in the days leading up to and following his murder. If, like they say, he was on foot someone might have some dash cam footage. A long shot, I know, as most is recycled if not saved for any specific reason. We need to track Hurst and Bostock's brother even though he believes he's dead."

"What about this knife and butcher's glove?" Owen turned the file round. It showed a clear image of the knife and the glove attached to the straw bale.

"With Forensics now. Neither knows how it got there. Bostock assured me it wasn't there earlier in the day but then he can be a stranger to the truth when he wants to be. You'll have noted the initials on the handle – *BHB*?"

"Bill Hurst?" Shakti offered. "No idea about the last letter unless he liked things in balance."

"This is getting muddier the more we investigate. I could do with getting my backside on a lounger for a couple of weeks."

"Marriage and honeymoon are you suggesting, sir?" Shakti giggled.

"On second thoughts let's just grab a brew, I'm spitting feathers here. Let me know what you and Forensics discover and keep everything updated. And Shak, spend time with Belinda Bostock when she's in. Woman to woman, she might just tell us more when he's not about."

***

It took Penny a while to decide whether to make her planned visit to the retirement home. She knew Leonard was not deserving after his episode that morning but something within her, something she would not describe as fear, more like uncertainty, brought about her change of mind. The walk had been without incident and she was relieved when they reached the conservatory. Karl stood and welcomed them both. As usual, Leonard needed the toilet and he happily went down the corridor giving her time to explain briefly what had occurred that morning. Although showing concern, Karl had smiled. "Leave him to me, Penny. You rest and recuperate. I'll send tea and my paper in there. Some people are sitting in the garden, feel free to join them, you know most of them by now. We need to plan that birthday." He leaned and kissed her cheek. For the first time that morning she felt cherished and cared for. Goodness, did she need it.

Her eyes were closed when Karl brought Leonard into the room. He put his finger to his lips but as before Penny was only resting. Leonard immediately came across to her and took her hand before looking at Karl, he then looked back at his mother. "Sorry for frightening you. I don't know my own strength. Sorry. I promise not to do it again." As soon as he had finished, he looked at Karl for his approval. Karl smiled and nodded.

"Sit there, Leonard. I want to plan something with your mum. You know what it's about. We're just going through to the other lounge. If you move from your chair, we'll not be able to do what we hope to. I'll be able to see you and you'll be able to see me. Are you happy with that? We'll then feed the bearded dragon, it's your favourite of my pets, I know."

Leonard sat, brought his fingers to his mouth and grinned before nodding. He was fascinated by the idea of releasing live insects into the vivarium and Karl had kindly allowed him to visit the room in his apartment where all three pets were kept. On the first occasion, he was spoiled for choice but soon settled for the dragon. It was the name. He would sing *Puff the Magic Dragon* over and over again as the reptile moved freely. Being diurnal meant that Leonard saw it active unlike the snake and the spider. It's size and that of the vivarium had also made an impression. However, the dragon was the one pet Karl would not allow Leonard to touch.

***

Karl had not long entered his apartment when he heard his phone ring in the jacket hanging by the door. Fumbling to retrieve it from the inner pocket it stopped ringing. Four missed calls showed on the screen. All from Jo. He dialled.

"Love must be a wonderful thing to throw a man of mature age, a man of the world, into a spin. First not locking the door and then leaving a personal item behind." He heard her chuckle.

"Sorry again for the door. You women hold us in your thrall. Now, what personal item?"

"It's a small photograph of you in uniform and some others. One's holding a snake. When was it taken?" She did not wait for a response. "I know your game – you're hoping for a matinee performance, as you once called it." It had amused her at the time and she chuckled again at her remark.

"Now that would be exciting but I have a job I must do this afternoon and tomorrow I'll be away all day."

"So, who's in the picture?"

"You really don't want to know, a right bunch of nutters. Surprised you spotted me "

"It was the big snake." She chuckled again.

"Very funny."

Chapter Fifteen

Billy Hurst sighed as he opened the door to the cottage and collected the mail that had built up. It was the usual leaflets and flyers apart from two letters. He had deliberately left his case in the hallway. His feet ached and he was tired. What he needed was to piss and then make tea. Coniston had been everything he had hoped for. The weather had been kind, he had enjoyed some trapping and some shooting. Laying the traps for the foxes had been easy. The farmer owning the cottage he had rented was only too pleased with the results.

Leaning back against the cabinet he checked the mail again, keeping what he believed to be important. The rest went in the bin. It was as the kettle was beginning to whistle that he saw the framed photograph propped up on the table. He did not immediately move towards it but lifted the kettle from the gas. Knowing the picture had definitely not been there when he had left, he felt a tingle run down his neck. He scanned the rest of the kitchen. His eyes stopped at the knife block. Two were missing. Listening carefully he heard nothing but the occasional bird call. He slid the largest knife remaining from the block and ran his thumb across the edge of the blade. It was sharp, a throwback to his apprenticeship as a butcher. The blades had certainly had some use and had been sharpened many, many times to the point where they had changed from their original shape. He glanced at the initials on the handle, *BHB.*

"Billy Humphrey Butchers, Chadderton Manchester. Not Hurst, but Humphrey." The voice was light and nonthreatening, seeming to come from the lounge. "You mix and match those names to suit your present lifestyle I imagine. Don't you get confused, Billy? You were never the sharpest tool in the box."

Billy dropped the knife but quickly bent and retrieved it, his grip now stronger as if ready for a fight. He moved cautiously through to from where the sound had emanated.

"Unlike you to be timid, Billy boy. Always swift with the blade when you were in the fields with the lads, if I recall. See the photograph did you …? Bring memories flooding back did it? Memories of your old mates? Have you asked yourself how they're getting on these days, Billy, have you? Remember that specific day and the year?"

Billy stopped in the doorway. The sun streamed into the cottage, highlighting the thin layer of dust on the glass coffee table next to the chair. His heart was pounding and he felt fear course through his body. Perspiration seemed to drip slowly from his temples and onto his cheeks, his hands were sweaty too. His senses were vibrant.

"Good holiday? I've been waiting patiently. Knew you were back today but unsure as to the time. However, I've all the time in the world. Retirement is the best job anyone could have, providing of course, you keep yourself amused and you have a bit of brass in the bank."

Hearing the voice but not seeing the person speaking was disconcerting. The visitor had turned the chair, the back to the door and so he was unseen. Only the top of his head was visible but that was covered in what appeared to be a light blue hood. The voice filled the room. It was strong and defiant. Bill walked around the very edge of the room his eyes never leaving the chair. He stopped on seeing the blue foot protectors that were on the visitor's feet. The same light blue covered the lower legs.

"Who the fuck are you and what do you want? You're trespassing."

That brought a chuckle. “Trespassing, Billy? I’m doing more than bloody trespassing. But then so were you if my sources are accurate. Still up to your old profession I hear on the grapevine, but mixing it with our European neighbours. Funny how the rats always find the shit.” As he spoke, he stood and turned to look at Hurst who was now partially silhouetted against the light from the window. The lowered .22 was directed at his head. “Shall I call you Billy Hurst or Billy Humphrey?”

Billy frowned. “Humphrey, no, the name’s Hurst not Humphrey.”

He knew exactly what was pointing at him, he had used them enough. He had even handled that one, but the hood and the medical type mask covering the person’s nose and mouth, the full body coverall, confused him. It was clinical and surgical and extremely threatening. He began to move forward when a gloved hand was raised. “Not a good idea when facing a man with a gun. Knife, gun, gun, knife. We both know who’ll win … I digress. Let’s talk about Ramsgill, Mr Hurst, let’s call you Humphrey as that’s the name you used back then. Lovely part of Yorkshire, Nidderdale, most of the time, but not after you and your evil bastard friends had their way. Short of brass are we or are you just doing it for amusement, checking the old butchery skills are still there? It’s not the first is it? It’s growing in popularity too!”

Billy looked the stranger up and down and his fear transmuted to anger. “Who the fuck are you and what’s my business to you?”

“Missing your old pals?”

Hurst frowned. “Buddies … Fuck you, and there’s no money here so what do you want? Have I met you before?”

“Not always been an honest man, have you, otherwise why would Humphrey become Hurst? I’ve just one question for you.

It's simple. It's either a yes or a no answer, a bit like tossing a coin, like life and death but unlike the creatures you dealt with you have a chance. I asked your pals, Peterson and Lyons the same question." There was a long pause.

Billy allowed the knife to shift in his hand as if rearranging his grip. Fear had now been replaced by confusion. He felt a prickly heat flush through his body – the adrenalin surge brought with it bravado. "And the fucking question?"

"Do you know who I am, Billy, because I clearly know you?" The gloved hand that was held out, palm facing upwards, tugged the mask, fingers gripped the edges and the covering was slowly brought below his chin. "I made sure I was facing the light so that you could take a long, clear view. I'll even smile if that will help."

The sarcasm was not lost as Hurst leaned forward taking a close look at the stranger's features. "No fucking idea …"

As he spoke the word *no,* a finger pulled the trigger and the .22 round penetrated Billy's right eye at a rising angle. It swiftly traversed the cranial cavity, passing through the frontal lobe before lodging in the parietal lobe. The knife fell first, sticking vertically into the wooden floor and, like a partially hewn tree, Billy seemed to hover as if neither standing nor falling. It was as if in death he could not make the decision as to his next action. He wavered, blood and brain matter dribbling from his chin before his knees buckled and he collapsed to the floor. His body hit the protruding knife and the tip snapped with a loud click and was immediately hidden beneath the body.

Carefully, returning the mask over his mouth and nose, the intruder laid the gun next to the body before entering the kitchen. He lifted the photograph and smiled behind the mask. *Three questions, three correct answers*. He took the framed photograph with him, retrieved Billy's car keys and left.

***

Shakti ensured Belinda Bostock was comfortable. She had brought two ceramic mugs of coffee into the police station's public lounge, a room kept to be more conducive than the bare and emotionally cold interview room. A yucca stood in one corner and prints depicting Harrogate were displayed on two walls giving the room a more friendly air. As they were about to study a selection of facial images Shakti had prepared, they sat facing a large computer screen. It had been found that people sitting away from and not directly in front of the screen had a better chance of identifying a suspect. It was a positional thing. As the trainer had said, *how often do we face people a foot from our own face?*

The photographs started to appear, were paused briefly and then changed. Shakti held the remote control and could now stop, rewind or still the images at any time. Neither spoke. Halfway through the prepared images Shakti was growing anxious.

"Stop! Please hold that one." Belinda leaned forward. The photograph was of a man looking directly at the camera, his face contorted. Two others were to one side but neither was looking at the camera. He was obviously photographed outside and he wore a woollen bobble hat, his collar up and the lower jaw covered.

"Do you recognise him, Belinda?"

Turning to look at Shakti she put her mug on the table. "It's not the man at the front but … but the guy to his left." She moved towards the screen and scrutinised it. "I think it's him."

Shakti enlarged the image but in doing so she found the clarity was reduced. "It's pixilating, sorry." She picked up her phone. "Quinn. We might have a positive on image 2016/6/BedaleHunt.127. Can you get it sharpened? Face is partly hidden by a hood and some sort of scarf. I need to talk later. Collect all the contact details we hold for that image." Shakti could have done that immediately but she was conscious of the need to try to obtain the information Owen had requested.

"Let's just go quickly through the rest, there aren't many and he might appear in other shots." She let the images roll across the screen and chose her moment. "Forgive me, but I was aware of your concern when your husband learned that your DNA was found on the keys. Did you know Peterson better than you've made out?"

Belinda laughed. "He was seventy-seven years old for goodness sake!"

"Twenty-five years ago he wasn't." Shakti waited, knowing immediately she had hit the right spot. The pause was palpable.

"In confidence?" Belinda looked at Shakti. "It will go no further?"

Shakti smiled. "Total confidence."

"When he worked full-time, he was a fun character, he had quite a reputation and if the rumours were right, had a lot of women too. He always had a great physique for a man of his age. When you're isolated as I am, no kids, just the farm, you can get, let's say, distracted. You have a lot of time and when he was working in the yard my imagination took over. His sweaty torso, shiny and lithe was a bit of a turn on to be honest. To answer your question, we had a bit of a fling."

"Bit of a fling? An affair you mean?"

"We fucked a few times but I was always worried Ted would find out and you've experienced his temper. I was also frightened in the early days that I might get pregnant. We'd tried, Ted and me, I mean, but without success and I thought that he might be sterile. Ted could breed sheep, even cattle, goats and chickens but he couldn't produce his own offspring. Back then, these problems were and still are a taboo subject. Even now men won't talk about it, let alone go and see a professional. We often wondered about his parents when you consider the age difference between him and his brother. Probably an outside contract there for Trevor as they were like chalk and cheese. Well that's what Ted said when they fell out. I went and had tests unbeknown to Ted. They informed me that there was no reason why I couldn't conceive. I didn't tell him as it would have put the blame directly onto him and this way he could still believe that it was down to me. That's what he told folks in the pub. Ted then just wrapped himself up in the farm, saying that kids were time consuming and expensive but I know he felt bitter."

"When was the last time between you and Peterson?"

"About five years ago."

"Ever in the car?"

"No, definitely not."

"So, the keys and your DNA?"

"When he came to the farm, he'd drop them in. If Ted wasn't there, we'd have a quick kiss and a cuddle. Nothing else. I'd move them so Ted wouldn't see them if he came back. Sam would go off on the tractor or in the pick-up. He'd collect them at the end of the day. I'd leave them on the front wheel or if I was about, in the car. You must understand that it was the excitement."

"Did your husband ever suspect?" Shakti moved a little closer. "Enough to want to get some kind of revenge?"

"Kill him? Definitely not. Found it hard killing crows and jays. Needed Sam for that. Sam could kill anything and not even blink. If I'd have ever told Sam that Ted hit me, he'd have shot him. I know that."

***

Owen's mobile rang, the old familiar ring tone. He saw it was Dan Grimshaw. He listened. A call had come in from a member of the public who had identified one of the people in the photograph posted on social media. He listened as Dan told him the elderly gentleman knew him as he robbed him of £2000 in 1984. "He was to lay a driveway and offered a discount if he paid up front. Strangely enough, he paid and the man never returned. Interestingly he kept the flyer and the contract. *Driveways Direct.* I've checked the files for the period and fraudulent trading seemed rife and was reported a number of times."

Owen grabbed a pen and jotted down the name. William Humphrey. 1984. Formerly a butcher and greengrocer in Chadderton Manchester before becoming a fraudster. "Bingo! Where is he now?"

Owen frowned. "We don't know? Electoral list? Do we have an age for William Humphrey or Hurst?" Owen signalled for April to come closer. "Putting you on speaker."

"He was in his late thirties then so he'll be early seventies. They said he had a fancy car and smart suits back then. A plausible and credible salesman."

"Obviously."

"From checks, he sold those previous businesses, the car and the flat and simply vanished."

"Have you looked for any Humphreys living in the area? If he's flipping between the two names that's the reason he's slipped through the bloody net."

"That's next. If he's the butcher with the knife marked *BHB* and the glove found at Bostock's, we might be too late. Check with your caller. Get hold of the flyer. He's obviously held a grudge for a long time so he might be able to help more. Try for a description of the man and anyone else who might have worked for him. If they were con men, they usually work in pairs, one the workman, the man on the ground and the other, the salesman. See what you can dig up. Go yourself. I'll get it cleared with Greater Manchester Police." Owen put down his phone as the call finished.

April had moved away and was searching for the Humphreys within a fifty-mile radius. She added the approximate date of birth. "Jollies in the Dean Cottage, between Grassington and Hebdon. Lives alone. A William Humphrey." She swiftly called control for immediate action and requested a direct link to monitor progress. She checked to see if he owned a vehicle and then linked the registration with ANPR before giving a thumbs up to Owen.

Owen moved and stood behind her chair reading the details on the screen.

"Is that all there is? Work, any history on file?"

"Adding details into HOLMES for possible links now."

***

The killer drove the car towards Grassington before pulling off the road. Placing the framed photograph on the dashboard he quickly left the car and walked a hundred metres from the vehicle before stripping off the protective clothing and stuffing it into a small bag. It would take ten minutes to walk to Grassington public car park and his own car. Out of curiosity he drove back towards Hebdon and the cottage. His heart fluttered as he saw the flashing blue lights of a police vehicle approaching. Surely they were not going to the cottage, not so soon. He slowed as the car flashed by. His curiosity getting the better of him he pulled into the first available lane, reversed and returned towards Grassington, ensuring he did not slow down as he saw the police car parked outside the cottage he had not long left. *Shit! That was a close call*, he said under his breath and instinctively looked away as he passed. He knew they were connecting the threads and his heart fluttered more erratically.

Chapter Sixteen

Owen drove as April watched the countryside flash by; it was hypnotic and she felt her mind drifting. Neither said much, aware of what they were going to witness. She could see why Cyril often arrived feeling nauseous; the blue lights now clearly visible on the otherwise plain police vehicle seemed to bring out the worst in his driving. The thought of a cyclist or animal around the next blind bend made her close her eyes and hold her breath, only relieved when the road ahead was clear. He slowed as he approached the junction at Greenhow Hill, glancing at the church to his right and then at the yellow painted bicycle chained to a wooden telegraph post. A group of cyclists sped past in the other direction.

"Wonder if The Stray will ever recover from the World Cycling Championships," he mumbled. "Right bloody mess. Heavy vehicles and soft ground are a recipe for disaster."

"It's grass, it'll grow, that's one thing we can be assured of. Ask every gardener in this country. Ralph certainly doesn't mind as long as there's the odd puddle he can roll in; he'll even settle for mud!"

Ralph was her Great Dane, a dog she had adopted after the owner had been murdered. Owen always believed its DNA had more in common with that of a donkey than a dog but he too had a soft spot for the animal; they were both gentle giants.

The CSI were present on their arrival and they soon found themselves chatting to one of the four North East Home Office pathologists. As Julie was away Owen had presumed that it might be Caner. On their first meeting Owen had reserved judgement about the man. He always felt he had a condescending air, as if there was a permanent bad smell beneath his nostrils, aloof and arrogant with the less experienced in his company. It was only when he had been welcomed to the autopsies that their friendship developed.

Caner was just removing his protective clothing as they approached. “Owen, the cavalry has not saved the day on this occasion, I’m afraid, although I have to say from my initial tests you were closer than on many. The body was still warm when the first officers arrived. One went and checked the immediate area but found nothing. Time of death maybe no more than an hour maximum! I’ll know more when I do the full tests. So, Bennett and my colleague are sunning themselves in beautiful Barbados.” He let the last syllable run on his tongue. “Whilst we mere mortals have to deal with the sins of man. Lovely place for a honeymoon, mind. Have you been?”

April looked at Owen and then back to Caner. Both shook their heads and she wondered if Owen was thinking of Rodcliff Massiah, a friend and fellow officer who had inspired Cyril to book the holiday.

“You know DS Richmond?”

Caner smiled. “Indeed. We always seem to meet in such unpleasant circumstances. April, if my memory serves me correctly.”

April smiled.

“Billy Hurst, I’m informed, although the cottage is rented by a Humphrey. Shot in the head with a small calibre bullet .22. Penetrated the right eye. Reminded me of the case of a famous boxer. He was found in the rear of a car in a back street in Blackpool with an air gun pellet through his eye. Found sitting with the rifle pointing upwards. Never caught the person who did it. A long time ago so before my time, but I digress. Projectile will still be present in the skull as there’s no visible exit wound.

We'll get that as soon as he's on the table. However, I feel sure that it will match the gun that was to his side."

Owen looked again at April. "The missing gun from Peterson's place. Then there's the knife, probably removed from here. If that's the case we know it's the same person who killed Lyons and Peterson."

"Forensics noted three knives missing from the knife block. Each marked *BHB.* However, one was found under the body. Looks like he had it as some kind of defence. You'll get a clearer picture once inside. Nothing's been moved. Will be in touch."

As Caner walked away, Owen read April's facial expression and jumped quickly to his defence.

"Before you say anything, I used to feel the same about him. Trust me, he's fine."

"I'd have labelled him under the category of 'T'."

Owen chuckled and nodded.

Before entering they added the compulsory protective overgarments. In the lounge, Owen crouched near the body and tilted his head. The blood had congealed around the eye socket but the face below it was streaked with blood and matter. There was surprisingly little pooled below his face. He then noticed the chair placed at an unusual angle, as if deliberately positioned with its back to the door; it seemed out of place when he looked at the room's general layout. There were indentations in the rug to the right suggesting it had recently been moved from its regular position. The CSI confirmed it had been resited. It would be photographed and measured for a full ballistic examination.

"We need to see if this gun matches the one taken from Peterson's. Priority DNA testing after ballistics, please," Owen instructed. "We also need to do comparative DNA with the other two houses and with the Bostocks"

April had left the room on feeling her phone vibrate. It was Quinn. Humphrey's car had been located a five minutes' drive away and as they were close by, he requested they take a look.

Owen drove. The car for which they searched, a silver grey Mitsubishi Shogun, was parked partly on the grass verge. A police car was positioned across the road preventing access.

Owen showed his ID as the officer approached.

"It's one way, sir. Leads to a fish farm of all things. The keys are in and there's no sign of forced entry. There's a framed photograph on the dashboard. You can see it clearly."

Both slipped on overshoes and gloves for the second time before approaching. They took it in turns to look through the windscreen in an endeavour to keep the site forensically secure. It was April who spoke first. "That, if I'm not mistaken is the size of the picture missing from Peterson's, but that's not of the horse race, it's the one we found in the box beneath Peterson's body, the one with the faces removed." She grabbed her mobile phone and took three photographs. Checking her screen she enlarged the image to get a clear view of the faces. "If I'm right, those are the same four men taken years later and in different positions but ..."

Owen looked and nodded. "Indeed. Whoever is responsible is playing a bloody game."

As they were leaving the CSI arrived. Owen approached the van. "There's a framed photograph on the dash ..." He did not finish his sentence.

The investigator smiled and quietly replied, "As soon as?"

"Indeed. Thank you." He tapped the van roof. "Appreciate that!"

As they passed the cottage they saw the black van marked Private Ambulance parked next to the CSI's vehicle.

"Let's hope Caner can find some answers too."

***

Karl had not been in long and he needed a shower. He checked his postbox on entering and collected the mail. Flicking through the letters, he placed each one on the small hall table; they all appeared to be bills. The last one did not have a stamp; the pink envelope was quite a contrast and was addressed with one word – Karl. He reached for the letter knife and slid the top of the envelope before retrieving the single sheet.

Dear Karl,

I do hope you don't mind my communicating in this way but it's difficult when Leonard is with us. After a good deal of thought I feel I must let you know a little about Leonard's history, respectfully to put into perspective my response to the kind offer you proposed for Leonard's birthday.

Many years ago, when Leonard was having difficulty developing and maintaining relationships, I decided to let him keep a puppy, a King Charles Spaniel. We had talked about his responsibility and although he would be protected from many of the general tasks associated with the care of a young dog, he knew that his kindness, gentleness and appropriate behaviour were essential if he were to keep the animal.

The first few weeks he was a changed person. He was happy to walk her, would play on The Stray, even interact with people who came up to his dog to make a fuss. I would often just sit and watch him and I believed with the help of the young dog that he had turned another page in his personal and emotional development. However, I started to notice a more sinister change. When he thought I wasn't looking he would drag the dog by its lead or whip it if it didn't immediately do as instructed. The final straw came when I heard the dog crying. I dashed into the lounge to find he had the dog in the corner and his hands were round its neck. He told me that she had tried to bite him but there was something in his eyes, an anger I had never seen before. I'd seen fear and distress on many occasions but there was a venom, a cold and disturbing expression. As you can imagine, the dog was returned and from that day he became his normal self. He never mentioned the dog ... but I think I've told you this before, I'm sorry.

I believe buying him an animal that he could handle would be unfair on the creature. I couldn't trust him when I wasn't there. You've seen him follow your rules when handling spiders and snakes but you've always been there as you were when you first met when walking your friend's dog. The only suggestion I can offer is a fish, he wouldn't handle that. I would be happy to buy a small fish tank if you wanted to buy him a fish. I would leave that to your expertise.

You might like to send me a text message, you have my number. I must say, Karl, that since we met all those months ago, you've given me a good deal of hope, but more importantly I appreciate the time we've had to talk and meeting the people there when he is with you, I feel human again for the first time for many, many years. I feel now that I have a true shoulder to cry on, someone to share my fears and I sincerely thank you for giving me the time and space to be me … Bless you!

Karl reread the letter and the last paragraph three times. He put the sheet down. He had recognised she was a strong woman from the time they had chatted together but suddenly he now realised that even though she had an iron façade, there was a growing vulnerability and a developing weakness. Although she was not old by any means and she was an attractive woman, she was trapped. She was in many ways a caged animal, her freedom since giving birth to Leonard had been curtailed. She loved the boy, she always had and always would but her life was leaching away. He had allowed her some respite, to see the light. He also thought about Leonard. Karl had known some cruel people in his time, not only those who traded on a person's emotional weakness but those who relished physical harm to both animal and humans alike. He collected his phone and prepared the text.

***

"It's like ten green bottles. Now there's only one, Bostock." Owen checked the notes. "British army five years. Served in Belize, Cyprus and Northern Ireland. Can we get a picture of him from that time on social media? There must be people out there who knew him and might have kept in contact. If they have they might know his whereabouts."

Grimshaw came into the room waving a flyer. Owen turned. "What did you find in Manchester?"

"According to the guy, Peterson may well have been a partner of Hurst who was then Humphrey. He saw the picture we have of Peterson taken in 1986 and he immediately identified him. There was no doubt. I just need to get that confirmed. Peterson only started to work for Bostock over the last twenty-five years, so that's a possibility. Two are linked, so what's the connection? We have the hunting picture but the faces are missing. Can we assume it's the same four? Could it be to do with animal rights? We know Belinda Bostock identified the person who called at the farm after the car was taken. He was looking for Peterson and was involved in the anti-hunt protests and we know there can be some right nutters amongst them, mind you, the same goes for those on the hunt. They bring some right bastards as protection."

Owen moved across to look at the image that was once the faceless four but now, after locating the photograph in the car, they could see that there was a match. He also checked the image of the man identified from the hunt. The partial facial covering made him doubt the accuracy.

Shakti opened the door. "Two things. Forensics say there are two photographs in the frame, the one we have there," she pointed to the photograph Owen had been looking at, "and beneath that was the one from Ripon races. We know that was once on Peterson's wall. Now whether they have just been changed around and they were both there originally is only a guess but they both hold his DNA. More importantly, so do items found in the boot of the car of, shall we say, 'H' to keep ourselves from repeating Hurst and Humphrey now we know they're one and the same; overalls, wellingtons and a head torch. There's a match too to the prints lifted from the field after the rustling incident at Ramsgill. All the evidence suggests he was involved."

"Was there a knife or a chain butcher's glove?" Owen asked.

"No, only rubber gloves. Here's the list and the images taken as they were found and removed."

Owen took the list and read it.

Chapter Seventeen

The aircraft shuddered as it momentarily penetrated the white cumulous cloud. Cyril rubbed his eyes. The eight hour flight had been comfortable but he could not settle to watch a film nor read. His mind kept going over the case details with which Owen had furnished him. Glancing out of the window he looked down on Stockport and he mentally arranged the roads and railways into his mind's map. Within minutes he felt the undercarriage drop and lock bringing a shudder through the airframe. Julie instinctively reached out and took his hand. She leaned over and kissed his cheek.

"That was so special, Cyril. I'd heard a great deal about Barbados but never did I think I'd fall in love with the place like I did. Thank you."

Cyril felt guilty. He had enjoyed it but he also thought ten days would have been sufficient. As one of his old colleagues used to say after a shift of nights – *You can have too much of a good thing!*

If he found the flight tedious, the wait around the carousel seemed eternal. Everyone's luggage arrived quickly but there was no sign of theirs. He checked his watch, shook his wrist and looked again. A nicotine patch had helped him get through the flight but he was desperate for a vape. He thought of having a crafty couple of intakes behind a column but then thought better of it.

"Trying to speed up time, Cyril?" Julie chuckled. "They'll come. I've contacted the taxi and he's ready to meet us so you'll soon be back righting wrongs."

Ninety minutes later they stood in front of their home in Robert Street, luggage at their feet. Cyril found the key and opened the door. "I should really carry you over the threshold Mrs Bennett but …" He quickly bent at the knees, grabbed Julie and swept her off her feet before whisking her into the hallway. They kissed and Cyril felt a warm glow. "It's been special, you've been special and I'm just …" He did not finish as Julie kissed him again.

They heard a cough outside as if someone was trying to attract their attention, then a dog barked and Cyril felt the animal pass through his ankles. He knew just what it was and who was at the door.

"Congratulations to you both. We thought we'd just pop over and bring these just in case you hadn't made provision." The Germanic tone immediately informed Cyril it was Mrs Pfeiffer from across the road. The eyes and ears of the street. "We've been keeping our eyes open Mr Bennett, and now of course Mrs Bennett, and I note your big friend has been checking too. Kept seeing the occasional police car pop down." She moved inside the door and put down a small cardboard box. "Some milk, bread and six eggs. Just a thought." She smiled. "We'll not keep you, I'm sure you have much to do. Come on Hercule, leave Mr Bennett be."

"Thank you very much for the groceries, that's so kind," Julie remarked and they both bent and rubbed the Dachshund's ears, their actions bringing frantic movement to its tail and the whole of its back end.

"He'll stand that all day. Come on. This lovely couple have things to do." The dog reluctantly left.

"You bring the cases and I'll take these gifts in and get the kettle on. Tea never seems to taste the same when I'm away and I've longed for a good brew since boarding that aircraft."

When Julie came into the lounge Cyril was holding the wrapped painting. She put his cup and saucer on the coffee table. “To my wonderful husband. You can open it.”

Cyril untied the ribbon before slowly removing the heart patterned paper. As the final piece fell, he held it out at arm’s length. Julie had moved to the side to see his face as he viewed it for the first time; she was not disappointed.

“It’s a Whone. Herbert Bannister Whone.” He turned to Julie. “How did you get this? It’s perfect. You know he was a viol ...” He did not finish his sentence. Julie put her finger to his lips. “You like it I take it?”

“It’s just perfect. Everything about my life is in that picture. You knew that didn’t you?”

Julie smiled.

“I love you, Julie Pritchett.” He kissed her.

“Bennett. Julie Bennett. Your big friend got it for me at auction. I was worried at one point you might have been bidding against each other. You on the phone and Owen there. Luckily for me, you weren’t.”

***

It had to be said that Cyril felt decidedly jet lagged as he walked up Otley Road the following morning. He stopped to admire the needle-sharp spire of Trinity Methodist Church rising above the trees’ foliage. Somehow it seemed as if he had never been away other than for his lethargy and feeling a little chilly. He called into the usual shop to replenish his menthol vaping fluid, some atomisers and a newspaper. Even though the sun was high bringing early morning warmth, after Barbados temperatures he felt as though he needed his waxed jacket.

After a momentous change in his circumstances that he had not undergone without a good deal of thought, he realised that life went on. He stopped and looked at Harrogate Police Station – modern, efficient and in some ways a little soulless when you considered the architecture of the previous police building. Nothing was different. The squashed beer can was still lodged in the hedge where it had been when he had left a fortnight ago. Whether it was his jet lagged state or just his present mental euphoria, he pondered on the thought of death. If he had died a fortnight ago there would have been a funeral and not the wedding but life would go on. Just as it did when Liz Graydon was killed, life and the work of the police here in Harrogate continued. He suddenly felt human, almost insignificant, possibly mortal.

Quickly mounting the steps, he entered. The desk sergeant immediately sprang to his feet as did the others working behind the glass. Their welcome was as warm as the Bajan sun he had left behind twenty-four hours ago.

His office was no different. The *Welcome Back* banner across the door brought a smile. On entering he placed his jacket on the hanger and took a brief look around, his eyes travelling the full one hundred and eighty degrees. *It's good to be back,* he whispered. It was then that he noticed the wrapped parcel on his desk. He looked outside. The desks were unusually empty for that time of day. Had he missed something? Was there an early briefing? His attention was again drawn to the parcel. He read the attached label.

To Julie and Cyril on your wedding – well to be accurate – after your
wedding.
Proud to have played a small part.

Owen and Hannah
xx
(Hannah added those!)

Cyril laughed out loud. *In church he offered to marry me if Julie didn't turn up and now, he's frightened of a kiss,* he thought as he unwrapped the gift. The door opened as he held the statue at arm's length and loud cheering broke the moment of magic in its own special way.

"Welcome back, sir!" the chorus of voices announced, with Owen's voice booming over the many.

"Hope you like it. Strangely, it's called *Liberty* but I suppose that will depend on how you perceive marriage." Owen moved across and shook his hand before the rest of the team filed in. Within five minutes they were gone leaving April and Owen. It was business as usual and Cyril needed that.

"It's all there," Owen presented. "This is a strange one with threads running to and fro with various items linking one death with another. No particular pattern other than the four people now seen in two separate photographs. The more we investigate the more it seems to be linked to animal rights, certainly there's a strong link to animals from the very start. Awaiting Forensics from the latest murder case."

April spoke. "This guy has been using two names, Hurst and Humphrey, but you'll be reading that in the files. There's been a confirmed link between him and the second victim – they worked together and committed crimes together in the past. Also there's forensic evidence linking him to the slaughter and butchering of thirteen sheep near Ramsgill and as you know rustling's been on the increase across many counties."

"Bit of a jack the lad. Any links with the first case to that?"

"Their ages are quite disparate." Cyril turned to look at Owen, surprised at his vocabulary. "Lyons, George Lyons was the oldest of the three."

"So, what ages do we have?" Cyril started to open the files. He knew Owen preferred screen to paper but continued. "Lyons, eighty-three, Peterson, seventy-seven and 'H', as he's been labelled to save confusion was seventy-three."

"Disparate?" Cyril said. "Only ten years, Owen. Not much in a lifetime."

"Tell that to a twenty-year-old who has to teach a ten-year-old sibling ... sir."

"Point taken, Owen."

"The fourth, and we haven't located his whereabouts as yet, is the youngster of the gang of four, a Trevor Bostock. He's only sixty-six. Peterson worked for Bostock's brother for twenty-five plus years as well as being involved before that with 'H'. Peterson was also possibly linked to Lyons and so too maybe 'H'. It's a web of intrigue. However, there's another face been added to the equation and possibly the face of the killer. We know that it's not Trevor Bostock as he's in the two photographs we hold."

"Facial recognition?" Cyril asked, knowing he was treading on thin ice.

***

The bell on the shop door rang just as Joanne Taylor had sat down to lunch. Karl had suggested she close for thirty minutes stating that even prisoners and her pets got a lunch break. It brought a smile but now it made her realise that he was right. Taking a bowl from the cupboard she slipped it over the plate in the hope that it would at least stay warm.

There was a man in the shop, his back towards her as he inspected the gerbils in the gerbilarium. She knew him. He turned and smiled.

"I've seen these little critters in the wild, the desert rat. Once had one, and of course called it Monty, until it produced a litter of pups, so probably had two somewhere!"

"Thought you were only back on Friday?" By now Joanne had forgotten about her lunch.

"Slight change of plan so thought I'd come and see my companion, Lilith, sooner and let you know I'll still need her to remain here until Monday. I'll pay for the full board period, of course. Wouldn't have it any other way. Just need to get things ready at home."

"I love the fact that she's your companion and not your pet. Why Lilith, should I know?"

He dug into his pocket and withdrew a wallet. Inside the clear plastic side was a postcard of a painting. "A few years back I went to *The Grand National*, bloody evil horse race. I was staying in Southport as that's easy travelling distance. It was busy and I could only get a B&B but I called at the museum and gallery, The Atkinson. Facing the entrance was this painting, it was huge – can't remember who painted it, probably on the back. It was the constrictor that attracted me."

Jo looked at the image of the beautiful naked girl, red flowing hair to her waist, her milky white skin entwined by the snake. She chuckled. "Most men wouldn't see the snake. Didn't think you were the horse racing type."

"I like a flutter every now and again and Aintree is anyone's race." He put the postcard back in his pocket.

"I get many people in here who feel the same about cats and dogs but few who feel that way about other animals and especially reptiles. You give me a warm feeling. As I said when you left her, I wouldn't be confident handling her now she's the size she is. Four-foot constrictors are my limit and she's getting to be a little too big. You can see she's cared for." She smiled and led him through to the back room and the largest glass tank. "I'll leave you two together, my lunch will be getting cold. Just shout up when you're leaving and I'll see you Monday. I'd rather keep her a week than a fortnight as my gran used to say. She has a good appetite."

He reached into the tank and allowed the snake to slowly wrap around his arm. "I've missed you, Lilith."

***

The briefing room was full and the files had been distributed. The fuss made when Cyril entered had caused a delay but April quickly managed to restore calm and make a start.

"Firstly, we have results from Peterson's car, DNA checks for all the deceased and also the Bostocks. We have others too but as yet they haven't been linked. Of course, the Bostocks, if they are brothers, will probably only have a fifty percent match owing to genetic recombination."

"Army records?" asked an officer who was leaning near the whiteboards.

"Biometrics are relatively new, DC Chatterjee. DNA samples only taken from 1992, so our lad missed it by miles. However, we do have bodily fluid samples that match and no prizes for guessing whether front or back seats, but when I say Bostock and Bostock and Bostock and Peterson, we get an interesting picture. According to Shakti's interview, Mrs B never used the vehicle. The DNA is of a sibling and not that of Ted. And Chatterjee, if you're unfamiliar with genetic recombination or familial DNA you need to refresh your knowledge."

The young officer smiled nervously and acknowledged the advice.

"She admitted having sex with Peterson but not within the last five years and I don't believe it was a regular thing, more spur of the moment. If I may suggest, lust. However, the samples taken were not that old according to the lab results."

It was Cyril's turn to speak. "So, what do we have and what do we still need? Open minds everyone. Let's try to focus and get a direction. When we confront Mrs Bostock she only needs to know we have a sample from a Bostock, we'll let her work herself out of that."

"We have four white males, three now dead. One, Trevor Bostock is missing, his history is on file but his whereabouts unknown. A man who was seen at the farm and subsequently identified in footage taken at the Bedale hunt in 2016 but that has to be confirmed," came the response from April without hesitation.

Chapter Eighteen

Karl had waited until the time Penny had suggested before calling. As usual, he knew Leonard would be in bed; she had given him his usual sleeping tablet. Having him up in the night had always been a worry, especially if she had experienced difficult and long days with him. People in the early years had suggested respite and carers but she was young and proud and only now did she realise that she might also have been foolish. She had agreed to the small fish tank and two fish as a gift for Leonard's birthday, as Karl had assured her there was little he could do to harm them providing the freshwater aquarium was set up properly, they fed the fish correctly and followed simple rules.

"I'll set the tank up now and I'll pop round every month. We'll change some of the water together and monitor his level of interest and care. If this works, we can think of getting a gerbil. Tomorrow morning, if you keep him out of this room, I'll collect you both and take you to the pet shop. Jo, the owner, you'll like her, Penny, will show us some of the animals there. We can then return to show him his presents. As I've suggested, there's one I want him to see."

Karl put the small tank on a metal stand. He had bought it second-hand along with the aquarium and Jo had sold him the fish; he had bought six Bettas, the easiest fish to own. He had also bought a ship wreck and a diver to put into the tank, as well as greenery. Adding the light made the difference, giving the tank and the room a lovely green glow. Bubbles from the filter added to the nautical impression.

"He'll love that, Karl. Thank you so much. I'm looking forward to meeting Jo. It's so good to get out and make new friends." She leaned over and kissed his cheek. "You've been so kind to us both. You've given me a purpose again."

"I hope you don't mind my saying this, but remember you're an attractive woman and you've worked wonders with that boy of yours. Many people would have thrown in the towel by now and placed him in a home of some kind."

Penny found herself welling up and had to turn away. "If you hadn't been so kind," she whispered as she wiped her eyes, "there would only be the two of us for his birthday. I've made a cake and promised candles. Maybe later we could all walk to yours and let your friends make a fuss of him and he can see your animal friends."

Karl put his hand on hers. "It will be a pleasure. I'll see you at eight tomorrow."

***

Quinn and Shakti pulled into the farmyard and as if on cue the barking started, however, on this occasion there was only one dog.

"Unusual, usually two or none."

Mrs Bostock came from the farmhouse. She was wiping her wet hands on her apron as the few chickens ran towards her, thinking there might be food. They were quickly disappointed and slowly went back to their scratching. "What now? Found the man who called?" Her voice carried across the yard. It was obvious her husband was out.

"Just need a private word. We can do it at the station or in the car or …" Quinn pointed to the house.

"More questions! I'll put the kettle on. Ted won't be home until one. Out at the Farmers' Market."

Once inside, Quinn sat down, stirred his tea and left the questioning to Shakti.

Mrs Bostock fussed getting biscuits and removing her apron but they both let her settle. They needed her to be calm but they required answers.

"During our conversation you mentioned that you and Peterson, well how shall we say with DC Quinn here present, were good friends?"

"I've told you and even though he looks but a lad, if he's a copper, he's seen it and been there. We had sex." There was a pause. "You said in confidence!"

"You said it, Mrs Bostock. How did Peterson come to get a job here in the first place?"

"That's some years back, as you very well know. He came recommended by Trevor, Ted's brother. Brought a letter, a kind of testimonial. Ted put him on a month's trial and after that rented him the cottage and gave him full-time employment."

"Was there any trouble workwise?"

"We've always maintained he was hard-working. He'd do anything. Ted was right, he was frightened of nothing, including hard work. With Trevor not on the farm he was a godsend. At that time, we were trying for kids and if they'd come along, we'd have needed more help. As it was, we were okay."

"So how are you managing now?" Quinn asked.

"We've cut back on the land we farm. Rent out acreage and that helps. We'll sort out Peterson's and rent that when it's appropriate to do so. We'll get by, always have and hopefully always will."

"This question might seem strange as we've already had this conversation. The Forensics on Peterson's car indicate your bodily fluid was found on the rear seat. My notes suggest ..."

"I know what I told you. Once or twice we'd go for a drive and end up ... you know. Bloody silly, two middle-aged folk romping in the back seat. Made us both laugh; cheered us up."

"Your husband never suspected?"

"No, we were careful. Mind on one occasion someone banged on the roof and shouted something, but we thought it was kids."

"What's strange, Mrs Bostock, is that there's also a sample of body fluid of someone, let's say with the name Bostock. We are talking semen DNA."

She wrapped her hands more tightly round her mug and her expression quickly changed.

"Ted? In the car? Who with?"

"So not with you?"

"Don't be bloody silly. Christmas! He could hardly manage me in bed let alone some floozy in the back of a bloody car." She picked up the mug and drank but then realised what she had said and blushed.

Quinn and Shakti let the silence linger longer than usual. "So, if it couldn't have been Ted and it's a match to the Bostock family, what about Trevor, Mrs Bostock?"

Her face flushed a deeper red.

***

Cyril sat at his desk. There was a large board spread out before him, containing images of all the items linked to the case. The carpet thread and the captive bolt gun, the .22 rifle, the photographs, the butcher's glove and knife. Strangely enough he added a photograph of the car. He circled each item before drawing lines linking each if there was a connection, then listed all the names. It was methodical. He realised that his team had been staring at the evidence for a couple of weeks and he now had the opportunity to consider it with fresh eyes; he was aware of that advantage. Reading the notes taken from the interviews he added his own single word annotations, aides-memoire. Finch, Holgate the paramedic, John Gornall the original finder of Peterson's car, Tony Calderbank the community bobby and the farmer Gill Cunningham, Ted and Belinda Bostock. He incorporated details from the history of those murdered, again, just single words. He steepled his fingers briefly and drew on his electronic cigarette. A curl of minty vapour hung momentarily before disappearing. He added Trevor and underlined the word twice before writing *Survivor! Methuselah or Murderer?*

***

Belinda Bostock hung her head then nodded. "Forgive me but I feel so ashamed. With Ted not being … you know and finding I didn't have a problem I just thought if I could get pregnant it would solve everything and the farm would be handed down another generation. I knew he had a reputation with women in town, he'd have anything in a skirt, but he was kind."

"Did you tell him the reason?"

She shook her head. "Why would I do that?"

"Why the car? Surely there are more comfortable places."

"If anyone saw the car it would immediately be linked to Peterson but we did it before that too, before Peterson arrived here, just before Trevor left. I'm a weak woman, surely you believe that. He was kind, called me Lilith and I thought it beautiful. He never forgot that, always called me by that name."

Quinn jotted down the word thinking he probably called all his girls by that sobriquet. Romantic for a farm boy! Changing the direction of the interview felt right now they had achieved what they had come for. “One last thing, Mrs Bostock. We cannot get the name of the man you identified in the photographs. We’re still looking. Can you think of anything else? Did he give you anything, did he touch any …” He did not finish, she was already shaking her head. “When Trevor came back, did he know the car keys were left in the barn?”

“I might have told him but I couldn’t hold my hand on a Bible and swear to it.”

“So, for your liaisons, who drove?”

“I did.”

In more ways than one, thought Shakti.

***

Cyril was holding the small bronze statue, *Liberty,* when Quinn and April approached. As he waved them in April went to the easel in front of his desk. They immediately recognised the key names and words alongside the images written on the large board.

“Bit of a conundrum, sir.”

“Mr and Mrs Bostock. What did they have to say?” He placed the bronze carefully back on the desk and swivelled his chair to face them.

It was Quinn who spoke first. “Mrs only. Her husband was at the Farmers’ Market but that’s what we hoped. The chat was rather personal and delicate as it was covering her infidelity with Peterson and now, we discover, with Trevor Bostock too. She had the most original reason for that.” He explained and April pulled up a chair. It was the word *Lilith* that caught her attention and she raised a finger before going to the computer.

She added her password and typed in *Chronicles of Jerahmeel Section 23* and she read out loud. "*Adam slept alone and the first Eve – that is, Lilith – found him and, being charmed with his beauty, went to lay by his side and these were begotten from her: ghosts, male demons and female demons in thousands and myriads, and whomever they lighted upon they injured and killed outright, until Methuselah appeared and besought the mercy of God.*" She looked at her colleagues. "I remember reading about this many years ago. However, what's rather strange is what you've written here on the board." She pointed to the words *Methuselah or Murderer* next to Trevor's name.

Cyril felt a cold shiver run from his neck and down his spine. "That came to me this morning purely because it means long-lived and had nothing to do with ..." He looked at April. Her firm Christian faith and dedication to teaching at Sunday school, linked with her all-encompassing knowledge of religion, had proved invaluable in the past and today was no exception.

"Something else I remember. Lilith was the demon of the dark and winds and as well as being a seductress and killer of men, she was considered the killer of new born children by depriving them of oxygen, of blowing away their breath." She moved away from the computer and added the name *Lilith* to the board.

There was silence.

It was Quinn who spoke first. "Does that mean Trevor Bostock is a hero and not a villain?"

"It means neither, it means we keep an open mind and build on what we know and not on what we think we know," Cyril replied.

Chapter Nineteen

Karl's alarm was set for six but he had been awake since the early light had penetrated the curtains. There would be no traffic noise for another hour or so. He was concerned, and, in some ways, he felt a strange sense of guilt. He wondered whether taking Leonard to his home to see his pets was the right thing to do but then a contradictory thought moved in and in his mind's eye he saw Penny; vulnerable and trapped by her loyalty to her son. He wondered what life would have been like if he had been born without his disability, if he had received all the oxygen he had needed.

He swung his legs out of the bed and stretched. Whatever he had started he needed to finish, for the sake of his pride and for Penny. Sometimes he wondered why life was so complicated. He had been overwhelmed by life's complications in the past, which was one reason he had needed the fresh start in a different place with new faces; now he was getting even further out of his depth.

Fortunately, the day was warm and the mild breeze uplifting. The early morning stroll to St Mary's Walk was pleasant. Leonard was waiting at the door and waved as Karl approached. The excitement in his eyes was palpable. His coat was on, which was a surprise considering the weather, and he wore his hat; a type of comfort blanket to hide his face from elements of the world with which he could not cope. Karl had always seen him arrive in a hat and coat so he should not have been at all surprised.

"Happy birthday, Leonard. How excited we all are to be going to see some special friends on this your special day."

Penny was just behind him, moving him onto the path. "I need to lock the door, love. Go and stand with Karl." She turned and pulled the kind of face that implied, *thank goodness you've arrived!*

They put Leonard in the middle. It seemed incongruous, his being the tallest of the three, but it was safe as Penny knew they would meet children on the way. They held a hand each and Karl made small talk about their route. It would take them fifteen minutes to arrive at Jo's.

Jo had been up since the shipping forecast. The routine was always the same but she never tired of it. She chatted away to the various creatures in her care. She had boxed and wrapped a small gift for her guest and placed it on the counter. She knew a great deal about him and had to admit to feeling a little nervous about how he would cope with so many creatures in such a small space. Her concern was really for them. Karl had given her every assurance he would be able to control his behaviour and they would play it by ear. The slightest sign of distress on either side would determine the next move.

***

Owen received the call as he was starting the car. He turned off the engine and listened. The Border Force had intercepted a white chiller van in Hull as it waited to cross to Zeebrugge. Three men, two Romanians and a Bulgarian were found to be holding the carcasses of thirty-two sheep without export or import papers. There was every chance that some of those had come from Ramsgill. He made a call.

It was Harry Nixon who answered. "Hull. Now, sir?" He noted the location and jotted down the contact details before replacing the receiver and rubbing his head.

"Not a happy bunny, Harry?" Grimshaw leaned across his desk and ruffled his hair. "Seek and you shall find, my friend, that's the policeman's lot."

"Fucking Hull of all places." He picked up the phone and dialled the contact. He needed to know if he would require a translator and their exact location for the rest of the day. He also wanted Forensics to search the van and their belongings before he arrived. He collected the file on 'H', photographs of the crime scene and the evidence.

***

As they opened the door the bell signalled their arrival at Jo's. The familiar smell greeted them. As they released Leonard's hands, he immediately pulled his hat down to just above his eyes as Jo walked into the shop. She smiled and clapped her hands. "A very happy birthday, Leonard, and welcome to my shop. I hope you like meeting all of my friends. I know you've met and liked Karl's."

He looked first at Penny and then at Karl.

"What do you say to Jo, Leonard?"

"Happy birthday," Leonard said in all innocence.

They smiled.

Jo came around from behind the counter and held out her hand. "It's your birthday. Come, I have something for you."

To Penny's amazement he took her hand and followed. They went up the stairs to her apartment and set out on the small table were four glasses of orange juice and a small cake holding one candle. Leonard's other hand went straight to his mouth and he turned to look at Penny. She watched as the saliva dribbled down his chin and she moved swiftly to collect the drips with her handkerchief. Karl could see the mother's love in her eyes and now here, with people who showed her son kindness, she was blooming.

They helped him out of his coat and put his hat on the chair. He blew out the candle, quickly had his drink and a piece of cake and was ready to see what Karl had brought him for.

"Your mum and me will stay here. We won't get customers as I've put the *closed* sign on the door and dropped the latch." She emphasised the words, *dropped the latch,* and smiled at Karl. It did not go unnoticed and he grinned. "Karl will show you my wonders of the natural world."

The gerbils and the Degus fascinated Leonard, especially as Karl had to lift the roll of twigs to reveal the curled up rodents. He explained that they were wrapped together as they liked company and felt safe, just as he liked a hug from his mum. He explained too that some were separated as they were different sexes, but Leonard showed no interest. It was as they moved into the room at the back of the shop he grew more curious. Here were the reptiles. Some were familiar but others were new to him. He loved the Desert Blonde Tarantula and he squealed with delight as Karl put it on his hand.

"Spiders have eight eyes, Leonard, eight. How many do you have?"

"Two." He instinctively pointed to them.

"And how many knees do you have?"

He did the same, laughing out loud. "They're like Tony. This one is pretty and this one too." He pointed to a Pink Zebra spider in the next case. As they moved round, Leonard settled as he became overwhelmed by the number of animals and insects collected in one place.

Jo turned to Leonard. "Some people don't like shops like this as they feel the animals should be free, but they help youngsters understand the beauty of the natural world. Without these places we would never see such magnificent creatures in Harrogate other than at the circus or a zoo."

As they approached the large vivarium at the end of the room, for the first time Karl sensed Leonard's reluctance to move closer. He lifted the cover and gently brought out Lilith, the four-foot constrictor and allowed it to wrap around his arm. "This is a constrictor, Leonard. It wraps itself around the things it will eat. She is like Kaa, only bigger."

Leonard moved closer and put out his arm.

"Not this time. She could hurt you and I don't want to hurt her getting her free from you. Just look for the moment."

***

Harry Nixon turned right at the roundabout on Hedon Road and followed the satnav instructions. His mood had changed as the traffic had been lighter than he had anticipated and the sound of the gulls' cries and the sight of the boats acted as a tonic, as did the view as he neared Hull. Once at the docks, he was soon through to the second security barrier. He leaned out of the car and pressed the communication button. Within seconds it was raised and he parked between two border force vans.

Custom House, the force's main building was not unattractive. On entering he received the obligatory lanyard denoting his visitor status and was then escorted to an office on the first floor. There was no one there.

"Mr Sullivan will be with you shortly, Mr Nixon. May I get you tea or coffee?" Harry smiled as he had followed the *Clive Sullivan Way* to get there. "Coffee, please. White, no sugar." He looked out of the window across the car park towards the dock. Two large cranes, like sentries, one blue and one yellow, towered way above everything else. Even though the view did not stretch to the ocean he had seen worse. As he craned his neck, the Hull-Zeebrugge ferry was clearly visible and the revving of wagon engines and reversing warning indicators penetrated the double glazing.

Chapter Twenty

"Mr Nixon, John Sullivan and before you ask, I'm not a relative of Clive. If I had a pound ..." He carried the coffee, a cup and saucer – Cyril would approve. "As you may know we have the facilities to hold these men for twenty-four hours with the support of the port police. After forensic tests on the van, the contents and the vehicle have been moved to temperature controlled storage. As you can imagine after the latest dreadful tragedy linked to this port, we have increased the number of checks not only for inbound but also for outbound. When you're ready."

The three men had been kept separately since their arrest and the youngest was the last to be brought into the secure room. The others had remained silent and disinterested. Harry checked his Dictaphone and the file he had brought with him after returning the items from the last interview. An officer from the Port Police stood at the door. Harry said nothing, he neither looked at the man nor made any attempt to speak. It had been established they all understood and spoke English, even though they had said very little in the previous interviews. Harry slid a photograph of Owen and Quinn across the table. They were both dressed in jeans and shirts.

"Have you seen these men before?" Harry assessed the man was in his early twenties. There was neither recognition nor any emotion shown as there should not be as he knew neither. Harry then brought out a recent photograph of Humphrey. It was found at the cottage on his mobile, probably taken within the month. As he pushed it across the table, he saw it immediately, the glance away, the immediate shake of the head. He slipped a photograph of the butcher's knife and glove found at Bostock's farm. He put that on top of Humphrey's photograph. The latest had been taken at the crime scene, it showed the wires hanging from the tree and the odd bloodied fleece close by. Harry sat back. He said nothing. The young man fumbled with the three images as he constantly shook his head and pulled the occasional face at the crime scene. It was the last piece of paper that Nixon brought to the table that had the effect. It showed a picture of a prison cell on one side and a boarding card on the other. Harry flicked it one way and then the other.

"You decide to work with me, and tell me who he is and what he's done, and you can go. Or we'll decide in court from the evidence we have. Considering what your friends have said, you'll be going here." He let his finger rest on the picture of the cell. "Whereas they," he turned the card over to show the boarding pass, "will be long gone."

***

Leonard was reluctant to leave Lilith. He kept saying the word over and over again but it sounded more like *Lilly* as he manoeuvred himself to look directly in the snake's eyes.

"It's looking at me, it's looking at me." The words he would normally cry when he saw a child were spoken with a softness. "It's like the seat in the park."

Karl knew to what he referred. A good number of the seats in Valley Gardens had iron serpents for legs; the head and protruding forked tongue below the bench and the dragonlike tail forming the backrest. The serpent had long-standing links to Harrogate.

Karl put the snake back and covered the vivarium. “If you’re good today, maybe Jo will invite us back to see her animal friends again.”

Penny and Jo had returned and Leonard turned and smiled. “If you’re good,” they said in unison.

Within half an hour the three were back at the house and Leonard was guided into the room; the curtains had been drawn to give the best atmosphere for revealing the gift. Penny had covered his eyes with her hand. They heard a slight chuckle mixed with the words he kept repeating – *happy birthday, Leonard. Happy birthday to me.* The light from the fish tank on the stand glowed brightly in the semi-darkness, spilling a warm turquoise tint onto the furniture.

“After three, Leonard. One, two, three!” Penny lowered her hand and waited.

“Happy birthd ...” He stopped, moved towards the aquarium and looked in, his face gaining colour the closer he was to the glass. He saw the colour change to his hands and laughed.

“Happy birthday, Leonard. The fish are yours. I’ll help you keep them safe, change the water and clean the tank. You must feed them and you can give them names. They’re relying on you to look after them properly like I look after Tony, Kaa and the dragon, Puff.”

Turning to look at Karl, Leonard’s smile slowly evaporated. He moved towards his mother, occasionally looking back at the aquarium. He went out of the room, collected his tiddly winks and started to play his solitary game.

***

Nixon waited. He had folded his arms and settled back in the chair. He felt the slight vibration of the man’s foot bouncing nervously on the floor. It was time. Nixon slowly leaned across and collected the photographs one by one, deliberately leaving the card showing the boarding pass to the end. He checked his watch and then nodded to the officer at the door who moved over and grabbed the back of the man's chair. As Nixon leaned across to collect the card, he heard the words he wanted to hear.

"Billy, his name is Billy, that's all I know. He *măcelar*, meatman, butcher, you say, yes?"

Nixon brought out the photographs again, spreading them in front of the young man. "Which one?"

The finger dropped straight onto Humphrey.

The meeting, made more disturbing by the recent news of the human trafficking tragedy linked to those very docks, played on Nixon's mind. Passing myriad articulated wagons spewing from the port made him wonder about the cargoes they distributed throughout the United Kingdom. Like a virus suddenly entering the bloodstream, these wagons travelled the arteries of the country. Most were totally innocuous, vital, in fact, to the development of business and society but every now and then ... the success rate in prevention and arrests was still high, but what about the ones that went undetected? They were only seeing the tip of the iceberg. When it had been opened at the dock, the van he was chasing only contained carcasses of dead animals. The other cases were far more devastating. It was clear that with the increasing number of people willing to risk all for whatever their reason to come to the country, further tragedy and criminality was inevitable. *The grass is always greener,* he said to himself.

***

Cyril was perched on the edge of Owen's desk extolling the virtues of the Caribbean and in particular the west coast of Barbados.

"Like all places, Owen, I'm sure it has a dark underbelly. After all, there was a snake in the Garden of Eden. People look at Harrogate and think that we're still living in the past, the quaint Victorian town untouched by present times. Only when they see people sleeping in doorways, hear the news of sheep rustling in the Dales and when reports of a murder hits the national press do they open a myopic eye and see what's truly going on." He let two of his fingers delve into the mug containing sweets which was positioned to the left of the computer. To his surprise, he managed to collect one straight away. "You don't mind do you, Owen?"

Owen smiled. "That's why they're there. We all need a sugar rush."

As he spoke Shakti waved, one hand clamped to a phone. "Nixon, definite ID on Humphrey as being a key player in the rustling ring. He's on his way back. Can we now presume his death was in some way linked to that or previous misdemeanours as far as cruelty to animals is concerned? Evidence points that way to him, Peterson and Lyons. And, sir, if that's the case what about Trevor Bostock?"

Owen advised, "Until we locate him we make no presumptions."

"Nothing from social media or the news bulletins?" Cyril asked almost knowing the answer. "It's strange. A while back we investigated a case of people trafficking, they used the Brunswick Tunnel as a means of controlling the people they abused. Following the news coverage, when it all came to court, the reports clearly detailed the cruelty these people showed to the animals and their human slaves. The cruelty to the dogs produced far more outrage from the public than the psychological and physical trauma the humans suffered. People will turn on those harming animals, of that I've no doubt. I also know the killer's one such person or persons who have a strong, if not misguided, belief in the way society should deal with animal cruelty. For that very reason we have a focus and the priority is to locate Bostock." He stood and went to find April.

The kettle had only just boiled as April poured the water into a small brown teapot. Cyril appeared at the door. "Could you squeeze two cups from that and pop into my office?"

April turned and smiled. "Five minutes. Biscuit too?" Cyril gave a thumbs up.

In his office, Cyril pulled two chairs side by side. "I was fascinated by your comments about Lilith, especially in relation to the Bostocks' alleged relationship. If, as we believe, she is being honest and I've no reason to doubt her, then there's a hidden relevance within the name. I've since done some reading and the idea of two Eves, a good and a bad, I see as a strong link even though it's a reversal from female to male, Trevor and Ted. I also have a suspicion that Belinda Bostock has an idea where Trevor is living. Now whether the relationship is still ongoing is anyone's guess but her reluctance to come forward with information from the very start of the investigation makes me think that's the case."

"Fear is a strong emotion, as is guilt. I believe, and so do Quinn and Shakti, that she experiences both within the relationship. I feel she's a lady who realised that she couldn't have what she wanted in her marriage but she was also in a position that she didn't want to relinquish it for whatever reason. As the cliché goes, *you make your bed and you lie in it.* Only she had a number of beds she chose to lie in."

As Cyril listened, he sipped some tea. "We've had no response from forces' groups, or his old regiment which is strange. I looked at his service record, nothing out of the ordinary. Difficult time then with Ireland, of that I have no doubt."

"With Lilith, sir, she was cast out of the Garden of Eden. She was made from the same clay as Adam but Eve was made from his rib. That's why Lilith was a free thinker, a free spirit or demon. That's also why modern feminist groups revere her as the first independent woman. However, according to some accounts, she was so jealous of Adam and his partner that she came back as the snake – the reason she is depicted with the serpent – to destroy their relationship. Now if we put that into the context of today's scenario what do we have?" She paused and looked directly at her boss, not giving him time to speak. "Let me ask you this. Who is jealous of whom?"

Cyril felt it was like twenty questions. He took a while before answering. "Trevor is jealous of his brother, Ted." He paused again. "For two reasons. Firstly, their father didn't trust him with any part of the farm. It went to the younger of the two sons. Secondly, Belinda. He saw how happy Ted was with her, even when they failed to produce children they stayed together, and on the surface appeared to be contented. It was after his gallivanting and his wild life grew stale that he realised what he might have had. A share in the farm, a wife and probably kids."

"You're not going to go Cain and Abel on me are you, sir? You're not likening their father to God and that Abel, Ted, the younger was favoured over Trevor?"

"I've known people in families fall out and kill for a lot less. Okay, at the time Trevor was too up his own backside to care. He was young, arrogant and defiant and possibly thought he'd show them all by breaking away completely and going his own way only to find later he'd not been as successful or as impressive as he'd once anticipated."

"Came back with his tail between his legs?" April said, almost in a whisper.

"Came back to put his tail between someone else's was more my line of thought, April. Back to cause trouble. So, if we were to go back to the beginning of this conversation, Lilith. Why would Trevor call her by that name? How did he know the name and if he did, was he aware of its significance?"

Chapter Twenty-One

Before they went to visit Karl, Penny had left Leonard with the gifts she and Karl had bought. She had enjoyed the day more than all the previous birthdays when they were alone. She was growing fond of Karl. His warmth and his kindness to her son helped her believe that there was still good in the world despite all the sadness she witnessed in the news and in her own life.

The walk and the visit went well. Karl had arranged for others to be present in the conservatory and they held a small celebration. Leonard, although shy at first, soon laughed and played. He beat everyone at tiddly winks which seemed to lift his spirits more highly than she had seen for some time.

Her evening was normal, they fed the fish to make it part of their daily routine. Leonard had his supper before going to his room. Penny settled with a book; it was one she had seen in the lounge at the retirement home. The author was new to her.

***

Cyril met Julie at the corner of Robert Street before heading towards *L'Albero Delle Noci* at the bottom of Cheltenham Parade. As the evening was warm, they called for a drink at *The Little Ale House*. Julie found two seats outside while Cyril went to the bar. Before long, even though they had assured themselves that shop talk was banned, the conversation turned to the case. Over the time they had been together, Cyril had grown to trust Julie's judgement and now she was Mrs Bennett he felt as though he could share more of his daily dealings with her. The gin and tonic was just perfect and the conversation flowed. She was fascinated by the threads, the items from the various sites being swapped and linking the different murders.

"It's certainly not threadbare. It's as if the person is leading you to the next victim and the way I see it that's clearly intentional. The question is, my handsome man, why would he do such a thing?"

"To give them a sporting chance, which is more than they gave the animals they were involved with maybe? Interestingly, and I'm sure you can see this from their records held at your department, they were all made to suffer in some way. The use of the weapon, in Lyons's case, was more bizarre than the others. Each attack was deliberate and the perpetrator would know that it wouldn't bring instant death if done correctly. The last victim, Humphrey, might have been the exception, as according to Caner, the damage to the brain would result in a quick death."

Julie nodded. "Had the shot hit the man's face or mouth, then you would have seen a good deal of suffering, but then it would not necessarily have brought about his death. Clearly the motive is to kill. You also said that had the officer arrived sooner, the situation might have been very different. On this occasion the killer just needed to carry out his plan and leave."

They walked down towards the restaurant. Umberto, the front of house, welcomed them like long lost friends. He kissed Julie with all the Sicilian gestures offering his congratulations on becoming Mrs Bennett. "Tonight, the meal is on the house. I reserve you the quiet table." He clapped his hands and a waiter brought an ice bucket and a bottle of Prosecco. He opened the bottle and poured two and a half glasses. Handing one to each he collected the token coupe that contained only enough to toast the couple. "Matrimoni e vescovati sono destinati dal cielo," he announced as the glasses rang. "Or as you say here, 'bottom's up!' But I never understand this, no."

***

Ted Bostock rode the quad bike across the field to the gate. Within minutes he was heading back towards the farm. He fancied a pint; it had been a long day. The sheep were all where they should be and he could relax.

Trevor Bostock walked across the footpath and waited by the narrow track, one hand resting on the dry stone wall. The lichen and grey stone surface retained the heat from the day even though the sun was now silhouetting the horizon. In an hour it would be dark. His other hand held a broad wooden staff, his thumb curled through the 'V' at the top. Crows called, breaking the silence rising from the copse of trees set well into the field, as if to signal the sound of the quad that was now just becoming audible. He raised himself, leaned further onto the wall and caught a glimpse of his brother as he drove quickly across the undulating grass. Belinda was correct and he did not have to wait long. He did not move but waited patiently, a skill he had learned in the army. *Everything comes to those who wait … everything* he thought as the figure and machine grew larger by the minute.

***

As usual, Leonard had taken his tablet and the glass of warm milk to his room but on this day, his birthday, he was not going to take his medicine. The milk, however, was welcome. He heard the slight continuous mumble coming from the radio downstairs. Talking. All she seemed to listen to was people talking. He flicked the wink with the squidger and it shot straight into the pot. It was almost automatic. The four others lined up in a row followed, one after the other. His thoughts were totally wrapped up in the large snake and the name *Lilly* kept coming to his lips every time the wink hit the pot.

He put the things on the shelf where they were always placed, took his trousers and pulled them over his pyjama bottoms. The pyjama leg rolled awkwardly up his left leg as he struggled to get them on. He removed the trousers and pulled down the offending leg before stuffing both into the top of his socks. He tried again, this time successfully. Pulling out a cardigan he slipped that over his pyjama top before buttoning it. The buttons and the holes did not match up but it was neither uncomfortable nor a problem. He slipped into bed ensuring the covers were pulled up to his neck. He listened and waited. The slight drone from below continued into the evening.

***

Ted saw the figure and his heart beat a little faster. He screwed up his eyes to try to focus more fully and opened the throttle. A single dog was positioned expertly on the box on the back, momentarily losing its balance with the change of speed but then quickly it regained its equilibrium. Trevor waved the staff as the quad approached and within a minute Ted realised who it was. He slowed as he approached and Trevor moved away from the wall, blocking the path. The dog leapt from the box and ran forward. A single whistle stopped it and it lowered, its focus directed on the man in the road.

"Good evening, brother. Still see you have my Terrier box attached to this old quad."

Ted flicked the lid of the front box but it was empty. “I do what I like on my own land. I protect it from the likes of you and the bloody evil bastards who know fuck all about living and working in the countryside. They think it’s a bloody playground, a killing ground for their pleasure. You’re one of the bloody worst. Tell us why you left the army.” He paused and leaned forward on the handlebars. “You’re no brother of mine. You chose a different path in life. You took, put nothing in and buggered off. According to Dad you gave nobody nowt apart from bloody grief.”

“Your lass, Belinda, wouldn’t say that, nor a few others in the area. Shame about Peterson … Did you do it? Find out and killed him in a jealous rage? Found out he was a better man?” He emphasised the word, *better.*

“I did nothing, the police have been and are happy with my story. I know your game. You’ll try to break up what’s good; you always did. He worked for me, rented the cottage and that’s it as far as I’m concerned. Maybe someone collecting what he owed. He could spend faster than he could earn, always could, just like you. If you’d have got this place it’d be gone by now on some nag at the races.”

“You don’t know much. You don’t, but you know how to get people to kill for you. Peterson was good at that, I believe. He knew how to keep a woman happy too. Maybe that’s why he was murdered, little brother. Brothers share things and if they don’t, then they certainly should, so I’m just sharing things as brothers would.”

Ted was growing confused and angry. “Just what has Belinda got to do with all this, with you and Peterson? Why are you back here like a bloody bad smell? You were trouble when you were a kid and you’re trouble now. Just fuck off and leave us be!" He revved the quad, giving another signal to the dog which reluctantly returned and jumped onto its perch.

"Did you never think about the glove and the knife? Never thought about the missing car? Never thought how dangerous those quads are? They cause loads of accidents on farms." Trevor stepped to one side and waved the machine through. "Drive carefully, little brother. Don't forget to remember me to Belinda."

***

The thrum of the radio had stopped and he heard the door gently close. Penny had looked in as she did every night. He had fallen asleep even though he had been determined to stay awake. He listened as the sound of the water running in the bathroom indicated that she was cleaning her teeth. It stopped and he paused. He could hear the sound of the occasional car but otherwise all was quiet. He heard the toilet flush. Within minutes all would be silent again.

***

Apart from the vibrant red and orange cut slashed into the lower western sky, night had fallen. The quad pulled into the yard. Ted drove quickly allowing the four wheels to slide and skip across the cobbles before entering the corrugated iron barn. He did not lock it but removed the key which was attached to his wrist on a red cable, a precaution in case he fell off the machine. The dog stayed by his feet until they reached the cage and the kennel. It obediently entered. In minutes he was back with food for both dogs. He changed their drinking water before returning to the kitchen.

“You’re late, Ted Bostock. I was getting worried and you left your phone on the table. Much use it is there!” She moved towards him to kiss his cheek. “Have you been drinking?”

Ted said nothing. He went to the cabinet and took out a whisky bottle and a glass. He poured a large measure and drank it before pouring a second.

“What’s the matter?” She placed a hand on his shoulder but he moved away, taking the bottle and the glass. He sat in the chair that they considered his.

“Ted?”

“Met a friend of yours and a nemesis of mine earlier tonight. Told me that he and you were, shall we say, close.” He turned his gaze and stared her in the eye. “What do you think he meant by that?” He looked back at the glass before bringing it to his lips.

“What old friend? Who are you talking about or is this simply ale talk?”

“Peterson was also mentioned in this conversation.” He downed the next full glass. “I might be a simple fucking farmer but I’m no fucking fool.” He filled the small glass a fourth time.

“Peterson’s dead for God’s sake. You found him. So, Ted Bostock, who’s my old friend?” Her voice was now raised and she threw her apron onto the table. “Well? If you’re going drink yourself daft, talk shite and shout, I guess we can both do a bit of that.”

“I came from the top field, by Jonty Wood, Dad’s favourite spot, and guess who I saw on the track?”

“Now let me guess. The ghost of your father? No? Well what about Snow White and the seven fucking dwarfs? How the bloody hell do I know? Stop playing games, it’s late and I’m tired.”

“I’m serious!”

"You're bloody drunk."

He turned, putting the bottle and the glass on the hearth. "Neither, although to be honest with you, I'd have preferred to have met either of those." He turned and looked directly at Belinda and she could see that he was not only angry but he was confused. "It was Trevor. And he told me things. Truths about him and you and about Peterson."

Belinda felt her legs go weak. She had believed that going *weak at the knees* was purely a saying, but at that moment she realised the truth in the words. She grabbed the edge of the table to steady herself.

Chapter Twenty-Two

Leonard had been downstairs in the night before, usually at Christmas to see if Santa Claus had been. On those occasions, he had misjudged the moment as, in his excitement, he had gone to bed early in the hope the morning would come sooner and Penny had still been in the lounge reading or asleep over her book. Tonight, however, things were different. He had a goal. Looking out between the slightly parted curtains he could see the turquoise light in the sky to his left. The street lamp was still on and he knew it was time to go. He had a strange feeling deep in his tummy, a bit like the feeling he experienced when he knew children were about, a mix of fear and apprehension. An involuntary scream erupted from his lips and he immediately brought a hand up to his mouth.

He managed to negotiate the stairs quietly, carrying his shoes, and found himself in the hallway. Orange light leached through the transom window enhancing his nervousness. Sitting on the bottom step he slipped on his shoes, checking they were on the correct feet. He took hold of the Velcro straps and pulled tightly before collecting his hat and his coat. Within minutes he was ready. He could not remember a time when he had gone alone through the front door and beyond the gate. Taking a deep breath, he slowly slid the chain from the door, something he had been shown how to do in case there was ever a fire, turned the Yale lock and opened the door. The morning was deceptively warm and that was reassuring as he stood on the step before allowing the door to swing shut. He heard the lock catch. On reaching the metal gate he paused again. Here was the crossing point. He had often ventured this far alone, to look up and down the road, a dare to himself to see whether he could do it. On each occasion he had experienced a tingle of excitement when he returned safely inside. To be there alone was an adventure, as there was always the fear of a child appearing. He paused, resting his hands on the cool metal of the gate and turned to look at the now closed door. He would have to knock and wake his mother should he change his mind. He then thought of the snake, Lilly, his friend, alone in that long box. *She needs you,* he said to himself. *She's all alone*. Within moments he pulled his hat down. He tugged at the gate and stepped onto the pavement and into the unknown. His hands found his pockets and he was on his way. In his mind he had drawn a picture of the route he had to take, small vignettes that would aid his progress. He walked quickly until he approached the building that housed Karl's apartment and then slowed. From here the route was unfamiliar.

***

Jo slipped out of bed and immediately grabbed her dressing gown. It was Friday, as if that made any difference where the care of animals was concerned. She pressed the button on the radio and the gentle sound of classical strings was buoyed by the dull grey light that was beginning to penetrate the room. Stretching momentarily, she found the slipper that was missing. She moved to the bathroom, splashed her face with cold water and immediately felt brighter. The shipping forecast would not be long. The routine was instinctive as she made her way down the stairs. She looked into the shop, all was quiet apart from some of the animals moving within the confines of their cages. She paused. That familiar sound was one of the rewards of the job, that and making sure they were well looked after. She moved into the store room and it was then that she heard it. It was light at first and she paused, moving back to the stairs to try to identify its location. It was there again, only this time louder. It was coming from the shop. She moved in and rested on the counter, her ears tuned away from the familiar. She paused before looking to check the ceiling. There was no dripping water so she had not left the tap running upstairs which was a relief. She then looked around the floor. In the past she had experienced the odd hamster going astray and considering their size they could make a great deal of noise. Reassured that all was well, she was about to turn and leave when the bang sounded, a desperate crash which made her turn anxiously. It was then she saw the face appear simultaneously at the door. She screamed, an involuntary reaction that brought silence to the room. Although startled, and even though the man's face was compressed awkwardly against the glass, she knew immediately who it was. She moved to open it as the familiar voice of the shipping forecast drifted into the room.

Forties, Cromarty, Forth, Tyne, Dogger south or south west five decreasing three at times, showers thundery for a time occasionally moderate. Fisher, German Bight …

The light from the shop illuminated Leonard's face, pushed hard against the window, contorting his features and squashing the brim of his hat to cover his eyebrows. She could still see the desperation in his eyes as he mouthed the word *Jo* followed by *please*. His palm moved away and tapped the glass one more time as the door opened.

She stared at the face. "Leonard?" she said, finding it hard to believe he was at the shop so early. She opened the door more fully and let him almost fall into the room before quickly checking outside in the expectation of seeing his mother. To her surprise, the road was empty. "What are you doing here? Where's Penny?"

Tears filled his eyes, "I'm scared, Jo, I'm all on my own but I had to see Lilly. I promised her I'd come back. She looked at me. I know she liked me and Karl said I might hold her if I was good. I was good. I ate all of my tea and I blew out the candle and made a wish. Mum said I should make a wish and I did." He started to move towards the counter. One hand went into his mouth as if to stop himself from crying. She knew just where he was going but she put her hand on his arm.

Bailey, Cyclonic 5 to 7, occasionally gale 8 at first. Very rough or high. Rain. Good, occasionally poor.

"Stop! Leonard you can't go in there, it's not safe! Lilith shouldn't be handled. Leonard!" Raising her voice she pulled at his arm, suddenly realising somewhat foolishly that she was no longer dealing with a child. As he turned to look at her, his innocent expression changed. She recalled the conversation with Penny and how she had seen a change in him since meeting Karl and his pets. Whether he did it deliberately or accidentally, the result was the same as he pulled her closely towards him and then thrust her away. She lost the grip she believed she had of his coat sleeve and felt herself falling to the side. Her head connected with the corner of the counter top and her arm hit the RSPCA collection tin sending it in the opposite direction. The noise was drowned by Leonard as he screamed, uncertain as to what had happened. He watched as Jo's head struck.

And the Shetland Isles, southerly or south westerly 5 to 7 occasionally 4 at first perhaps gale 8 later in the far west drizzle at first and showers later, moderate or good, occasionally poor at first.

The second impact was Jo's head hitting the floor. She twitched slightly and blood began to pool around the side of her head. Leonard moved his hand to his mouth and began to cry. Tears and saliva mixed before dribbling onto the floor.

And that is the end of the shipping bulletin at ...

Neither heard the words streaming from the upstairs radio as Leonard moved towards the prostrate figure. With wet fingers he tried to open her right eye. The blue eye stared blindly and he allowed the lid to close. He tried prodding her arm but she remained motionless. "Sorry, sorry." A curious gurgling noise emanated from between his saliva-bubbled lips. "Jo, wake up. It's alright. Sorry. I'll be good. I didn't do it, it's not my fault, you fell."

She remained motionless. Leonard stood and looked at her face. "Sleep tight. Don't let the bed bugs bite," he whispered, determined to believe that she was only sleeping. He moved towards the back room, his concentration now fully focused on Lilly. "You sleep. I'll look after the animals for you. It will make you better."

***

Cyril stood at the window. The venetian blinds tilted to allow him to look out onto Robert Street. The street light had automatically switched off fifteen minutes previously and the room was slowly becoming bathed in the gentle light of morning. A faint snuffle and the occasional snore made him turn to look at Julie. The duvet was tightly pulled to her neck but a leg dangled from the side of the bed. It was, she had assured him, her method of controlling her temperature.

He inhaled the minty vapour of his electronic cigarette before sipping his coffee. His mind had been active most of the night, not only with the murders and the links between the dead, but also with Trevor Bostock, the missing person from the photograph. The longer he was missing, the more likely he would turn out to be the killer. He was also suffering from his copper's nag, the knot that appeared in his stomach when something was not right – when they had missed something or considered it irrelevant. He needed to be at work, he was solving nothing here. He hastily showered, dressed and wrote a note for Julie. She would not need to return to work for another two days.

Within the hour he was staring at the bronze figure of *Liberty.* He let his finger run around the base, the cool of the metal was soothing. *Freedom,* he whispered to himself. *Freedom, Mr Bostock? Not if I have anything to do with it,* before typing his password into his computer.

***

Ted Bostock could not sleep either, the dry mouth and the pounding in his head had made any pattern of sleep difficult. He had stayed in the chair. Belinda had denied everything. Her words rang in his head but also rang true. *He's always been a troublemaker, a liar and a cheat. He caused all the rifts on this farm and now he returns out of the blue and you, like the soft sod that you can sometimes be, believe every damn word that he utters.* She had a point. They had a good life here, they had enough to live well on, the home was theirs and they were cutting down on the farm work. People would give their eye-teeth to be in this position at their time of life. If he sold the farm he would be a very wealthy man. Belinda had mentioned this on a number of occasions. It seemed to always crop up when they were considering their wills. They had no kids and few relatives. Her argument of cruising and holidays and getting some money spent had very little appeal but he also knew that when they both passed away the farm would be sold and others would quickly fritter it away.

He crossed the yard and the dogs made a few welcome yelps as they pushed themselves against the bars. He opened the gate and they sprang out trying to wrap themselves around his feet. Needing time alone, he stroked them before returning them to the kennel.

The morning sun was ready to make its way into the barn as he swung open the door which groaned, protesting on rusty hinges. The sun's light followed. The large space had its own familiar smell and that, for Ted, was comforting after the night he had just experienced. How could he possibly split from Belinda and sell what had been in the family for generations? If only he had been able to have children this dilemma would not have presented itself. Moving to the post where the glove and the knife had been left, he ran his fingers along the vertical mark made by the blade in the wood. He had given up wondering why the items had been left there.

"She told you I was lying, causing trouble didn't she, brother. Denied everything."

The voice from the hay loft startled him until he saw the legs dangling over the edge. "Jesus Christ!" he exclaimed as he stepped backwards.

"Far from it. I'm a Bostock and not a particularly honourable one at that. Whatever happened to good morning?"

Thin beams of light penetrated the holes and the cracks in the cladding, needling and illuminating the dark areas. Particles of dust floated aimlessly within the beams.

Ted said nothing but stared at the boots dangling about ten feet above his head. All he wanted to do was to leap, grab and pull but he knew what the final result would be if he could have made such a move. All their sibling fights had always ended the same way. "The police would like to talk to you about Peterson and the other deaths we've read about in the papers. There's a link and you're part of that for some reason. You're on the police website, I'm told. Missing, hiding. Did you kill them, Trevor? You're capable of it, dad always said so after stopping you trying to kill me when we were kids. I remember his exact words to mum, *He'll kill someone someday our Trevor. Can't control his aggression. See it when he deals with the flock."*

"That's why I joined the army. They trained you to kill but also gave you discipline. Strategy and planning, little brother, that's what they gave me. I killed no one, not then and not now. It's true about me and Belinda and what I said about her and Peterson but he's no longer here to confirm it. Did your job when you bottled out. Couldn't kill foxes and you couldn't fuck, is how I see it. Peterson was up for both. Don't know about the others who died. Maybe your lass got shut of them to stop them opening their mouths. You know how village gossip works."

Ted grabbed a pitch folk and swung it at the boots but missed by about a foot. He threw it down, removed his phone and dialled. "Let's get the police here and get this thing sorted out once and for all. You've more to lose than me."

The barn went quiet but then the faint sound of a ring tone and someone speaking broke the silence. Trevor jumped, springing from the upper level, and landed just in front of his brother and within the same movement brought out his fist; one punch floored Ted. The phone instantly left his hand, tumbling through the air before it clattered along the dry cobbles. "Don't you dare fucking move or I'll fucking kill you!" He moved towards the phone and crushed it beneath his boot.

Chapter Twenty-Three

The sound of voices drifted in and out of Jo's consciousness. Her body was stiff and her head pounded. Instinctively her hand went to the back of her head and she could feel the crusty covering of congealed blood. She looked at the transferred fluid on her fingers. Rolling onto her side she tried to stand but the room began to swim and circle before she felt the nausea rise. She stayed put for a moment in order to regain her composure. Her thoughts turned to Leonard and then Lilith. If he had taken the snake it was quite capable of killing him out of stress. She had to find it but first she had to get onto her feet, a task that was proving more difficult than she had anticipated. Had it not been for the early customer she was unsure as to how long she would have remained on the floor. Three attempts to right herself had proved unsuccessful.

On seeing her, the customer had remained calm considering the pooled blood that was now spread after Jo's attempts to get up off the floor.

"Just get me to a chair, please," she had whispered, her head pounding and a constant feeling of nausea flooding her body.

She neither remembered the customer ringing the emergency services nor hearing the siren but she did recall the paramedic asking her for details of her next of kin. The concussion brought total confusion but she could say the names Leonard and Lilith before she was removed from the building once the police had arrived.

***

Cyril had been drawing circles on the whiteboard in his room as Owen popped in carrying his mug and a bacon sandwich. A globule of brown sauce poised on the edge of the foil in which it was partly wrapped.

"Morning, sir." His mouth, full of partly masticated bread and bacon, ejected the odd morsel in Cyril's direction. "Venn diagrams again?"

"Do not enter my room with that otherwise it will turn into a crime scene. It's leaching fluid of some description and it's not going to land on my carpet. Leave it outside or eat the offending article and return." Owen pulled a face, lifted the wrapper and spotted the leak, lapping it up with his tongue. Turning, he left immediately, meeting April en route.

"Bloody hell! He's back and marriage has done nothing for his morning persona." He took another bite followed swiftly by a swig of tea.

April watched as his jaw worked the food. "Attack at Bostock's. Received a 999 call but only background conversation and sounds were recorded. Tracked to his mobile number and we're working to get the exact location." She handed him the tablet containing the recording.

Owen stopped chewing momentarily, putting down the mug but forcing the remains of the sandwich into his mouth; he was going to listen, not speak. He tossed the screwed up foil towards the bin but it landed a good foot off target. April followed its trajectory and shook her head. The word *men* came to mind but she said nothing as Owen lifted the electronic tablet and listened.

"Don't you dare fucking move or I'll fucking kill you, it sounds like but it's faint." April nodded. "What was that noise I heard at first?"

"Not sure. But the latter is the phone hitting and skidding along a hard surface, probably the ground. We've sent a car to the farm and also authorised armed officers considering the connection with the three murders and the discovery of the knife and butcher's glove."

"Has *Flash* heard this?"

"Just going. Sent Quinn and Shakti out there just in case the threat was executed."

***

The paramedic's estate left through the farm gate and the two firearm officers were climbing into their vehicle as Quinn approached. "All must be well, if they've gone before an ambulance has arrived," he said to Shakti. He switched on his blue strobe lights momentarily, to signal *police* if they had not already recognised the vehicle. He pulled up by the marked police car. Lowering his window, he smiled and raised his eyebrows. "All good?"

"We've given it all a three sixty and there's nothing. Domestic but one offender's gone. No firearms were stored on the farm which is unusual. It's all yours, an officer's inside." He pointed to the other car.

There was silence from the caged kennel. Quinn had a quick look to make sure that the dogs were not loose before leaving the car. Belinda Bostock appeared at the farm house door and beckoned them.

"There's an officer with him and those two with their guns and fancy clothes frightened the living daylights out of me. Ted's in the chair. Trevor was here this morning, here last night too. Can I have a word with you, love?" She looked directly at Shakti. "The cat's out of the bag as far as ... you know what is concerned. Trevor spilled the beans, told Ted about our dalliances and told him about me and Peterson, although how he knew that is anyone's guess."

Quinn approached a chair where the officer was tapping a statement onto an electronic tablet. Bostock looked the worse for wear. Bruising had coloured the left side of his face and a paramedic had dressed the cut on the back of his head. Both turned to look at Quinn.

"Looks worse than it is."

"When we were kids, he did far worse," Bostock muttered through a thick swollen lower lip. He kept raising a finger to see if it were still bleeding.

Quinn addressed the officer. "Do we know where he is now?"

"He appeared late last night. For all Mr Bostock here knows he might have stayed in the barn overnight."

"What about the dogs? They even bark at whispers."

"Quiet all night. In the kennel when I went out today. Seemed happy enough. They'd have let me know if we'd had a visitor, believe me."

"So, you've no idea where he might be staying?" Quinn watched as Ted tentatively shook his head. "Any other barns on this property, empty cottages, derelict or other?"

"Top field barn, derelict roof but we keep an old caravan in there for early lambing, when the weather can be poor. I've not been up for a while, a month, maybe longer."

"Even with all the rustling?"

"It's well off the road. I'd have seen tracks."

Quinn moved away, brought up the map of the farm on his phone and began searching for the buildings; he selected the satellite image for clarity. He took it towards Bostock. "Where on here?"

"Bloody hell, officer, I'll need me lamps for that. They're on the table." He pointed to a pair of spectacles.

"There. See, told you it was remote."

Quinn called it in. He wanted a drone and pilot there as soon as possible. It would be easy to check the building for heat and movement which would save a good deal of time. If he were there, they could enter; he did not want to scare him away.

Belinda and Shakti nursed mugs of tea, it seemed to be the default setting whenever people were agitated; tea, a good brew, was the universal panacea. Belinda explained what had happened the previous evening. There were a number of protracted pauses as she collected her thoughts. To Shakti it was as if she were mentally shuffling the playing cards she had been dealt, but whichever way she looked she failed to find a winning hand. It was clear in her expression. Shakti had seen desperation and hopelessness before.

"You knew he was here, Belinda, and you've been sheltering him. The question is, for how long?"

"Too long or not long enough, depends where my mind is at the time. I saw him outside last night. Ted had finished the bottle of whisky and then decided to fall into a drunken stupor. I wasn't sure if it was delayed reaction to the knock on his head or the booze but either way he was out cold. It was then I heard the dogs. Call it women's intuition but I just knew who it was. The dogs recognised him too as they quickly went quiet. I looked out and there he was. Funny, but I was so pleased to see him. He helped me get Ted into the chair and put a blanket over him. We sat for a while and then he left."

"Where to?"

There was another pause as she seemed to check her mental cards again.

"Let's have the truth. I know you're worried about him with the murders that have been going on, and you know we've been looking for him because of the photograph but there's more to it."

"As I look after the money, I managed to help him rent a small cottage under my maiden name, Phinn. He had nothing. He's been back eight months. Before that, who knows where he was. Once he left the army he probably just roamed."

Shakti looked up, certain they were finally getting the truth. "I take it we have an address?"

Belinda nodded.

Chapter Twenty-Four

It took exactly an hour and forty-three minutes before the report including the word *Lilith* appeared on April's computer screen; a coincidence maybe, but the fact that it was a report generated in Harrogate brought a clear relevance – the HOLMES computer was doing its job – connecting vagaries from the multiple reports placed nationally onto the system every moment of the day. It had coincided with a frantic call received at Control from a worried parent about a missing son. However, at that time, there was no link and the latter had been directed to a different department.

The connection with the word *Lilith* was, as far as Cyril was concerned, strong enough to warrant a personal visit to the shop. April's knowledge and conviction that there was a definite link to the murders had convinced him to always keep an open mind. Besides, he did not want to drive his desk all day.

On arrival, CSI were already checking the building. The RSPCA had been contacted to ensure the security and the safety of the animals in the shop until the owner could return. The initial hospital report suggested that would not be for at least another twenty-four hours. Cyril checked his watch, shook his wrist and checked again. It would be another forty minutes before they would be allowed inside. There was no damage and nobody had died but something nagged at Cyril. He needed to see for himself.

***

Penny, after initially searching the area, had walked towards Karl's apartment and the retirement home but there had been no sign of Leonard. All she could think was that at least he had had the sense to take his hat and coat; his name and address were stitched into the lining of both items of clothing should he be found lost and anxious.

The officer who had been assigned to speak with Jo at the hospital had reported that the person entering the shop was known to her and his name was Leonard Ross of St Mary's Walk. The snake in question was named Lilith. That had been the vital link. Details about Leonard's disability and his description were quickly posted on the North Yorkshire Missing Persons website and owing to the man's vulnerability it was fast tracked to hit the television and local radio news immediately. A family liaison officer had been sent to support Penny and a recent photograph, one taken at his party the previous day, was issued with the reports. Jo kept protesting it to be an accident as she had opened the door to him and that he was only a child at heart.

Karl had received the news directly from Penny on her return from her fruitless search and he immediately thought of Jo. He had telephoned the shop and her mobile phone, but in each case, had only connected with the answerphone. He knew that she would have been up early, she always was. He thought it best to see Penny first and once reassured that she was okay, they would go to the shop. As he prepared to leave his phone rang.

"Karl, it's Penny." Her voice was tight and tearful. "I have a lovely police lady with me. They're doing everything they can but I wondered if you could help find him? Check the garden at yours and then the shop. I know he wouldn't go far. It's the shop and the snake, call it a frightened mother's intuition. He talked about it constantly when we got home. And Karl, don't try to stop him physically if you find him, he's very strong. Please let Jo know he's about as I feel sure he intended to go there." She started to lose control so swiftly thanked him and hung up.

As requested, he checked the garden but there was no one apart from the gardener who was preparing to start his day's work. Karl explained the situation and described Leonard. He insisted should he see anyone fitting that description during the morning to call him; he handed him his card. He took one last glimpse before stepping out of the grounds and onto the pavement. Instinctively he looked in both directions and then began to follow the same route they had taken together the previous day.

On turning the corner of Cold Bath Road and Cold Bath Place, he saw the CSI van and a dark coloured car parked outside the shop. He paused; his heart suddenly began to pound. This was the last place he wanted to be. He moved slowly, looking carefully to see if he could spot Leonard or Jo. The police tape strung across the front of the shop made him even more anxious. A few people had gathered even though it was still early. Two of them, he assumed to be officers, were leaning against the car. Pausing again, he considered turning round and continuing his search. It was clear Leonard was not there. He needed to make a quick decision but then thought of Penny. He wiped his hands on his handkerchief and crossed towards the car. Introducing himself, he explained what had happened the previous day and his concerns for Leonard.

"Is Jo, the owner here? She could tell me if she's seen him," Karl suggested.

"Sorry, Jo, Ms Taylor isn't. She needed some hospital treatment." April could sense his genuine concern. "Are you alright? Did you know her well?"

"We were partners I suppose you could say. Is she badly hurt?"

"Concussion. She'll be in for a day just to monitor the situation."

Once he had composed himself, Karl repeated the conversation he had recently had with Penny.

"Is he a danger to others?" April questioned, turning to look at Cyril and then back at Karl. Cyril's attention was suddenly sparked.

"You have to put his behaviour into context. He's a child in a man's body. Imagine a six-foot tantrum when he can't have his own way. His mother, Penny, has been growing more concerned about him and she's been shaken a few times, physically I believe, but a mother's love is very strong and the thought of his going into a home to receive specialist care is not even a consideration at the moment, although after this ..." He did not finish but seemed to change tack. "There's another worry. He was shown a four-foot constrictor, a snake ..."

"Lilith?" April interrupted.

"Yes." A look of amazement appeared on Karl's face as he looked at the two officers. "You know?"

"And the point is, Mr?"

"Sorry, Karl, Karl Leslie. I'm a friend and I've kept snakes for a number of years but nothing like the one they had in the shop, other than when I worked abroad. The snake, if handled incorrectly, if it gets stressed and anxious, will wrap for security. It will not be doing that to kill, you understand, purely in self-preservation. Most snakes will only attack when frightened. However, like all generalisations there are some exceptions where they are just aggressive and strike for no reason."

"And this one?" Cyril asked.

"It's a constrictor, it wraps."

"Wrap, you mean coils itself around a person and squeezes?"

"Or a tree branch. A constrictor doesn't asphyxiate as such, the pressure it exerts closes down the blood supply to key areas. Owing to its size, the real worry is if, in fact, he's taken the snake and wrapped it near his neck, then it could kill him. Or if he's let it go out of fear and someone else ... You can see my point."

"Where was the snake in the shop?"

"It was in the back room in the largest vivarium there is. Its name is scribbled on a piece of paper above it. It was being looked after for a client whilst he was away, I was told."

Cyril went to the shop door and spoke with one of the officers who immediately went to check. He returned. "The snake's missing." He did not need to speak to April as she was immediately onto control relaying the information for those searching for Leonard. The idea of the missing snake was, for the moment at least, to be kept quiet.

April moved Karl into the privacy of the police car, took his details and instructed him they might need an extended interview later before letting him continue his search.

Cyril looked at April. "We recently had deaths as a result of snake bites in Knaresborough, now the potential for another victim here in Harrogate and to cap it all, a different type of snake. And to think the adder was supposed to be the only snake in the UK that could harm you. You couldn't make it up."

"Lilith, sir. The seductress, the killer of men. Who do we know with a name like that?"

Cyril turned back to her. "Surely you're not thinking ..."

"Not just the name but the link. Remember Adam's two wives and the idea that Lilith was put into the story a thousand years later to introduce evil into the Garden of Eden, to justify the wicked behaviour of the sons of Adam and Eve, Cain and Abel? If you transpose that idea with what's going on at Bostock's farm – one woman with two men, two brothers, in fact."

Cyril scratched his head. "Simple policing, that's what we used to have and now ... When they've finished," he pointed to the CSI's van, "I want any results immediately. I want DNA, I want the lot. There's more to this than Bible stories. I don't mind the odd coincidence but not when they're fed to us like kippers on a plate. If we get this wrong that's what we'll look like in the eyes of the press and, therefore, to the general public."

Chapter Twenty-Five

Owen, Nixon and Smirthwaite arrived at the front of the cottage. The dirt track, dry and rutted, ran past the cottage and through to a large copse of trees a quarter of a mile beyond. It was evident that whoever lived there was allergic to gardening. A grey van was parked on a piece of ground to the right and that too seemed to have received the same care and attention as the garden. Owen sent Nixon round the back as Smirthwaite approached the door, then stood on the track, where he had a clear view of the upstairs windows. He nodded and Smirthwaite knocked on the door.

Trevor Bostock stood, his back against the bough of an oak tree. He had enough of a view through the trees and bushes in front to observe the visitors to his cottage without being seen himself. A flush of nervousness ran through him but he remained immobile. During the jungle training in Belize he had felt a similar flush, a mix of excitement and fear; adrenalin, his sergeant major used to announce at the top of his voice, was the best free drug in the world. The more you got, the more you wanted. Like now, they were then training to escape and evade. Whoever these three were, his instincts told him he needed to stay well clear. To Bostock, this was not training, this was reality.

Owen nodded again and Smirthwaite checked the door – it was locked. He moved to the mullioned window and peered in. The low-slung ceiling and dark wooden beams seemed to prevent the light of day from penetrating the far recesses. He shook his head. The upper rooms were no different. The curtains seemed partly drawn and there was a general air of neglect. Owen focused on each one to check for movement. There was none.

Nixon called in the van's registration number and waited for the response, ensuring his phone was on vibrate against his thigh. A ring tone now would be unprofessional. He too moved and checked the back door and then looked through the only window. The yellowing, nylon curtain suspended on a drooping wire made it impossible to see anything. He felt the phone. "Who?" He listened to the rest of the information. Hanging up he came around to Owen. "Van there is registered to Mrs Belinda Phinn and to this address. Insured third party, also to her. She must pay the utility bills. Expensive sex. Hope she gets her money's worth."

"Other drivers?"

"That's the funny thing. The other named driver is Edward Bostock, that's her husband, but according to Shakti's report, he supposedly knew nothing about this place or the van. More importantly he was unaware that allegedly his sibling was back in the neighbourhood."

"I wonder if he knows where his driving licence is right at this moment. I bet I do, though. Seems he trusted his missus a great deal more than he should."

Bostock continued to watch. The activity at the front of the cottage caused him concern, particularly when all three went across and inspected the van.

Within the hour Ted and Belinda Bostock were cautioned and driven to Harrogate Police Station.

***

Karl only had a cursory glance as he walked along Cold Bath Place. There had been building development at the bottom of the road as it reached Back Harlow Moor Drive. There was now only one way you could go but Leonard would not know the road to be a cul-de-sac; he must have hoped it would take him to the park. Time, he needed time, and he needed to see Jo. Decision made, he would check the park's perimeter and then get up to the hospital.

Karl had looked through the foliage and called Leonard's name a few times but felt foolish. He saw no one apart from the odd motorist. He walked towards the park entrance near Swan Road and called a taxi. Walking was out of the question; it would take at least thirty minutes and he had spent too long already.

Within four minutes the taxi had arrived and he was making good progress until they reached Knaresborough Road. A car had broken down on the junction and he could feel his anxiety building.

***

It had taken a degree of persuasion for the nurse to allow him five minutes with her but explaining the circumstances and reassuring them that he would only need ten minutes did the trick.

Jo smiled when she saw him. "No flowers?" she giggled. "Only kidding."

Karl was relieved to see Jo looking better than he had expected. She was sitting in a small lounge just off the ward when he arrived. He sat with her, his hand in hers. "I have no grapes either, I'm afraid." They both laughed. "I didn't know what to think. Leonard is normally so placid but to be honest you can see he has a temper. I've tried to find him but he could be anywhere. I just hope he's done nothing daft with the snake."

Karl bent and kissed her. “Sorry, I thought I was doing the right thing bringing him to yours. The wonder of the animal world. You know I like to spread the gospel as far as animal welfare is concerned.”

“No sign of Leonard then? He was just so eager to see the bloody thing, that was the problem. If I were to be honest, Karl, I was taken aback seeing his squashed face at the window. It scared me at first until I realised who it was, and then to find him without his mum seemed strange. I had to let him in. I don’t think he meant to hurt me, he was just so excited.”

“Penny has been concerned lately. She feels he’s changing, becoming less compliant and I’ve told her she needs to talk with Social Services or her GP. She’s not old but she’s not getting any younger either.”

He saw Jo’s expression change. She too seemed to have felt sadness for Leonard’s predicament and believed the introduction of a pet might help both him and Penny. It was then that she rested her hand on Karl’s knee and sat up leaning towards him.

“I’m hoping to be back home tomorrow and they’ve told me they have someone who knows small pets in the shop to check, feed and close up. Lilith’s owner is supposed to be coming in today or tomorrow to collect it. I’ve had it for five or six weeks and nothing happens and the day before he’s due to call it goes missing. If only he’d taken it when he popped in. He’ll be heartbroken, he told me it wasn’t his pet but his companion.”

“I could inform him, Jo. Do you have a contact address?”

“It’s at the shop. His name is Trevor, Trevor Phinn, but I can’t recall his address, sorry. I’ll have to do it when I get back in. If I think I have a headache now I’m sure I’ll have one when I need to make that call. He was, I believe, a good herpetologist.”

"Trevor? Right. I could go and see if it's still in the shop. Where did you keep his address?"

"In the red book under the counter but you don't need to, love, you've done enough."

He leaned over and kissed her forehead. "For you, anything. I'll grab your mobile too and bring it in later. Bedside cabinet as usual?"

"You know me too well." She paused. "Remember when you left the door unlocked?"

He nodded and sighed. "Will I ever be allowed to forget it? Yes!"

"You dropped a photograph, or else if you didn't someone pushed it through the letter box." She immediately saw Karl's expression change.

"Photograph? On the floor of the shop?"

"Yes, a customer found it. It's just come to me when you said *spread the gospel as far as animal welfare* ... I thought you'd dropped it as I recognised a very young you but it said on the back *Tommy Goff.* I thought that was the other chap pictured. You looked very dapper in uniform I have to say. Must have been the knock on the head that reminded me about it. I put it under the counter." She smiled, but Karl's demeanour had changed. The muscle in his leg tightened as he looked away.

Chapter Twenty-Six

The morning run so far had been easy for her, it was the warm and dry weather that made all the difference. Waking to rain had a tendency to kill her enthusiasm. The last three months had seen Ruth's stamina level increase as her weight had dropped. She had started with what she would call her morning shuffle but steadily she had increased to a jog. She always ran the same route. That way she could judge her progress by the time she achieved. Being rather conscious of her weight she stuck to the park but not an area that was too isolated.

She had entered the park by Ebor Rise, rounded the tennis courts before moving across the pathway towards The Sun Pavilion, her favourite part. Even at this hour the same dog walkers would pass and that was always reassuring. Keeping parallel with Cornwall Road, she would cross onto the lower path. She was then half way. It was as she followed the path, passing the model boating pool and entering the Japanese Garden that she paused. Something had caught her attention, leaning against some stones, the legs spread across the path at the other side of the ornamental pond.

The sound of early morning traffic and the occasional bird call was all she could hear apart from her breathing. The man seemed to be asleep; a hat was on the grass close by his coat which was wrapped tightly around him, belted and twisted as if it were keeping him from moving further.

"Hello," she said, her voice barely above a whisper as if she dared not wake him. She moved closer. It was something about his hands, the way they fell to either side of him palms uppermost, and his shoes, they were dug into the dirt as if he had been struggling, that made her stomach quiver. “Hello,” she repeated more forcefully. There was still nothing. Bravely, she went to the small, wooden bridge and walked towards the figure, constantly hoping someone would come or the man would move. Keeping low and still fearful she might startle him if he were, as she suspected, a sleeping drunk, she touched his left hand. It was neither cold nor warm and this confused her. He did not move. As his hand was facing upwards, she felt the inner wrist, manoeuvring two fingers to locate a pulse. It did not feel as though there was a pulse but then she could never find her own. Taking off her Fitbit she slipped it around his wrist and watched. There was nothing. She looked up as the sound of pounding feet grew closer, another runner came into view. Standing, she waved him to stop.

“I think he’s dead.” Her voice showed more control than she would have thought possible under the circumstances.

Without hesitation the runner came and lifted back Leonard’s head. The eyes, partially open, stared blindly as his tongue lolled from the corner of his mouth. He then slumped to the side, his head hitting the pathway hard. “Jesus! Ring 999.” He took the phone from his sleeve and handed it to Ruth. Slipping off his light jacket he placed it over Leonard’s face and shoulders. Ruth began to cry and handed the phone back. Within minutes of the call being made, the runners moved away to a respectful distance and waited.

***

Cyril knew that it would take at least twenty-four hours even with the new fast procedure for securing DNA tests but at least he had set the wheels in motion. Ted and Belinda had been kept separately since their arrival at the station, standard procedure with domestic issues. It was clear that neither was in the mood to talk to the other. Cyril had decided that Owen and April would question Belinda Bostock and he and Quinn, Ted. From the reports to date Ted might well be the innocent in all of this but Cyril had seen many cases where still waters ran far more deeply than they appeared to.

Belinda fidgeted as she sat in the Interview Room. The officer on the door neither smiled nor spoke. The general sounds of people on the floor above were barely audible but could on occasion be heard. The door opening suddenly startled her. Owen tossed a file onto the table in front of her and grabbed both chairs opposite. He and April sat. He looked up and then back at the file. April started the digital recording giving details of date, time and people present. The formality brought beads of sweat to Belinda's brow. She shuffled nervously on her seat but remained silent. She really seemed unsure as to what to say or how to act.

"Trevor Bostock. Tell us what you know, the whens, the wheres and the hows. In other words, Mrs Bostock, from the beginning." Owen spoke first but did not lift his head from the file. He could sense her anxiety – her dilemma.

Belinda talked nervously at first, unsure if he meant from the first time they met, but as soon as she realised she was required to give the full history, she relaxed a little.

"When I was courting Ted, I met him a few times. He was older, brash and not very nice. I knew there were always rows between him and his father to the extent that he left. I heard that he had joined up, but if he had we never saw him when he was on leave. I believe that his father paid him a monthly allowance to stay away and he lost all rights to the farm. Ted was different. He was always industrious and loved the farm, working alongside his father up until the old man passed away. We were married by then and his mum lived with us. That wasn't easy. Never felt like we had a real marriage. Another set of eyes and ears in the place meant you were never really free. You couldn't be spontaneous if you know what I mean, and at the beginning of a marriage you need that."

Owen's thoughts suddenly went to Cyril and Julie being spontaneous but he quickly cast the image aside. He could never believe his boss had a spontaneous bone in his body.

"She was like that king who lived forever, you know the one? And even though she was ill … creaking gate and all that."

April wrote down the word *Methuselah,* the name Cyril had written alongside the word *murderer* on the Incident Room boards, and underlined it.

"I sometimes wondered if that's why Ted could never have kids because his mother was always there in the next room."

Owen and April continued the interview until they brought up the cottage and the van.

"Trevor had always been into hunting, the horses, dog racing and country sports both legal and illegal. Went around with Peterson when he came back and they, believe it or not, were more alike than he was to Ted his own brother. They were exciting people to be with, spontaneous like. I needed that spark, and to be honest, I needed the sex."

April was growing a little frustrated by the prolonged justification for why she had strayed and wanted to know the details. "So, when did he return? Tell us about the cottage and the van."

"When he came back, he stayed in the caravan in the derelict barn and it was then that we met by accident. I didn't recognise him at first but then … well we sort of clicked. A friend had the cottage and I rented it with no questions asked as she didn't want the tax man to know. The van I bought cheap. He was using Peterson's car on occasion but once the tax ran out that stopped."

April tapped Owen's shoe under the table as if to signal honour amongst thieves. It was a wasted kick.

***

Ted Bostock seemed extremely crestfallen. He kept seeking reassurance that Belinda would not contemplate doing the things his brother had suggested and occasionally broke down.

"Things had been fine since my brother left. I'd heard whispers, of course, that he was back but I'd heard them before and he'd never shown up at the farm. Strangely, the rumours came when there was some trouble in the area. Like now with the rustling, I should have put two and two together. That's him all over. Him and Peterson, poachers the pair of them."

Cyril was the first to present information that Bostock would find difficulty in comprehending. "Are you aware that your brother has a cottage not four miles from your farm?"

Cyril watched the frown furrow his brow. There was a pause as if the information was slowly percolating through his consciousness. He shook his head.

"Is that a yes or a no, Mr Bostock?"

"No."

"Therefore, you were unaware that he'd lived in that cottage rent free for just short of eight months?"

"No. What are you getting at exactly?"

"We know who paid the bills. In fact, as we speak, Mr Bostock, we will have police officers in that cottage taking a good look round." Cyril paused.

"It has nothing to do with me. I didn't even know he was there."

"But your wife did. She's been paying the bills. Correction. You've been paying the bills, unbeknown to you I grant you."

A look of puzzlement flashed across Ted's face and Cyril saw his lower jaw sag. He was genuinely surprised and Cyril made a mental note. They had hardly started when an officer popped his head around the door. "Sorry! Important, sir. Mr Black needs to see you."

Cyril collected the papers from the desk and moved to the door. "I'll be back shortly, Mr Bostock. My staff will make sure you're comfortable."

"I've a bloody farm to run. I can't stay here all bloody day, man!" By the end of the sentence he was talking to the officer on the door. Cyril had disappeared.

Chapter Twenty-Seven

Cyril and April met outside the interview rooms before heading towards the car park. "I don't think we've done much for strengthening that marriage," Cyril said. "Are we sure our *Mr Black* is Leonard Ross?"

"The description is the same and the name and address found in the hat next to the body confirms that."

"Lilith, the snake?"

"Not found as yet. The RSPCA called and their snake charmer will be in the area shortly."

"Remind me to drop a few bob their way when this is over."

Within fifteen minutes they parked just outside the park on Valley Drive. A gate set in the hedge and fencing allowed easy access. Already the area was busy and that entrance was closed. A PCSO stood blocking the way but quickly moved as Cyril showed his ID.

"To the left, sir."

"Any snakes?" Cyril asked as he passed.

He watched the officer look around his feet and then back. "Not that I'm aware of. Should there be?"

Cyril smiled, walked past the model boating pond and ducked under the police tape. A blue and white pop-up tent had been erected over the body and almost into the narrow Japanese pond. The same CSI he had met at the shop was busy. Two vehicles had entered the park and were positioned on the grass to the right. The Crime Scene Manager came from the tent, waved a gloved hand and crossed the ornamental bridge.

"Morning, Cyril. From all accounts he's not been dead long, an hour at most. No rigor mortis present. Body's barely cold. The weather helped maintain that, as you know." He did not state the obvious to Cyril and went to the facts. "Dr Pritchett's with him."

Cyril looked confused. Julie should only start back the following day. "Julie Pritchett?" he asked, knowing full well there was only one doctor and pathologist with that name in the north east. The officer smiled. "Right. The two runners who found him are in that car. They're giving statements and then they will be released. Not a pleasant start to the day for anyone. The young lady is particularly upset. The paramedic who was the first responder has checked them both but she might need some professional support otherwise she'll not be running in the early mornings again, he feels."

"Any sign of the snake? I assume you were briefed regarding the possibility."

"Nothing as yet and from the expert, that's the lady who owned the shop, they are active in the day and can move a good distance when the need arises but the likelihood is it will be looking for a warm place, possibly dark and warm. She also said that they are beautifully camouflaged too."

Cyril scanned the park, all seventeen acres of it. He knew the extent of the general layout and the pine wood in the upper area. However, there were gardens that backed onto the park too, adding to the search boundary.

"Do they bite?"

"They will do but they're not venomous. The experts suggest we notify owners of small dogs and cats and parents of young children to be extra vigilant, unless you feel we should temporarily close the park."

“Keep it open for now but ensure warnings are posted. The more people we have in here the greater the chance of finding the damn thing.” Cyril noticed Julie exit the tent with Hannah.

He found it strange looking at the woman emerging from inspecting a corpse dressed in protective clothing, and knowing she was the same woman who had snuggled warmly against him less than four hours ago. For their professional integrity, he would have to separate the two. He felt a glow of pride. She saw him and raised a hand and then five fingers as she spoke with the CSM. She crossed the bridge, dropped her mask and raised her safety glasses so they were positioned on the hood of her suit.

“We’ll have to stop meeting like this Bennett or people will begin to suspect.” A broad grin forced laughter lines around her eyes. “And before you say anything, they were short staffed and my husband had left very early for work. Missed it like you, I guess.” She stripped off her gloves and thrust them into a yellow biohazard bag.

“Well, Doctor Pritchett, what do we have?”

“Male, mid-to-late thirties. I found spot hematoma to the right eye but no bruising to the neck. Initial findings suggest asphyxia and maybe a loss of blood flow to the brain but there is no evidence of hand strangulation or that of a rope or scarf. If this were the result of the constrictor, I believe they apply the pressure gradually, so when the prey breathes out they increase constriction as they move most of their bulk to the neck area. The victim finds it more difficult to inhale. It does what its name suggests – it constricts the blood vessels and the trachea until you pass out and in turn, die. It’s their natural hunting instinct. People often underestimate the strength of these creatures, even one measuring a couple of metres. If a person were inexperienced it would soon overpower them. As it’s a warm morning it might not have wrapped to gain warmth, but rather because of anxiety and poor handling."

Cyril listened as Julie removed more of her protective clothing.

"I'll know more later today. If he's taken the snake it looks like a case of misadventure to me. I'll check the lungs and have a definite for you. Coming yourself or sending Owen?"

"I think there's something on TV I have to watch." He winked. "See you tonight."

Chapter Twenty-Eight

The taxi dropped Karl on Cold Bath Road and within minutes he was at the shop. The tape had been removed and the *Closed until Further Notice* sign was clearly displayed. It saved him a job. He was exhausted. The initial anxiety had drained him and he returned to his apartment. He needed tea and breakfast before calling in to see Penny. His only hope was that Leonard had been found. He felt more like a social worker than a retiree. However, things could be worse.

Penny had been calm until the officer came to bring her the news about Leonard. She had become distraught and for a time inconsolable. All she could do was stare at the illuminated fish tank and whisper his name as if in some vain hope he might suddenly return. The experienced police liaison officer managed to bring some sense and calm to the situation. Karl had volunteered to go and identify the body. It seemed logical as Karl had looked into Penny's eyes and been greeted by an emptiness, a void of uncertainty. It frightened him. What would she do? Say? He moved and squeezed her shoulder. She turned to face him directly and the sign of a slight smile broke across her lips, albeit momentarily but it was there – she was not totally broken.

***

It was lunchtime before Cyril and Owen stared at the Bostocks across the tables in the Interview Rooms again. Cyril wanted very much to release Ted. His story and his responses told him that he was a man with problems but he was neither a killer nor an accomplice to murder, whereas his wife seemed to retain more information than she had disclosed to date. He had suggested to Owen that all the evidence needed to be wheedled as subtly and as soon as possible but considering Owen's facial expression he knew he had chosen the wrong term.

"We need answers, Owen, bloody honest ones."

Owen fully comprehended his boss's wishes and smiled knowing that a reluctant interviewee was doubly time-consuming and frustrating and they needed answers, honest answers. They had swapped briefly, Owen to interview Ted and Cyril, Belinda. Owen even had doubts as to whether he should trust her judgement about the mystery male whom she had identified from the images of hunt saboteurs. By four pm they were both driven back to the farm. There was nothing concrete, all was circumstantial at best. All he hoped for now was that Ted would not show his true colours and beat his wife senseless for her infidelities. It was a risk he had to take.

It was just as Cyril was packing to leave that the call came in. The snake had been found. It had taken refuge beside the metal railings, enjoying the sun's warmth, two hundred metres from where Leonard was found. It was now in the safe keeping of the RSPCA.

***

Owen looked down onto the table, a view he was now familiar with and one that brought neither fear nor nausea. Julie was again dressed for the part and her professionalism shone through. There was little time for chit-chat as she removed the lungs and weighed them.

"As I thought, they weigh twice what they should. Our man here was asphyxiated. Time of death was about six this morning. No physical damage to the neck or throat. It was the boa constrictor. I've read through all the files on similar deaths and strangely, Owen, they are not too common and many have the same identifiers. It's up to the Coroner but I'd say misadventure verdict. It shouldn't be long before we can release this poor chap. I'll be through here in thirty minutes. Are you going straight home or back to the station?"

"What time did Hannah finish?"

"An hour ago."

Owen raised his eyebrows as if to say *I wish,* whilst glancing at the clock set behind the glass screen. He calculated he had been at work for eleven hours already. "I should go back but I'm not. I'm done. It'll be early in tomorrow no doubt. I'll call Cyril and see what he's planning. Thanks a lot." He lifted his hand.

Cyril was just crossing The Stray when his phone rang. The sun was still relatively high and the shadows short. The fresh air had brought a spring back to his step. "Bennett," he answered, always abrupt and to the point.

"Just left the autopsy, sir. It's as originally suggested. No signs of foul play. Asphyxiation. What time do you want me in the morning?"

"Seven thirty, my office first, Owen. Briefing at eight. Have a good evening. And Owen."

"Sir."

"Thanks for your hard work today. Still nothing on Trevor Bostock; he's a will-o'-the-wisp it seems. I have a watch on the cottage for when, and indeed if, he should return. I've applied for a search warrant and that'll be through tomorrow. I'm in no rush. Rather find him in, so to speak, rather than out. See you tomorrow. I have a Black Sheep to rustle."

"Cheers. Might just find one myself."

Chapter Twenty-Nine

Karl was up particularly early. He had one task to do after feeding and boxing the pets ready for transportation. He finished his coffee before collecting the three travel boxes and started taping them together, leaving the carrying handle to the top. Quickly he checked the ventilation holes were clear on all three. He removed an item from the small wardrobe safe and checked it. Everything was in place. He removed his jacket from the peg in the hall. The envelope addressed to Jo was on the small hall table and he slipped that into his inside pocket.

Cold Bath Road was quiet but he expected nothing less at this time of the day. It would take five minutes to get to the shop. On turning onto Cold Bath Place, he was pleased to see the van outside and a light illuminating the back of the shop. The sign hanging behind the glass on the door still announced that the shop was closed until further notice. Putting down the boxes he put his hand to the glass and brought his face closer. Knowing this was the time the majority of the animals would be checked, fed and watered, he was not surprised to see the person in the back. His timing was perfect.

The tapping on the door startled Tony Turnbull, the RSPCA officer who had been tasked with the job. The shock nearly made him drop the water bowls he was carrying. On looking over his shoulder, seeing the face at the window of the door did not help. Putting down the items he entered the shop. "It's shut!" he shouted whilst pointing to the sign.

Karl lifted the three travel boxes and pointed to them. "They're booked in today. Arranged it with Jo weeks ago." He exaggerated his words so the person might read his lips.

Tony frowned and scratched his head. His instruction was to check and feed the pets within the shop, not run it. He turned the key and opened the door.

"I'm sorry but the shop is closed until tomorrow. I can't help you, sorry."

Karl smiled and then changed his expression to one of sadness. "Goodness. I'm leaving the country for a couple of weeks and I'd booked these three in with Jo. She boards them for me when I'm away. It's in the diary if you'd care to check."

Tony could clearly see the customer's predicament and Karl read his expression well. "If you can't take them my wife and I will have to cancel the trip. I've no one else to leave them with and I'll not leave them alone, they would die … please?"

He saw Tony look at the three boxes and then back and he took the opportunity to add more gravity to his expression. "Bring them in."

"Jo's looked after them before and as I say they're expected. They don't need anything today, I've already taken care of them." He placed them on the counter. "The diary is usually below …" he lied, moving around the back of the counter and bobbing down to look at the shelf. There in front of him was the photograph. Picking it up he quickly slipped it into his pocket. "No, it's not there. If there's been a problem then maybe Jo's taken it. Can I leave you this?" He handed the envelope to Bill. "It's for Jo. Maybe you can pop it onto the table in her flat."

Within five minutes he had left the shop. Tony scratched his head and looked at the envelope, the name *Jo* written in bold black ink. Karl tapped the breast pocket of his jacket and smiled. He had only one more errand to complete.

***

Owen's phone bounced along his bedside table before it dropped onto the floor. The sound of its alarm and a droning, dull vibration eventually penetrated his waking consciousness. His hand instinctively hovered as if sweeping the table's surface but without success. "Hell's bloody bells!" he cried from beneath the duvet. Within a minute he had found the offending article. He quickly squinted at the screen. It was Cyril. Putting the phone to his ear he grunted, "Morning … I think."

"Sorry, Owen. It's been light for hours. Thought you'd be wide awake and eating your breakfast." He received a long growl that could have been interpreted as a grunt.

"Seriously, it's important. DNA results have been sent through to us more quickly than we could've hoped. We have two common samples found throughout this case, matching within each of the homes of those murdered and also at the shop where Lilith was taken. One we know to be that of Trevor Bostock but the other is a bit of a mystery. It's not showing on the National Database. What's interesting is that samples found at the shop were found not just downstairs but upstairs too. Shall we say samples of a more personal nature. DNA is a bit like looking at stained glass windows, Owen. Pass a church in the daytime and from the outside looking in you often see nothing. Pass at night when the church is lit and everything becomes beautifully clear." Cyril heard another groan.

"Sorry, sir, but I haven't a clue what you're talking about. I'll get dressed and be with you ASAP." Signing off, he threw the duvet to the side and staggered to the bathroom, scratching an itch on his right buttock as he went.

***

Karl removed the photograph he had retrieved from below the counter at Jo's. He looked at the two young men who stared back defiantly. "Tommy Goff. Just look at you there!"

The cottage was quiet as Karl moved to the front door and slipped the photograph through the letter box before knocking loudly. A curtain moved upstairs and Karl stood back to allow the observer to see him. He waved and smiled. Within two minutes Karl heard the door lock turn but then nothing. Cautiously he pulled down the handle and pushed the door fully open knowing he was silhouetted against the light. He said nothing, allowing his hand to move to his jacket pocket before he entered. The room was not only deplete of light, owing to the small windows and the low ceilings, but it also lacked the morning's warmth.

"Close and lock the door." The words came from the dark recess that led to another room. "I wondered how long it would take. Thought it was you the other day but obviously I was wrong."

Karl closed the door and locked it as instructed but then remained by it.

"Not seen that photograph for years. You do keep some crap. Fucking *Tommy Goff*. Tommy Goff, the local's nickname for that bloody snake you were handling. I remember. Hell, you frightened everyone shitless. The most dangerous and angry critter you could meet and you waltz in with it. A fucking pet you said."

"Everyone wanted to be photographed with the most venomous snake in Belize, like the brave squaddies we were if I remember right. You included. The Fer de Lance, a stunning creature, they only kill to live unlike you. And yes, you're right, known to the locals as *Tommy Goff*. Like all the animals you met out there you quickly killed it when I released it. I listened to your stories and escapades, Trevor, and knew one day the time would be right to bring about a change. The world is altering, it needs to as it's been raped enough. I really don't think you fully comprehend the passion people feel for the natural world. We witness the greed, the nonchalance or the cavalier attitude towards our environment, the casual way life is treated as if it doesn't matter. I see and read the results of these so-called hunters killing in the wild, slaughtering creatures bred so the wealthy can come along and destroy them from a place of safety and are then photographed with their kill. You watch it on the Internet but now you see not only men but women and children too. I despise that, Trevor. There's no chase, no fear, no them and us and worst of all, no hunger. They are not killed for food but purely as trophies ... for selfish pleasure."

Trevor laughed and then grunted. "It's always gone on and always will. Like fishermen and hunters here in this country, they protect the rivers and countryside. The landowners hunt but put so much back into the land. It's a trade-off. You were naïve then," he waved the photograph, "and you're naïve now if you think you or some of these so-called animal rights people can help or even change anything."

"We're talking not only of the rights of human beings, but also about the rights of animals. You can see that vegetarians and vegans are growing in numbers, businesses are catering for them, plastics are now frowned upon and the government is beginning to heed the calls to protect this environment of ours. There will be change but the change is slow. Soon, we hear, there will be prison sentences of five years for illegal hunting in this country, not the paltry fines that are easily paid. You're wrong to believe that as individuals we can't change things. You don't know this but after the army I went back to Belize and worked in a wildlife sanctuary. I then worked in zoos, caring for the very things you and your buddies enjoyed killing. But now, Trevor, look at your friends, Lyons, Peterson and Humphreys. Ask yourself if they'll kill and slaughter again. The hunters became the hunted. You'll never know the strength of feelings people have for animals. They would sooner see a man killed than an animal and, Trevor, so would I. They taught us well, her Majesty's armed forces. They taught us to escape and evade, to seek and find. We both did that. Remember, Trevor? As I recall you were a shit then and from what I've discovered about you since, you've not changed. Did I kill them? Yes, like a spider with a web I threaded my way from one to the other, linking them all so that those that followed would know each was related. I led a path to the farm; the knife and the glove was genius even if I say so myself. I did it so that you would firstly be exposed for the shit that you are. I wanted them to discover more of your duplicitous ways and it's worked, I feel.

Those here the other day would be the police. They know that you are the missing link but they are also unsure as to whether you're the killer or the next victim. I felt sorry for Ted. I did when you talked about him way back then. You believed everything should be yours, being the elder. Ted was good, just like Eve, and you were Lilith, the sinful one. That came to my mind when you killed that snake, the one in the picture. You wouldn't understand that. You never read, never learned other than to drink, shag and gamble and let's not forget … to kill!"

They stared at each other in the gloomy light, both men taken back in time, one man confused as to where the future was heading.

"I remember you saying you'd come back and you'd take her from him. That he had taken the farm from you and you would take her, take Belinda from him, you would make him suffer. Your own flesh and blood. You would break him. Do you remember that, Trevor?"

Trevor moved quickly from the corner where he had remained since Karl had entered. He could run through the kitchen and out of the house but then what would be the point?

Karl removed a TT pistol from his jacket. "You'll be familiar with this, used on the farms by you and your dead mates to destroy. I found this at Peterson's. Well that's not strictly true as it was in his car."

Chapter Thirty

Owen went straight to Cyril's office. April and Quinn were already there. A spare chair had been added. He checked his watch. It had been forty minutes since the early morning wake-up call.

"Thanks, Owen. Right." Cyril pointed to the chair and Owen quickly sat. "DNA. The first link is fascinating. Saliva samples taken from the shop door, the counter and the floor are identified as those belonging to Leonard Ross."

Quinn looked at April as if to say *that's hardly surprising as he was known to be there*. Cyril glanced sideways catching the look on Quinn's face. "We know he was there but what's interesting is that there's a match, a familial match to a Trevor Bostock."

You could have heard a pin drop in the room as Cyril glanced at each officer in turn. "We know that he was renowned as a womaniser in his youth. We know the father did a runner when the true extent of Leonard's medical condition was revealed. I know that they were never married. He was the result of just another fling."

"Does Leonard's mother know this?"

"I've sent the same liaison officer round. Hopefully we'll get some answers although what further we need to understand I don't know. I'm sure of one thing, she's probably not seen him since the early days after the birth."

Owen stifled a yawn. "What about the other DNA that you mentioned at that ungodly hour this morning, sir? The one found at every murder site but not on the database and the one found at the shop?"

"Semen found on the sheets belonging to the shop owner …"

April immediately jumped in. "Karl … what was his name? Came to the shop early looking for Leonard, friend of the family but mentioned that he was Jo's partner, the shop owner. Goodness I have the memory of a hen. I thought at first business partner, otherwise he'd have been there that morning. I looked him up. His address, if I remember, is on Cold Bath Road. Leslie, that's it Karl Leslie. May I?" She stood and Cyril nodded. She left the office.

She looked through the notes on her desk before picking up a pink folder and returning. "It's here. Karl Leslie, sixty-six. Here's the address. I checked. He has no previous. He owns an apartment in a retirement complex."

"Quinn, take Nixon for a visit. I want him in here. I think he'll have flown the nest by now if he's the killer, so be careful. Owen get the car, we're off to the cottage rented by Trevor Bostock. I want armed backup. In thirty minutes."

They left leaving April nursing the pink folder.

"I find it strange, April. Call it copper's nose or gut feeling but something's not sitting correctly. I want you to see Penny, find out as much as you can about Karl Leslie, then go to the retirement place and see when she and Leonard first appeared. Find out if there was ever a carer involved for Leonard. All this time without a break I find difficult to comprehend. I want you to dig."

April smiled and left. Cyril collected his jacket and tapped his pockets. The words *spectacles, testicles, wallet and watch* went through his head. If his assumption was correct, he was going to need some kind of divine intervention.

***

Quinn and Nixon discovered that Karl had logged out early that morning. It was nothing as simple as signing out, just a log of the activation of his alarm. Quinn called Owen who answered hands free as he was driving.

"Leslie checked out before five this morning and there's no sign of his return. Want us to wait and see if he comes back?"

"Wait an hour, then leave an instruction for someone to call should he return."

***

"I believe there's something else that you've been running from, Trevor, from a time when you seduced young girls, girls who gave you everything and then you left them. I know of one such woman. You'll have forgotten, as I'm sure each would blend with the other. That's why photographs help us to recall. The races, remember the races? When was that?" Karl took another photograph from his pocket. "It's a copy I'm afraid, but you'll remember." He sent it across the room.

Trevor picked up the photograph and smiled. "Ripon, 1986. I was twenty-three and care fucking free. Won a few bob that day. Went into Harrogate."

"And in Harrogate, what?"

Trevor lifted his eyes to Karl and grinned. *"Met a girl as cute as can be ..."* He hummed the words to the song.

Karl squeezed the trigger and the shot rang around the cottage as the bullet ran clean through Trevor's right shoulder. His body was instantly thrown against the wall behind. Milliseconds after, the bullet embedded itself a metre away into the plaster. The released photograph fluttered to the floor. A stifled scream followed by a loud groan seemed to echo the fired shot as both sounds filled the claustrophobic room.

"That's what you do to life, Trevor, you simply use it for your pleasure and throw it away. Do you remember the girl's name, the cute one?"

Another groan emanated from the figure now sitting propped against the wall. A thin red line ran down from the bullet's impact and continued as a smudged line against the rough plaster, marking the body's slow descent.

"Shall I remind you? This was not one of your dumb animals. This was a girl of sixteen. You saw her a few times by all accounts, went for the same thing and when she was pregnant you hovered. I believe that you actually liked her. I know you told her you loved her, even bought her a ring, a cheap one granted, but at least it was a token. I've seen it. She kept it, Trevor, it was a token of your love for her and for your child. Did you know she treasured it? Do you care? She also told me that you promised her the world. Was that just to get into her knickers?" Karl paused, looking for any expression of remorse. There was none. "Were you shagging Belinda then too? And if so who else, Trevor, who else?" The second shot hit the sole of Trevor's boot, the bullet removing his big toe before lodging in his lower hip. The devastation brought another cry of agony.

"Jesus Christ, man. I … don't fucking know …" Trevor was now on the ground. His head on the floor. Blood pooled by his shoulder and the light reflected red. The blood flow throbbed through his foot, burning as it pulsed.

"Are you still with me?" There was a grunt. "Let me remind you. You told me all about her when you were drunk and boasting. Penelope, Penny to you, Penny Ross. And your son, what about his name? The poor unfortunate bastard. Bastard's right isn't it, Trevor? A bastard child formed from lust and not love. What is his name, the boy, the result of your wickedness? You see how you're suffering now, your friends suffered too. Nothing quick. They didn't know me. I asked. It was the last question they ever answered. *No,* they all said and even though that was the correct answer they still died. Why? Because they were all cruel ... that was so true ... but that was not the main reason, it was because they knew you and they knew what you had done. How did you feel as one by one they met their maker, Trevor? As the noose approached? As the hunter grew closer to the wounded and confused creature that you are." He raised the gun again. "Well, your son's name?"

Trevor spoke through clenched teeth. There was still a note of defiance. "Which one? I neither care nor fucking want to know. It was a long time ago."

"Looked a bit like you but sadly the lad never stood a chance – father buggered off, scared I assume – Lilith took the oxygen from him at birth, caused dreadful cerebral damage. Lilith, the taker of the breath of the new born, you wouldn't see the connection or the significance."

Trevor lifted his head from the floor. "Lilith, I call all the girls by that name. Saves confusion at key moments ... they hate it when you call out the wrong name when ... need I say more?"

"Somehow I knew the subtleties of all of this would be lost on you." Karl checked the pistol.

Chapter Thirty-One

Owen let the blue strobes flash as he parked the car a hundred yards from the lane where the cottage was situated. The police firearms team climbed from the van and moved quickly along the lane, taking cover behind the low hedge that ran to the side. The sun had brought shadows along the lane's edge, offering cover for the black-clad firearms officers. Cyril followed, watching the lead figure. They used only hand signals as they split into two units, one taking the rear the other the front. They would now go onto coms.

The shot rang out loud and clear and Cyril immediately saw the group at the front of the cottage stiffen and then lower themselves.

"Armed Police!" The call was sharp, clear and decisive. It was repeated. Another shot rang out followed by another in quick succession. The officers, along with those in the rear, checked the door. It was locked. An officer removed a stun grenade from his jacket and threw it through the nearest window to distract those inside as the door was being forced. Cyril heard the multiple shouts, *Get down, Police, Down!* come from the confines of the building before one of the officers appeared at the door. Light grey smoke from the grenade curled round the intimidating masked figure before disappearing quickly. The officer signalled Cyril and Owen over.

The room's opaque light still brought an eerie hue and the smell was pungent, causing a tightness to the throat and a sting to the eyes. A figure lay on his back, a pistol resting a short distance from his side. Owen leaned over and saw that the man's lower jaw and the rear of the head was missing. The second figure had also been hit directly in the face. Cyril knew both. Glancing at the photographs he removed his phone and took a picture of each.

"Seen this image before, Owen. The races, 1986 if my memory serves me correctly."

He put his head in his hands and rubbed his eyes before leaving the cottage. Taking a deep breath, he sighed. "I need to talk to April," he informed Owen. Cyril thanked the firearms team and trudged down the lane. The building would be secured and Forensics called. He wondered if Julie would be the one to deal with the aftermath.

Cyril and Owen both sat in the car. A group of bystanders had already appeared but so too had three police cars. Officers were already setting up the cordon.

Owen spoke first. "You had an idea back at the station that Karl Leslie was involved. You had a suspicion he'd be here too."

Cyril nodded. "The DNA, Owen, the stained glass I mentioned. It allowed me to see the light, see what previously wasn't there. What I don't know is the true motive for killing four men and then himself. I can understand how people can be fanatical about animals and even put themselves in harm's way to protect them, but to kill for that?"

Cyril's phone rang. "Bennett." He listened, occasionally nodding and looking at Owen. "Right. Dig more deeply and get back to me."

"Quinn. According to a man at the home, Karl Leslie served in Belize and on checking the records he was with Trevor Bostock for a time."

"There's an age difference," Owen said. "A large one at that."

"Not everyone is the same age. Some enter late, some early but they all find themselves posted together, but you're right, Owen. You're right."

***

April arrived back at the station with Penny. She had volunteered to accompany her. She put her in an interview lounge with a female officer and a large mug of coffee. She had also called the duty doctor. It would be fifteen minutes before Cyril entered the station and signed in by tapping his finger on a fingerprint screen reader. He shook his head, never understanding why they employed expensive equipment when all that was needed was a pad and pencil. Grabbing his lanyard he popped it over his head. April was hovering when he arrived at his office.

"What about Penny Ross?" he asked as he hung his jacket behind the door. Owen came in with a cup and saucer and a mug, placing Cyril's drink on his desk. He looked at April and pointed to the mug. She shook her head.

"She's downstairs. Although she's not the instigator of this series of deaths she feels as though she's the catalyst."

Cyril sipped from his cup, his eyes not leaving April's. If truth be known he was not surprised but asked, "How's that? Before you explain, let me tell you that Leslie has just killed Bostock and then shot himself. Both are well and truly dead."

"Bloody mess it was too," added Owen.

"A year ago, Penny met Karl. They were walking back from town. Leonard was with her but he seemed to take a liking to Karl. Karl was walking a friend's dog, something he did at that time and he allowed Leonard to stroke it and throw the ball.

Anyway, she invited him to tea and then he'd call when Leonard was in bed."

"Sex?" Owen said. Both April and Cyril turned and looked at him.

"I asked that, Owen, but in a more, shall we say, a more subtle way. The answer was no, well not initially. However, from being a lifelong carer to being with someone who cared turned the tables even though she knew that Karl was in a relationship with Jo from the pet shop. She told me she felt his relationship with her was strong and that she was disappointed. She had hoped she might have found a man who thought her attractive, saw her as a woman and importantly, Leonard's mother. However, although she realised that she had found an occasional lover, she was convinced she had found a true friend. As time went on, they talked about their past lives. It was then they realised that they had a mutual acquaintance." She paused and as if on cue both Owen and Cyril said the name.

"Trevor Bostock."

April nodded. "Apparently, when they were in Belize, Karl saw the true side of Trevor and they soon fell out. On meeting Penny and hearing her story he discovered other things. People talked in the shop about animal rights and animal support. Jo was very anti-blood sports and Karl tagged along. I've had someone call at Bostock's farm with a photograph of Karl taken at Leonard's party and Mrs Bostock can confirm that it was he who called at the farm regarding Peterson. It was him she identified at the hunt. But it wasn't Leslie who suggested retribution, it was Penny Ross. She wanted to teach Trevor Bostock a lesson, she wanted him broken and scared and so they plotted. The photograph from the Ripon races was the starting point."

"How did that work?" Owen asked.

"The evening of the races was the night Trevor met Penny. He'd had a good day and was splashing the cash. He got her drunk and they ... well. Anyway, the next day, he showed her the photograph and because she thought he loved her she kept the paper and she's had it ever since." April took out a transparent sealed envelope in which the news cutting was preserved. "Someone has written the names around the side, obviously, him. Here faintly you can see he has written *To Penny*, then were added: *Lyons, Peterson, Humphrey and me*. There was also the word *Hurst* written beneath Humphrey in a different hand."

"She showed this to Karl Leslie?"

"Karl said he should pay and so he did his research and found out about each man's past and began to weave each to the other."

"The snake, the one that killed Lyons. Did he own that?"

"No, but I think I know who did."

"Jo?"

"We'll soon know."

Chapter Thirty-Two

Cyril moved to an interview room and both the police doctor and April sat in. April cautioned Penny explaining that she was under oath but at that moment she was not under arrest.

"Ms Ross." Cyril spoke quietly. "My name is DCI Bennett." Both his hands were clasped on the table. Penny looked up and stared him directly in the eye. He introduced April.

"I have some more bad news for you I'm afraid. Karl Leslie killed himself this morning." He deliberately did not mention Bostock. Penny's facial expression did not change. Cyril waited.

"Did he kill that bastard ... Leonard's father, Trevor Bostock?" Her eyes were cold but optimistic.

Cyril looked at April and then at the doctor.

"If Karl is dead then I know he's done it. He has fulfilled what we set out to do. We set out to find and trap Bostock, that's all I wanted. Karl wanted the others too, for the animals, to make a stand for Jo."

"What about Leonard?"

Penny smiled. "Planned, we planned it together. He would get what he wanted and I ... Leonard had suffered enough. What would happen to him when I couldn't care for him any more? He'd been getting more difficult year on year."

Cyril saw a deepening, callous coldness grow in her eyes, as if the words were coming from elsewhere, an emptiness magnified as if now she had succeeded, she had erased the errors of the past or at least smudged them until they were illegible. He looked at her without blinking. There was more written in her eyes than he could read but he had seen the look before when he had interviewed killers. Was she the catalyst, had she manipulated the whole spree? Had Karl been coerced and if so for what?

"I loved that boy, so much so I sacrificed my life for him. Can you imagine the life I've had because I opened my legs when I was but a child? It might be classed as rape today but then? I was a silly girl. The man was always right. He could lie better and boys will be boys in a man's world. No. It's beyond anyone's comprehension. When your parents don't want you, you live from hand to mouth. You crawl your way up being respectful but at the same time being rebuffed because you had a bastard child who was different from the rest. Tolerance is a rare commodity in today's world but this was more than thirty years ago. Bostock beguiled me. I remember this quote, 'To beguile is to deceive or lead astray, as Lucifer beguiled Eve in the Garden of Eden.'"

April felt her emotions get the better of her and at one point felt she might have to leave the room. "Could you not have shared his care, Penny?"

The response was slow and deliberate, matching the way their gazes met. There was a deepening resentment in Penny's expression. "Are you a mother, Officer Richmond?" Her question was deliberate and strategic. Cyril noted her control.

April flashed a quick look at Cyril. "No, and I can't imagine the struggles you have had. What I do know from the time I've been involved with this case is just how strong a mother's love can be but to …" She stopped herself.

"According to Karl, the constrictor would have killed my son gently and calmly. Leonard loved that snake even though he'd seen it only the once; a planned birthday treat," she emphasised the word *planned* and deliberately turned her gaze to Cyril.

"You knew he went out that morning?" Cyril said immediately after her response.

Penny nodded and there was a hint of a smile. "I knew his every move. When you have a child like mine you are constantly prepared. I heard him go down the stairs, heard the front door. I looked out as he hesitated, like a timid chick about to take its first flight from the nest. I followed him before waiting outside the shop. I saw him enter and I saw Jo look out. I saw him leave with the snake at arm's length. I checked on Jo; she was unconscious but breathing; she didn't know I was there. I watched him go to the park … to the oriental garden, as if to the Garden of Eden with Lilith. I watched my son die and I held his hand." She smiled and closed her eyes, allowing her hand to move across the table and touch Cyril's fingers.

Cyril did not move.

"You are under oath, Ms Ross." The doctor spoke quietly.

"I know. If you'd not sent the liaison officer and then this lovely lady here to my home, I wouldn't be sitting here, I would be with my son and with Karl." She withdrew her hand. "This man knows that."

"Doctor, a word. April please stay, I'll send another officer in too."

Outside the room Cyril requested psychiatric assessment and that Ross be kept secure. The potential for suicide was clear. The review and assessment would take priority over all else. He would request the CPS use the power at their disposal to seek further evidence and that Penny Ross be moved to a safe place until decisions on the correct legal process could be made.

Chapter Thirty-Three

Cyril refused a lift home even when it included the offer of a pint. He needed time to think, clear his mind and try to understand the minds of those with whom he had been dealing. He crossed The Stray and stood before the snicket that led to Robert Street. Even on the warmest of days a cool breeze moved through the enclosed space. He leaned against the wall and thought of his mother and the strength of love she had shown for him. He then brought Wendy, his stepmother, to mind. Her selfless kindness caused a lump to form in his throat. He thought of Penny, a woman broken by a love she had cherished and a hatred that had been fuelled by sadness, and the tears began to fall. Had his mother not done the same, plotted and planned for the sake of her child?

Julie was home when he arrived and she could immediately see he was distressed. As she wrapped her arms around him, he allowed the flood gates to open. He realised, probably for the first time in his life, just how lucky he was. Pulling away briefly he kissed his new wife.

"Please never allow me to take anything for granted. I'm so lucky. I know that more now than ever before. I've seen and heard things today that show the strength of human love and that maybe, just maybe, you have to be cruel to be kind. I should have seen that sooner but it has taken what I've experienced today to see it with a sharper clarity."

***

One week later

The report came through that Jo had kept the Russell's viper illegally but as it grew she had become afraid and had asked Karl if he could give the snake to a Zoo where he had once worked. As far as she was aware, he had complied with her request.

She had broken down after hearing the news about Leonard and Karl. Having a clear police record, she was allowed to return and run the shop but with regular checks on the animals within her care.

Penny was moved to a psychiatric hospital for further assessment and the case was left pending with the CPS. In Cyril's mind, what Penny required more than anything now, was a huge helping of human kindness and specialised care. She neither needed to stand for murder nor manslaughter, and that was unlikely to be the case. In his eyes, she was now no longer a risk to anyone but herself.

***

Three weeks later

Cyril arrived at work early. The sky had been grey but the rain had kept off. He handled the statue, the wedding gift from Owen, Hannah and his team. He allowed the cool metal to fall on the palm of his hand. *Liberty,* he whispered. It is perfectly named. He then saw the note attached to his computer screen. He pulled it away and read it.

Sorry to inform you, sir, but we have just received a report advising us of the suicide of Penny Ross. Full report on file.

Quinn

Putting down the statue Cyril reread the note. He put his head in his hands. *Liberty,* he said again to himself. *Liberty, for the love of Leonard she's now free, bless her.* He sighed a breath of relief. Justice had been done. Momentarily he thought of his mother and the strains of *The Lark Ascending* came to his head, the cry of the fiddle, the sound of a mother crying for her son.

Taking a deep breath, he checked his watch, shook his wrist and looked again. He put the note back on the screen and left his office. He had a briefing to attend.

Featured Artist

At the end of all my books I like to write a little about the featured artist. On this occasion there were three but I'll cover two of those in brief.

I was fortunate to visit the exhibition held at the Mercer Art Gallery in Harrogate of work by the artist William Frith, the people's painter who was born not far from Harrogate. This exhibition has to be one of the best I have ever experienced and I congratulate all those who worked to bring so many paintings together. Should you ever get the chance to see any of his work then I politely urge you to do so.

There was another piece of work mentioned, the bronze of *Liberty* presented to Bennett by Owen. *Liberty* is a small sculpture made by Thomas Taylor Bowie (1931–1983) in 1966. Bowie was born in Scotland before moving to Canada. However, he returned to work on a number of commissions including the Robert the Bruce Memorial at Bannockburn.

***

Herbert Bannister Whone (1925–2011)

However, it is Herbert Whone I want to concentrate on for this section, as here was a man who fascinated me when I was researching for 'Threadbare'. He was a perfect foil for the role. To find a Yorkshire self-taught artist who not only captured the Dales so freely in his work but who was also a professional violinist, playing at the Royal Opera House and the BBC Symphony Orchestra, was a gift. I could imagine that he and

Cyril's mother might possibly have worked together at some stage; after all, that is what fiction writers create, a possibility of matching the real with the imaginary that I find enchanting. To have a painting given to Cyril as a gift from his new bride, a woman who had nurtured him through emotional and difficult times, seemed perfect.

Whone retired and moved to Harrogate, another twist of fate, and not only continued to paint but began to write, having nine books published. This is the ninth book in the Harrogate series! Once living in Harrogate he became a guide at Fountains Abbey. If you recall, this was the spot chosen by Cyril to propose to Julie.

I am keen to search for a perfect Whone painting and one day I feel sure that I will find one.

Acknowledgements

The quote from Penny:

'To beguile is to deceive or lead astray, as Lucifer beguiled Eve in the Garden of Eden' – Joseph B Wirthlin.

'Everyone has a book inside them,' I have often heard, but to be honest I had my doubts. Yet here I am concluding book nine in the Harrogate series, book ten overall, as I think of 'Bridging the Gulf', my first attempt at writing a novel. I also remember it is only three years since my then publisher brought out this series – only thirty-six months and this, I feel, is an achievement of which I should feel proud.

Writing is a selfish pastime that allows only me to travel to a fictitious world. I have a wonderful time creating the characters, researching the crimes and the elements that make up all aspects of the writing but there comes a time when the ink is dry that I need others to help and therefore, without the interaction from the readers, I do not believe I would achieve the same degree of satisfaction. It is clear to them, from our chats, that for me, Cyril and Owen are real, to them too. They trudge the streets of Harrogate, drink in the same pubs as them, admire the spectacular Stray and breathtaking Yorkshire Dales whilst delivering justice. I try to make them live and breathe.

For this to happen, however, I'm grateful to many people and I would like to tell you about some individuals and some groups. Obviously, I cannot name them all and if any should slip through the net, my apologies.

My wife, Debbie, is first to be mentioned. Her dedication, patience and understanding are limitless and I could not do this without her. Thank you x

To Helen Gray, my sincere thanks for casting your professional eye over each and every word.

Thank you to Kevin Graham for the cover photographs and to Craig Benyon at *Create Print* for ensuring everything on those nine covers has the same professional appearance.

Caroline Vincent, from *Bits About Books* who has been with me since the beginning through thick and thin. My guardian angel and true friend and to whom I shall forever be grateful.

What would we authors be or do without the blogging community, those prolific, enthusiastic readers who turn a pleasure into a profession, my thanks to each and every one. To the reading and book groups who spread the word; just remember how vital you all are.

My ARC readers who kindly give accurate and honest feedback on the books I write: to Stef O'Leary, Kath Middleton, Carrie Heap and Lindsay Muir, my thanks.

Always at this time my thoughts are with Emily Shutt – a princess, a warrior and a little angel … you are not forgotten.

Thomas and Lady Ingilby – Ripley Castle – for allowing the wedding to take place at your beautiful home.

Andrew Forsyth, Geoff Blakesley, Gill Cleverdon, the staff at The Harrogate Library, Georgie and the staff at Cordings, Harrogate, my thanks for your continued and loyal support.

If I'm not careful this will turn into one of those Oscar speeches and that would never do. So, to close, as always, the last is not the least, I mention you, yes you holding this Kindle or paperback, the reader, for without you I would not be here. Thank you for buying and reading book nine in the series. If you have enjoyed it then please mention my work to friends and family, as word of mouth is the best way to see more people find Bennett and his team.

Until book ten,

Thank you.

Malcolm

The Harrogate Crime Series
Malcolm Hollingdrake
MALCOLM
HOLLINGDRAKE
TREBLE CLEF
The Harrogate Crime Series
"Hollingdrake is to Harrogate what Rankin (Rebus) is to Edinburgh - able to build a realistic landscape to portray his characters against - which is even better if you are familiar with the landscape. I have just read the first 3 books back to back - I love the way the characters are evolving, the pace is good (I often just stop books as I get bored), and the plots compelling - enjoy!" - John Robson
ONLY THE DEAD
HELL'S GATE
FLESH EVIDENCE
GAME POINT
CROSSED OUT
THE THIRD BREATH
www.malcolmhollingdrakeauthor.co.uk

Printed in Great Britain
by Amazon